how
we got
to
today

Ben Ellis lives in Worthing with his wife, son and step-son.

You can find Ben online at www.b3n3llis.com.

how
we got
to
today

BEN ELLIS

ACCENT

First published in Great Britain in 2020 by
HEADLINE ACCENT
An imprint of HEADLINE PUBLISHING GROUP

3

Cataloguing in Publication Data is available from the British Library

ISBN 978 1 7861 5972 4

Typeset in 10.5/13pt Bembo Std by Jouve (UK), Milton Keynes

Printed and bound in Great Britain by Clays Ltd, Elcograf S.p.A.

Cover images © bubaone, alazur, Bigmouse108 and Sentavio, all @ iStock

MIX
Paper from
responsible sources
FSC® C104740

Headline's policy is to use papers that are natural, renewable and recyclable
products and made from wood grown in well-managed forests and other
controlled sources. The logging and manufacturing processes are expected
to conform to the environmental regulations of the country of origin.

HEADLINE PUBLISHING GROUP
An Hachette UK Company
Carmelite House
50 Victoria Embankment
London
EC4Y 0DZ

www.headline.co.uk
www.hachette.co.uk

For Claire, Happy 1st Anniversary!

(PAPER!)
please don't be reading the ebook version

SHERIDAN

Chapter One

ONE YEAR BEFORE TODAY

I grip the bench. My foot taps out an urgent SOS in Morse code. I'm holding on tight because I can feel my world is about to get turned upside down.

This bench, 'our bench', in the middle of the pedestrianised high street of Wigthorn, is on display for all to see. I'm a dummy in a shop window.

All the moments in the past in which I've sat nervously waiting for someone else to direct the course of my life coalesce into one: outside the headmaster's office; at the doctors' with an ex, awaiting the morning after pill; in a little chair in the corner at home awaiting the return of my dad after breaking a window; job interviews; first dates; getting my eyes tested. Right now, this bench has all the ergonomic comfort of an electric chair.

The source of this anxiety? Heidi. My girlfriend, Heidi. Although, it's the 'girlfriend' part of that statement that is in jeopardy at the moment. The precariousness of my future lies in her thoughts on this matter. The past few months have seen imperceptible changes pass right beneath our feet, and only recently have we begun to notice them. Or rather, only recently have I begun to notice them. I don't see how these changes would fundamentally affect our relationship. We just need to take a pit stop, change tyres, refuel, and carry on. My sense of foreboding stems from the fact that I don't think Heidi's on the same track. Whatever the time after the 'honeymoon period' is called, well, that period has ended too.

Using motor racing analogies isn't going to help my cause either.

Yesterday, Heidi said we should meet here today. She's had twenty-four hours to think of reasons to leave, and I've had twenty-four hours to compose a miracle monologue on why she should stay. I wonder how she's done, because I've got nothing.

She's late.

I sit on the bench with my head down, avoiding all contact with the outside world. I don't want to catch the eye of any friends, colleagues or customers and have to conjure up a modicum of enthusiasm. I'm on hold, paused, frozen until Heidi shares her thoughts with me. This bench used to be fun. On our lunch breaks, we'd people-watch: judge strangers, evaluate customers and gossip about so-and-so from that shop sleeping with whodyamacallit from the other shop. Now it's me on display, every passer-by passing comment, every mannequin watching in silent judgement. People in glass houses, etc.

I haven't arrived at this defining moment unarmed. I prepared myself earlier and now have an ace up my sleeve – a surprise holiday. Unoriginal? Yes. Crass? Yes. Cheap? Metaphorically, maybe. Financially? Unfortunately not. Desperate? Hell, yes. The credit card bill is going to be hanging around a lot longer than the tan. Well, it's almost booked. I'm waiting for Angela from Holidays Plus to come over like the cavalry and confirm the five-star hotel in Dubai has been booked, as the computer system froze and it was getting late. I thought it would be a sweet moment, almost romantic, to have her come up to us on our lunch break to break the news, Angela a bejewelled, buxom messenger of hope.

I look east to search out Angela, but she's nowhere to be seen. I look west to see if Heidi's coming out of Candleina, but she's . . . yes she is. She's talking to a friend . . . and now she's coming over.

This is it.

I look east again, hoping to see Angela and my secret weapon. Nothing. I'm on my own, as I've always been. This is probably why I'm where I am.

Heidi is walking over, avoiding eye contact. Even without seeing her face, I can tell she's not in the best of moods just from her walk.

Hopefully she's had a really crap customer this morning or her camera's broken or it's something, anything, other than me.

There's plenty of room on the bench but I move over as a welcoming gesture. She flashes me an ill-drawn smile with darkened eyes before sitting down and coughing a little. She doesn't look good: pale, stressed, vacant. Am I the cause? Whatever's in me, is it in her? Does the reason Heidi and I got together have more to do with mirroring than love? Dependency, not devotion. Shadows on crutches escaping the night.

'I can't offer you anything, Sheridan.'

This is typical of Heidi, dropping a softly spoken bombshell into my lap without context or preamble. I try my usual first approach at diffusing one of Heidi's heavy-handed, open-ended conversation stoppers by totally brushing it off as something banal and mundane. Sometimes it works; lately it hasn't.

I raise my sandwich. 'It's all right, I've got—'

'I don't mean the sandwich, Sheridan. I mean, I can't offer you anything in life.'

'Oh.'

'There's no point pretending, is there?' Sitting with her elbows resting on her knees clutching a bottle of water, Heidi continually twists the lid like a dial, clockwise, anti-clockwise, clockwise, anti-clockwise. We watch, waiting for it to tune us both into the same wavelength. 'We're not kids, life's too short, people never change . . .'

'Are you gonna say something original?' I don't mean to be mean. OK, I do. I can feel parts of myself disintegrating, so I pick off something sharp and throw it at her, hoping it'll pierce the small talk and hit something truthful.

'What do you want me to say, Sheridan? We're over?'

Too sharp. 'If that's what you want to say, then say it.'

'We're over.' She glances at me. I try to cushion the blow. 'We don't know each other. I don't know *you*, Sheridan. Sometimes what you do and what you say are so far removed from what I want, I wonder how we even got here in the first place.'

'*You don't know me*' – that old chestnut. A few months ago it was

5

all, '*We're so made for each other*', '*We're soul mates*', '*We're two peas in a fucking pod*', but now it's all philosophical. '*You don't know me*' as in, how can anyone know anyone else? That's what you believe now because it suits your own needs, don't try and bullshit me. Your feelings have changed, not your personality or your past, and neither have mine, so don't go turning this into something deeper than that. You've changed your mind, you don't want to deal with it and you just want to walk away. *That's* the oldest love story in the world.

I put my arm on the bench, turning around to see if anyone from my shop, Twenty20 Opticians, is looking through the display of frames, sunglasses and special offers. No. I turn back and look at the shop opposite, Candleina, Heidi's workplace, and no one there is peering through the candles, pot pourri, and aromatherapy displays either.

Now is when I'd appreciate some help, but the world has turned away. I feel insignificant – a feeling I recognise all too well. I'm out in the open, exposed to a multitude of shoppers filing past during one of the most pivotal moments in my life, no one batting an eyelid or even performing the smallest of cursory glances. The mannequins' eyes glaze over. Apparently, we're just a couple having lunch on a bench in town. Perspective is everything. Trust me, I'm an optometrist.

I look for our reflections in a shop window. It won't do any good, not for me anyway. I change tack. 'Is there someone else?'

'Christ, Sheridan! You can be an absolute prick sometimes. Am I *seeing* someone else? When, Sheridan? When have I ever had the time away from you to meet anyone since we've been together? You don't get many straight, single guys coming into Candleina.'

There're one or two things I've never been able to see, and this termination appears to be another one of them. 'Is it because I suggested moving in with each other recently? Because that's not a deal breaker for me. If you want to wait, that's fine.'

Heidi looks me in the eyes for the first time. I try to keep her there, but she knows better. I can see she's twisted the lid on too tight and can't undo it again. Heidi's heart speaks in between the beats. Her face betrays what her mouth never does.

'This isn't a hurdle for you, is it? This is an exit, a chance of escape.'

She's given up trying to loosen the lid and is just tightening it up even more. I offer her an open hand. She puts the bottle into it.

'I can't give you a definitive list of reasons, Sheridan. I can't explain every little detail. It's just the way it is. I'm sorry. Really, I am, Sheridan.'

The lid is stuck; Heidi has always been strong. Or stubborn. I'm never sure where one begins and the other ends. I give her the bottle and keep hold of the lid. Now we're probably tuned into the same wavelength.

'I never realised things were quite this bad, that your reaction would be quite so . . . final. Christ, I feel like an idiot.'

She doesn't answer, she doesn't move. Nothing.

I must be an idiot. It's amazing how the brain can fool you. Mine fools me everyday.

Are Heidi and I mirrors for each other? Reflecting the soul we can't see for ourselves? Or did love lift us from mere dependency? I need to know if we're the same or different. Heidi may have become so skilled at hiding her lack of reflection that she's able to hide it from anyone, even me. It's possible, because I've managed to hide the same condition from her.

A couple of tears tread carefully down Heidi's cheek. I hitch a ride and pull out a tissue. 'Heidi, here, make-up's running.'

'Thanks.' Heidi takes the tissue and retrieves a pocket mirror from her handbag. With the tissue pulled tightly around her finger, she starts to clean up the mess I've caused.

It's quite clear: Heidi doesn't suffer from the same disorder as I do. She can see herself. Mirrors don't manifest a mystery. I never doubted a beautiful girl such as her had the equilibrium of a beautiful soul looking back.

She's nothing like me.

'What if we took a break, Heidi? Give us some space to figure out what's going on here and find out what we both want.' My enthusiasm for this idea fades as soon as I hear it come out of my own mouth.

'No, Sheridan. I want a clean break.' Heidi sits up rigidly, talking to me but facing the street as though she's giving someone directions. She is. 'Let's not prolong it. It'll just complicate things. A clean break is good for both of us, and it gives us both clarity moving forward.' She takes my hand without looking. I'm sure it's for comfort and not to reclaim the lid.

Clarity moving forward? What self-help claptrap did she dig that up from? She turns briefly to give me an empty smile, devoid of emotion or sentiment. I see nothing in her eyes. All the chemistry that bonded us together has dissipated, all the magnetism faded. All of a sudden, she looks like a stranger.

All of a sudden, I feel like a stranger interrupting this girl's lunch break.

What more can I say? How can I fill this silence with something profound or life-changing? Just something 'mind-changing' would do me right now, but nothing comes. She's made her mind up. She's not stupid. She knows what she wants. I'm probably the stupid one – got to be. The dumb optometrist who can't see what's plainly obvious, can't see the nose in front of his face. It would be funny if it weren't true.

Who was I to think this could turn out any different? A happy ending with a beautiful, intelligent, independent young woman? Ain't going to happen, son! Not here and not today.

'Sheridan.' Heidi crouches over in pain, grimacing as she brings her chest down to her knees before straightening herself back up and taking a swig of water. 'I feel like crap, if it's any consolation.' For the first time she looks at me as though we might have met sometime in the past and exchanged a pleasant word or two. 'I'm sorry.'

'Yeah.' I'm not sure I believe her, but I acknowledge the words. I can feel the faintest spark of *hope* flickering deep in the darkness, as it does in the heart of an optimistic fool. I have to leave. 'Look, I'll have lunch somewhere else, leave you alone in peace.'

'No, Sheridan, you stay here. I've got to go.'

Heidi stands up, and for the first time I notice she hadn't really settled on the bench for lunch like she normally does – no sandwiches, no magazine, no camera. It was a planned sit-and-go meeting: work, have lunch, dump Sheridan, go back to work. No fuss.

'Goodbye, Sheridan.' She leans in to give me a pained kiss. I half-offer a cheek. '*Goodbye, Sheridan*' is a little too final for my liking.

'See you later, Heidi.'

And that's it.

I watch Heidi walk away as I grip onto the bench, resisting the gravity dragging me towards her. If she doesn't glance back for one last look, I may never see her face again.

She doesn't.

Gone, disappearing into the smoky aromas and designer colours of Candleina without a second thought. Already I'm forgotten, lying here on the bench midway through a heart transplant with my chest clamped open, waiting for the replacement as a cold breeze rattles through my ribs, reality quickly sweeping aside the anaesthetic.

A jangle of jewellery alerts me to Angela from Holidays Plus approaching. 'Hey, Sheridan! I got you that holiday in Dubai for a bargain price. They're throwing in the honeymoon suite for free too, as they've had a last-minute cancellation.'

I crank up an industrial smile, the one I reserve for humouring customers' idiotic questions. 'Thanks, Angela, sounds great. I'll come in this afternoon to sort it all out.'

'OK. I thought you said Heidi would be here?'

'Yeah, she had to leave unexpectedly. Thanks, I'll see you later.'

Get up, Sheridan, leave! Go! Anywhere will do. Junk food? No, I don't feel hungry. I couldn't eat a thing; it'll just fall out of my open chest. Just walk. Where? Follow the breeze, it sounds romantic, the sort of thing a broken-hearted poet would do. I stick my finger up, an exaggerated gesture. Empty, futile gestures are for those without hope or reason. The wind's heading east. I head east.

I try to figure out what this is all going to mean for me, the big change from being with the woman you love, who you think you're going to be with for ever, to being alone. I shuffle along the street without getting any closer to getting my head around it, but there's one thing that might've changed for the better. Maybe I'm no longer alone in here, looking out upon the universe without being able to look down at my feet? Maybe remnants of the devastation left behind are being stirred up in a tail-spin, swirling around in the darkness, slowly coalescing into a rudimentary human being, clumps of life colliding with chunks of consciousness, getting bigger and bigger, until it forms all the attributes of a fully functioning human being and achieving a mass which it can reflect upon.

To see myself for the first time at my lowest ebb would be the sweetest of all ironies. Would I ever want to look at myself again?

Sudden traumatic events can alter a person's mental or physical limitations, causing a permanent change, sometimes giving them an amazing new skill or ability. Now I'm hoping this turn of events has been significant enough to jolt my optic nerve, give my occipital lobe a kick up the arse and shake up my visual cortex a bit.

Again, my foolish heart harbours the slimmest ray of hope amongst the onslaught of a dark future. I increase my pace, hold my head up, and search out a retail outlet providing easy access to a mirror. A women's clothes shop lies just ahead. I cross the pedestrianised street towards it, straightening my back, adjusting my jacket, preparing to meet a stranger.

The shop isn't too hectic so I can easily find room in front of a mirror, but I don't want to launch straight into it, I want to savour it.

Plus I'm scared.

A full-length mirror sits on a pillar in the middle of the shop floor. Next to it is a selection of jackets. I file through some of the jackets, pretending I'm shopping for the lady in my life. Why? I don't know.

I'm scared.

I end the useless charade and sidestep in front of the mirror with my head bowed down. I see my shoes. Raising my head, I see my trousers, belt, white shirt. Then I climb the stripes on my tie upwards

10

to the collar, my neck. I can't lift my head anymore. I don't want to. I've already skipped ahead, like a reader on the last page skipping to the last paragraph. I've already seen the familiar blur just above the outline of my chin. I don't want to look up any further.

I look up.

Nothing. No face. Just a blur.

Chapter Two

ELEVEN MONTHS BEFORE TODAY

If I lie here long enough, in freeze-frame, everyone will assume I'm dead and cremate me. Sweep my remains under the carpet and forget about me as my ashes seep into the cracks of the floorboards.

Sounds relaxing.

Consciousness compels me to search out Heidi every waking minute of every stinking day. Occasionally I'll drink something, maybe eat a little, but after that it's all Heidi. My hierarchy of needs have been shuffled and reprioritised, common sense has folded, and I'm on the turn. I'm tired. I crawl around the internet on my hands and knees hoping for a glimpse of activity from Heidi – stalking Snapchat, flicking through Facebook, tracking Twitter, infiltrating Instagram, perusing Pinterest. I've also created anonymous profiles on every dating site hoping to catch her moving on with her life, which for some reason seems to be something I need to see. The problem is she may have signed up anonymously because she knows her ex might be on these sites waiting to catch her. Which I am.

Make no mistake. I am a huge loser.

It's amazing what I've discovered online about my friends, her friends, friends of friends, people I've only met once or twice, but nothing about Heidi herself. I'm not the only person who's been left in the dark and I'm not the only person who's noticed her absence, but I think I'm the only one still looking. Coming to Dubai has been good in one respect: roaming charges make me think twice before texting her mum, her friends, her sister, or anyone else.

My mobile phone used to keep us connected when we were out

of sight of each other, but now it feels like a corpse. Her life used to light it up, some of her personality was contained in its little body, it was an extension of her, but now it's a dead shell. I push the button to awaken it and her face beams back but there's nothing more. This connection is dead without her. It's just a phone.

Cutting myself off from the whole world is preferable, shutting down, unplugging, disconnecting from every possible stimulant. Retreating into a void behind closed eyes.

Like a child.

But I'm not in a void, no matter how much I try to convince myself differently, no matter how tightly I close my eyes.

Heidi's absence causes me to think of her more obsessively in order to fill that very absence. Her lack of presence gives her omnipresence. She fills my mind, invading all corners, implanting herself into memories made before I even met her. I have a clear recollection of her dropping a test tube in my school science class – when I attended an all-boys' high school and I know, actually know for sure, she was brought up in a neighbouring county and is three years younger than me. My mind has been playing tricks on me my whole life and this is just one more: constructing a past that never happened, a present that has no place in reality, and multiple futures based on the strength of those foundations.

Heidi is gone, yet it feels like I'm in the centre of her world.

'Sherry.'

Please let that be a euthanasia doctor at my bedside . . .

'Sherry?'

Or the Grim Reaper to escort me from whatever world I'm in to the next . . .

'Sherry!'

A bright light, intense heat! Yes . . .

'Come out from under that parasol, Sherry, my son. There's birds aplenty round the pool!'

Mike. Best friend, confidant, and romantic-break substitute. There I was thinking I'll be an astute, modern consumer and skip the cancellation insurance to save money, only to be foiled by that

13

age-old adversary: fate. Mike insisted I go and that, since he was such a good friend, he'd be there to support me. In Dubai. In a five-star hotel. In one of the honeymoon suites.

'Come on, mate.' Mike sits on my sun lounger, cradling his fourth cocktail of the day. It's 11 a.m. 'I'll rub suntan lotion on your back.'

'I don't think that would be a good idea. One of the managers is over there.'

Two men checking into a honeymoon suite doesn't sit well, even in fairly liberal Dubai. Sharing a 'Texas King'-sized bed with Mike doesn't sit well with me either, to be fair, so the diplomatic outcome was a standard single room each with the money left over stuck on the bar tab. Mike's been drinking elaborately decorated cocktails ever since.

'Forget about him, Sherry, our love is real.' Mike places a hand on my knee. The duty manager halts his aimless strolling, sensing an extreme act of Western liberalism, and looks our way.

'Leave it out, Mike, you'll get us deported.'

'Ha, ha, ha, you need to lighten up, man.' Mike downs the rest of his cocktail, nearly choking on a flower. 'Come on, I've been doing some reconnaissance and I've got a shortlist of bikini-clad babes who don't appear to have any significant others. How about we grab some drinks, find the non-Brits so our stories sound fresh, engage in some initial *entente cordiale*, then do our civic duty of extending our hands in peaceful, diplomatic, sexual friendship?'

Mike smiles, a bright red petal stuck to his teeth.

Going on holiday has been the worst idea possible. Nothing to do with Mike, in fact – he regularly reaches into my melancholia and pulls me back into reality. Albeit *his* reality, but a reality nonetheless. The problem is, I want to seep into the cracked floorboards of Heidi's world.

'No. I'm going down to the beach for a swim.' I get off the sun lounger and slip into my flip-flops.

'Great, I'll come with you.'

'No.'

14

'Great! I'll get us some drinks, keep an eye on the ladies and prepare for your return.'

'No.'

'Great, I'll stay here and completely ignore you until it's time to go back to the airport in three days.'

'Great.' I head to the beach.

As I reach the other side of the swimming pool and am just about to open the gate to a sandy path leading down to the beach, Mike calls out, effeminately, 'Don't be long, honey!'

Please God, Allah, whoever, kick us out of this country so I can go back to my own bed.

I say Mike is a 'confidant', I've never told him about my condition. I've never told anyone though, so that's more of a reflection on me than him. Although, whenever I get close to thinking I might tell him, share the load and confide, he opens his big mouth. If I fully understood my secret then it would be easier to share, instead it feels like a shameful failing than a nugget of information. I have no family so this secret has been part of me for as long as I can remember, maybe that's why I never told Heidi either. If I revealed it, I'd lose a part of me.

The water of the Persian Gulf is only about a ten-minute walk away from the poolside. The horizon is a Rothko in blue, the infinite sky upon the ancient sea. Behind me, Bedouin tents have been crushed by a steel-storm of skyscrapers marching into the sea. Wigthorn this is not. This, a city embracing change, arming itself for the future, exploiting what it has today to rebuild for tomorrow; the other, a seaside town attempting to reignite its fire with damp driftwood. One trying to tame the fantasies of a monarch; the other trying to create dreams from democratic bureaucracy. Progress really is in the eye of the beholder.

Heidi would've loved it here – the colours, the rich mix of cultures, the architecture, the light, the futurism contrasting with the traditional, capitalism competing with religion for devotees. Her face would've been stuck behind that camera for the whole five days, a technological niqab from which to view this city.

I step out of my flip-flops and leave them on the sand. I don't care if they get nicked. What a difference sand makes to a beach! My heart almost pings out one beat of joy at the mere touch of its warmth and grainy softness. So much sand here amidst so much construction. They can't build these fantastical structures on sand. Where do they get their hardcore from? Can't the Dubai construction industry ship some oil tankers filled with sand to Wigthorn in exchange for all of our bone-crunching, skin-shredding pebbles? We could also exchange a caravan of camels for all of our giant, cafe-invading, ice-cream-eating seagulls.

A woman is sitting on a small stool on the water's edge in a full burqa, bending down to splash her two children playing in the water. An understanding barges its way through the Heidi traffic jam in my mind. A burqa allows the wearer to interact with the world without the world interacting back. Sounds perfect. I nod to the mother, hoping I can steer this gem of empathy across the Arabian breeze. She averts her eyes. Maybe she's wishing she could swap it for a swim-suit and jump in with the kids.

The water's warm, calm and clear. I walk until the waves gently break against my knees. I rarely go beyond this point as I can't swim, which is a sacrilegious statement to make in this day and age, I know. Maybe now is the time to try. Just keep on walking. I don't care what happens. The further I get away from civilisation, the better. I need to de-evolve, shed these limbs and re-grow fins, recede back into the water. Sorry, land, it was all a big mistake. Let's accept our differences and move on.

I march into the Persian Gulf, relinquishing my position at the top of the land-based food chain to become a non-swimming, air-breathing, flailing piece of prey, lower than plankton. I could be eaten before I'm over my head. Would that pull Heidi out from the shadows? Would she attend my funeral, for what the shallows left behind? Torture herself with what-ifs? Might her final words be 'If only I gave him some swimming lessons before I ruthlessly dumped him' before crying herself to sleep?

I don't want to die. Maybe I'd be willing to sacrifice a leg, an aperitif for a great white shark. I could still work in optometry supported by a prosthetic, but the whole traumatic story would probably make the papers back home. Who am I kidding? I don't even want to lose a leg. Maybe I'd save one of those kids from a shark . . . in shallow water. A great white so hell-bent on eating children it was willing to risk grounding itself in shallow waters to devour one. I'd be a hero both here and back home, entente cordial indeed. I'd land at Heathrow to a hero's welcome – banners draped over the terminal, a welcome party waiting to greet me as I descended the steps from the plane. The tabloid press could track down Heidi in an instance, phone-hack their way to her front door and bring her to mine for the ultimate love story, 'Shark Hero Optometrist Sees Love Again'.

Who am I kidding? They'd call me an optician.

Heidi never explicitly said, '*I want to be with you*'. I assumed everything we'd been through meant the same thing, though. It doesn't. '*I love you*' doesn't mean as much as you might think. It promises a great deal but delivers very little. It's a verbal pat on the back. Why would anyone gamble away their life on words? '*I love you*' is not a foundation; it's a hole in the ground.

Love let me down.

Arrrggghhh! What the fuck was that?

Just above the sand, in the clarity of the water, a school of tiny fish rhythmically dance through my legs. My focus readjusts and a sun-kissed silhouette of myself dances upon the water's surface, a smashed mirror on the tide. The focus of my immediate future needs to readjust as well. Heidi is gone; my reflection is still a blur – why?

I can't see my own face. This isn't a metaphor, an analogy, simile or a physical deficiency; it's true and has always been so. I cannot see my own face. I can see only the outer reaches: ears, upper forehead and the lower part of my chin. To me, my face is a blur framed by a hollowed out head.

I cannot see if I've got icing sugar on my top lip after eating a doughnut. I cannot see if my eyebrows are getting too bushy and wild. I cannot see if an errant nose hair has unravelled itself and is hanging out of my hooter like a jungle vine. I cannot see if a shaving cut has completely healed or when a spot appears one morning. I don't know what my confused face looks like, nor my face of aggression, shock, quizzicalness, happiness, embarrassment, apathy, or just after a school of tiny fish have rhythmically swam through my legs, scaring the living crap out of me.

I lack the ability to use a mirror as a doorway into the inner dimensions of my mind to search for meaning and self-discovery. There is no reflection of myself to reflect upon. A mirror may as well be a wall. The windows into my soul have been boarded up.

Imagine not being able to look into your own eyes or understand your own face. Imagine not being able to witness those moments of private introspection, when pure thoughts mould your face, the mirror translating and transcribing your innermost contemplations.

Now imagine not being able to see your reflection, your own image, via any medium: mirror, photograph, illustration, video, wood carving, or painting.

Inner beauty and all that crap is true to a point, but how much of your own identity is built upon your own face? Are scars not judged? Is beauty not discriminatory, both positively and negatively? Are personalities not constructed from interactions? Are interactions not initiated upon aesthetics from time to time?

Everyone knows roughly how 'attractive' they are, constantly assessing themselves against others. Upon entering a room of strangers, a person will immediately infer their own place within the hierarchy based on properties that can only be physical at that point. Of course, they'll probably place themselves in the wrong position, but imagine not even being able to do that. Only being able to picture yourself as others have described you – a portrait painted in words, written by other people.

I became an optometrist (not an optician, look it up) so I could look into the eyes of other people because I can't look into my own. It's that simple. You don't need to be a therapist to work out where I'm coming from here. I ain't a freak though, don't get me wrong. I'm not locking clients' faces into some kind of head clamp, supergluing their eyes open as I intensely stare into them hoping for self-discovery and reflection by proxy.

OK. I do look into them hoping for self-discovery and reflection by proxy, but I haven't got a head clamp and my rapport with customers is excellent.

One of the pockets of my shorts vibrates. Mike's FaceTiming me.

'Hello?'

'Where are you?'

'In the sea.'

'What are you doing in there? You can't swim.'

'I know.'

Mike raises a cocktail filled with a small rainforest.

'I've got another one of these with your name on it, plus a couple of surprises waiting for you back at base.' Mike turns back to face the hotel swimming pool. I look back out across the sea. A silence sails across the space between us. 'There's nothing out there for you, mate.'

'I know. I'll be back in a minute.'

I look at my phone, this extension of Heidi, this window into a virtual, unreal world, this claw that won't let go . . . and I let go. I throw the phone into the sea, wait for it to sink, and head back to shore – a little quicker than before, as the little fish appear to have stopped dancing and are now nibbling my toes. As I walk out of the sea, the mother meets my eyes and returns the previously ignored nod.

I shuffle into my flip-flops and head back to the pool. Mike is sat on a sun lounger with a couple of pretty, barely clothed, tanned surprises either side of him. I stand on the edge of the pool and look down, my reflection broken by the ripples and cracked by the sunlight. Am I trying to find a shipwreck hiding treasure or filled with skeletons?

Someone far smarter than me, with a name far more unpronounceable than mine, said '*the face is the soul of the body*'. Does that mean I have no soul? How can someone love anyone without a soul? How has my soul shaped my face? Has my soul deformed my face so badly that my brain fails to register it for my own safety?

These are the answers I should be searching for, not Heidi. I need to focus on myself, literally.

'Sherry!' Mike stands, passing me a cocktail. 'Sherry, meet Natalya and Tatyana, two of St. Petersburg's most beautiful daughters. I call 'em Nats and Tats.'

Of course he does. 'Hi, Natalya and Tatyana.' I hold a hand out and they both pull me in for a kiss on each cheek.

'Shezza, we're on the continent, don't be so English.'

'Dubai, but yes, we're on *a* continent.'

'Nats was just telling me about this nightclub, sounds amazing.'

I'm thirty-five years of age. No nightclub sounds amazing to me at this point in my life. 'I'm off to check out the souks later on today.'

Natalya's eyes light up. 'Buy gold, yes?'

'No, mirrors actually. Apparently there're some unusual ones around the—'

'Oh, jeez.' Mike performs the universal finger spin around the ear for '*crazy*'. 'This man just can't get enough of himself, always getting portraits and mirrors and stuff. Loves himself, he does.'

'Very handsome man.'

Thanks, Tatyana.

'We come, yes?' asks Natalya.

No. Please, this is a personal odyssey of discovery, a search into the self that you couldn't possibly understand. It's more fundamental than the question of who I am; it's the question '*what do I look like?*' I need to face this alone.

'Come on, Sherry, don't be so English.'

I soon demonstrate how English I am by crumbling in the face of public awkwardness. 'Yeah, sure, let's all go.'

Chapter Three

TEN MONTHS BEFORE TODAY

Beep.

A text message.

'Jesus Christ, Sheridan! Can you put your bloody phone down for two minutes?!'

Mike's asked me round to his flat because he's organised a surprise. I've been on edge ever since. I check my phone. 'It's Heidi's sister, Gemma. She hasn't seen Heidi either. Nor does she know where she is, what she's doing, where she's going, what led up to this, if I'd done anything wrong, said anything wrong or anything whatsoever at all.'

'She said all that? I thought she didn't talk much?'

'Well, she texted "*Fuck off Sheridan, you fucking loser*", so I think that covers all bases.'

'Is she single? I always liked her candidness. You know what my old man always used to say? "*Hold on tight to a girl with a loose tongue.*"'

'Remind me, what did he die of again?'

'Syphilis in extremis. Coffee?'

'Go on then.'

This visit to Mike's flat is meant to be social, but I arrived begrudgingly and I shall exit even more begrudgingly to put him off asking me again. Over the past few weeks, our Dubai tans have faded along with the promise I made myself of focusing on finding my own reflection and not finding Heidi. I've been lost in social networks, text messaging, phone calls, looking through photos, driving to old haunts, walking down well-trodden paths, all with

21

the aim of finding out what has happened to Heidi. All from the safety of my laptop, on my sofa in my darkened flat.

Heidi's not dead. Her mum and sister have told me that much. It was meant to put my mind at rest, but it hasn't. It means she left for a solid, bona fide reason. She wasn't snatched from me; she left willingly.

Disposing of my phone lasted all of about five days. What I didn't think about was the wonder of modern technology and 'the cloud'. As soon as I got a new phone with my existing number and logged in, all my photos and text messages magically resurrected themselves from their digital purgatory. Apparently we live in a disposable culture. Well, I want to live in a deletable culture. I performed a factory reset on my phone. Unfortunately, 'life' doesn't allow for such a clean break.

I'm slouched on Mike's sofa, devoid of poise or emotion, a bag of cement dropped into a sandpit, focusing on the patterns of the lounge carpet and hoping their wavy lines will weave their way through the worn-out patches and wine stains and onto a hand-stitched master plan. 'So, what's this surprise you've got me then? I can't sit around here for ever, I've got shit to do.'

'No you haven't.' He's *clanking* around in the kitchen, every scrape, bang, and slammed cupboard door grating against my impatience. I can't afford to lose anything more; this last layer of self-pity is all I've got. 'You've got the week off, and I know for a fact you've got nothing else planned other than sitting on that bloody computer all day waiting for a sign from Heidi. It ain't going to come. She went batshit crazy and fucked off. Good riddance, mate.'

'Shut up, Mike.' I know he doesn't mean any malice, he's just trying to make me feel better, but it does make me think. Maybe it is good riddance. I hope not, otherwise I'm wasting my time searching for her. Maybe it is a waste of time and I just need '*closure*'. Christ, now I'm quoting self-help claptrap. 'I've got an appointment later, so I can't sit here and listen to your bullshit all day.'

'OK, OK, Mr Busy, just sit tight. Your surprise will be here any minute.'

'It's a person?' Unwanted thoughts flash through my mind in a nanosecond.

Ding-dong!

'. . . and here she is.'

'She? If it's a stripper or someone like that, I'm leaving.'

'Jesus Christ, Sherry! Have some faith in your old mucker.'

My faith in my old mucker doesn't extend very far. He's shoddy, dishevelled, cuts corners, slapdash, make do . . . I mean, check out the coffee he's just left me. There's a touch of an old coffee stain on the rim and bits of undissolved instant coffee floating on top. Subtlety and sophistication are not terms of endearment you could accuse dear old Mike of possessing.

Mike and I have been friends ever since meeting for the first time at City University in London when we were placed next door to each other in halls, which was pretty remarkable since we both came from Wigthorn. We'd never met before, as we grew up on different sides of town, went to different schools and colleges, and never crossed paths upon the fields of sporting or academic competition since we both couldn't be arsed with that sort of thing. Our friendship grew from a rich dedication to drinking cheap beer, chasing unobtainable girls, and frantically helping each other out on assignments the night before they were due in. A lot of Mike's journalism assignments were eye-related due to him pinching the latest research ideas from my magazines, and in return, his eyes were more regularly tested than a fighter pilot's. I haven't tested them since. He claims he doesn't need it; he has an editor.

Mike returns to the lounge. 'This is Sergeant Malloy.'

A 'policewoman' follows.

'Oh shut up, Mike!' I get up from the crumb-infested sofa. A long-lost coin can be heard falling onto a long expired spring. 'I told you, I ain't in the mood for a bloody stripper.'

'No, no, no!' With Mike, you don't listen to him, you watch him. The way his face suddenly dropped and the speed in which he sidled up to me suggests there maybe a slim slice of truth somewhere to be found in this gigantic gateau of falsehoods. 'Seriously, Sheridan, this is *Sergeant* Malloy, from the Wigthorn Constabulary. A proper, bona fide officer of the law.'

Mike steps aside.

Hmmm . . . Her uniform is a little *too* authentic. Her face a little too plain for enticing punters. Her body a little too robust for straddling tied-up grooms and more suited to restraining drunken street fighters. The accessories on that belt look a little too useful and not one comedy vibrator or oversized dildo in sight.

'Mr Maddox, would you like to see my ID?'

I smile at the officer. 'I'm so sorry, Sergeant, Mike and the truth are not commonly acquainted.'

'I know what you mean.'

'Sergeant Malloy, can I call you Sue while in uniform?' Sue nods at Mike. I've never seen him so deferential. 'Sue's in the pub darts team. We got talking and she's offered to help you.'

'What? Find Heidi?'

'No. Put together a photofit of your own face.'

Sue places a laptop on the coffee table and tries to find a comfortable position on the sofa opposite. 'A strange request, not one me or the others have ever heard of before, but Mike said it might cheer you up and I could do with the practice as they've just updated the software.'

'And you lost a bet,' Mike replies.

'True. Mike got two lucky triple twenties and nailed the double sixteen. First time he's beaten me in months.'

Mike rarely gets one over on me, but when he does he lets me know with the dumbest grin. 'What do you think, old fella?' he says.

'I'm speechless.' It's true, I am. Mike has actually found a form of self-portrait I'd never considered before. A police photofit. An amalgamation of computer-generated facial attributes. Maybe this hybrid of foreign features will fool my brain into thinking it's seeing more than one person or something.

The search for my reflection has taken over my free time. It's become a channel to funnel my frustrations into, a sewer to flush my heartbreak down. I need to see what Heidi ran away from, see what my eyes are too scared to face up to. God! It sounds crap, doesn't it? Pathetic. I'm not even blind. If I were blind, it would be a touching, hopelessly brave pursuit, almost certainly destined to fail but noble nonetheless.

This is just a sad compulsion by an incapable fool. Knowing this doesn't shame my enquiring mind into ending its futile journey though. Conversely, Heidi's departure has only served to fuel its descent with more vigour.

Everyone needs a hobby, right? For the heartbroken, any hobby not involving their ex has to be good, so I'm looking for my face. It's a secret, though. I don't go telling people I'm looking for my face – I'd sound insane. I lack a sensory self-perception, not total self-awareness.

'Yeah, Sheridan is a bit of a narcissistic freak. He can't get enough images of himself.'

What Mike gives with one hand, he takes away with the other.

'I'm sure he has a simple explanation, Mike.' Sue opens up her laptop.

'Yes, Officer Sue, I do.' I've never been able to think of a single coherent explanation for my dilemma and the search for an accurate self-portrait. This is why I keep it a secret. Revealing the truth would be such a blow to my image as a sane, intelligent professional. Yes, my sense of self is exaggerated as a result of my lack of reflection, like a blind person with exceptional senses of smell and touch.

I try a variation of the old 'art project' explanation. Art nowadays is as much about bullshit as the stroke of a brush. 'It's an ongoing art project type of thing, blending in with my work as an optometrist. I'm interested in seeing if the wide variety of ways in which we can represent our self-image has any relation or influence on how our eyes perceive ourselves and the world around us. Do we see only one true image or rationalise a cornucopia of images into one image we can easily understand?'

Please buy it and don't ask any more questions!

'You see, Mike?' Sergeant Malloy looks up from her laptop.

Mike's deference fades. 'Huh? I didn't understand a friggin' word of that.'

I can't fault his logic.

I swiftly change subject. 'So, let's get this thing going. What's the best way of doing this?'

'Well, you aren't the best judge of what you look like . . .'

'I can't argue with you on that point, Sergeant.'

'. . . so you just sit over there whilst Mike and I construct your photofit.'

Mike plants himself next to Sue. 'Can we give him an eye patch and a handlebar moustache?'

I sit there looking at both of them whilst they debate the shape of my nose, compare lips, discuss my jawline, eyebrows, eye colour, etc. Unexpectedly, hearing this discussion about my face is more illuminating than any portrait. I should try to find non-visual portraits such as discussions like these or a written description like a radio broadcast or a news report so I can build up an image in my mind.

I should be recording this. I pull out my phone, open up the sound recording app, and press *record*.

Mike notices. 'Can you add a phone to this image because I've never seen Sherry without it.'

Who else could I get to describe my face? Who are professional 'describers'? A romantic novelist describing their hero? A sports journalist describing the attributes of a prize-fighter? How does a blind person understand someone's face without touching it? I should talk to a blind person. I have done before, surreptitiously. I was too concerned I'd sound like a nutter and never told them my full story, therefore I sounded like even more of a nutter and soon gave up. My ambition is greater now, my need more demanding.

After ten more minutes of discussion they finally come to a consensus: I have been photofitted. I should probably refrain from committing any crimes and going on the run, because a rather accurate representation has apparently been rendered and is currently being uploaded to the national database.

26

I summon up some positive vibes. 'Let's have a look, then.'

Sue spins round the laptop. Mike reclines on the sofa as though he's painted it himself. 'We've made you better looking than in real life.'

I lean forward and examine the image on the screen.

A blur. I can't see a thing. It must be my doppelgänger. 'Wow! It's uncanny, like looking in the mirror.'

'This new software has so many more options and an easier interface, which really helps put together a more accurate and realistic photo.' Sergeant Sue wants to sell me a copy. 'Some of the old ones we used to get were a joke and hindered more than helped.'

'Can you print me out a copy?'

'I'll email it to you, then you can do what you want with it.'

'Perfect, thanks. Here, I'll write down my email address for you.' Whilst I fish around in the drawers of Mike's coffee table looking for a pen and paper, I suddenly realise I've got an officer of the law here right in front of me, someone experienced in looking for people; how would she go about finding Heidi?

Then I remember: I've given up. Stop.

I hand her my email address scribbled on an old betting slip. I also take a punt of my own. 'Sergeant, has Mike told you about my girl-friend walking out on me?'

'He's mentioned it.'

She can sense what's coming next, like someone asking a doctor friend '*I have a slight pain in my knee, do you . . .?*' or a friend in IT '*My computer seems to have slowed down, can you . . .?*'.

'Do you have any idea how I might get in contact with her? I'm not a crazy stalker or anything . . .'

'That's what they all say.' Thanks, Mike.

'I just want to know if she's OK, you know, get some "closure".'

'She hasn't been reported missing, has she?'

'No. Her mum and sister have heard from her, but they're not telling me anything.'

'You've tried contacting her on Facebook, phone, text, Skype, and all that lot?'

'Yes. Nothing gets a response. It's weird because some of her accounts are either deleted or haven't had any activity since she disappeared. It's all a bit drastic and over the top, like she's hiding from an assassin or a violent ex-boyfriend.' I see Mike squinting at me. 'I'm neither, by the way,' I say before Mike can stitch me up any further.

'Yes, it does sound a little too . . . complete. Obviously she's got her reasons, but she doesn't want to tell you. If you feel you've done nothing wrong and you aren't deluding yourself, then I'd say she's protecting you from something.'

'What do you mean? There's nothing dangerous in our lives. I'm an optometrist and she worked in a candle shop. We were Plain Jane and Simple Simon.'

'I'm only going by what you've told me. She hasn't just cut you off; she's cut herself off. She's taking the danger elsewhere. I know it sounds ridiculous, but you'd be surprised the secrets people keep from each other, no matter how close they think they are. Mostly it's to protect the other person from knowing too much and spoiling their own image. Can you look yourself in the mirror and honestly say you've told her everything about yourself?'

Sergeant Sue is good. 'No, I suppose not.'

'And is that because you're a malicious liar or because you didn't want her to see a side of you that may harm that idealised image of yourself you like to project?'

'She's good, right?!'

Yes, Mike. I've already thought that.

'You could be on to something here, Sarge.' I've always wanted to say 'Sarge'. 'So, what should my next step be?'

'The family are blanking you. Friends?'

'Her closest ones are blanking me. The others haven't heard from her either.'

'What about her workmates at this candle shop?'

'Heidi wasn't particularly close to her work colleagues, except Chloe, but I've collared her a few times in town and she doesn't say much.'

'I'd try confronting her head on and having a proper conversation, not just stolen snippets as you queue for lunch. Her work colleagues would be with her for eight hours a day, five days a week. I would be surprised if she could hide everything in her private life under that level of scrutiny.'

'True.' I know *I* can't. 'Good point. So I should try and talk to Chloe in more depth?'

'Yes.'

'OK.'

Bollocks.

A new day brings with it nothing in particular. I look at the photofit on my tablet, adjusting the angle and light in an attempt to catch a brief reflection of my true self, but no angle or light wave exists to communicate such horrific information.

I ponder Sergeant Malloy's advice as I stand on the precipice of total disintegration. She's added fuel to my hopefulness, intensified the light, fired up the attraction. I'm just a moth caught in the turbulence, fanning the flames the more I flap my wings trying to escape. If I stop, I fall. I keep flapping. I flap harder. I'm tired.

Some tunnels don't have lights at the end of them. Some lights are actually fires.

I want to walk away, but I can't until I've exhausted every possible solution. It's my day off. I've got nothing else planned. Let's go exhaust some solutions.

I pull the visor of my baseball cap further down to shield my face as I enter the pedestrianised high street of Wigthorn, heading for Candleina. The shop lies directly opposite my own place of employment, Twenty20, so it's imperative I avoid being spotted and becoming the subject of gossip for the next few weeks. I walk through the doors and a warm rush of air blows down onto my cap before a riotous crowd of odours vandalise my senses.

'Sherry! Where you been, my love?'

Crap, the shop's empty and the staff are obviously bored, milling around what looks like a dentist's chair. Chloe has been made the new assistant manager since Heidi left and this extra power has added to her already overly friendly *'what-can-you-do-for-me'* manner. 'Hi, Chloe, how's business?'

'I know it doesn't look like it now, but it's pretty good. Here, come over and sit yourself down.'

'No, I'm fine—'

'That's right, just here.' She grabs my elbow and leads me onto the chair. I have no choice – I'm now plonked on the chair, staring at myself in front of a full-length mirror. Well, staring at the outline of my head. 'Ashia, your next client is here, a bloke!'

This catches everyone else's attention, not just Ashia's. Chloe steps on a pedal and the chair flips back 45 degrees and I'm staring at the ceiling.

'We're trialling a new service, Sherry. I had a brainwave last week while watching a documentary called something like *Techniques of Guantanamo Bay* . . . whatever. I'm sure you, a fellow retailer, appreciate the need for as many revenue streams as possible? Diversification and all that jazz.'

As I'm lying there looking at the strip lighting, allowing my sense of smell to vacuum up the scents of vanilla, herbs, flowers, and essential oils, I wonder why I'm sitting in a chair in a candle shop.

'I bet you're wondering why you're sitting in a chair in a candle shop, Sherry.'

'It had crossed my mind.'

'This new service is to compliment our current offerings, allowing us to cross over into the highly lucrative market of self-administered beauty treatments. You've heard of waxing. Well, where does wax come from? Exactly, candles. So I want to gain a sampling of customer feedback to present to HQ showing how our candles could potentially produce wax that not only removes hair but also moisturises and exfoliates the skin too, leaving it smooth and smelling gorgeous. And if our current products don't moisturise or exfoliate, then the boffins up at HQ can invent something. Amazing, huh?!'

'Self-administered?'

'Don't worry, Sherry, we're going to do it for you.'

30

And yet I'm still agitated and alarmed.

'I take it HQ knows about this. It's been risk assessed, safety measures have been put in place . . .'

'Ha, ha, don't be so nervous, Sherry! Relax, close your eyes.'

I hear a few packets being opened as well as the milling about and congregating of a few staff. I'm guessing not many guinea pigs have been as easily persuaded as I, and of those who were, none were men. Smooth and gorgeous-smelling skin is not really a top priority for blokes. Not this one, anyway. 'Seriously, Chloe, I'll pop back later. I just wanted to see if any of you guys had seen Heidi?'

'Lie back, and we'll tell you all about her.'

'You've seen her?'

'Are you going to play ball, Mr Optician?'

'Mr Optometrist. Yes, OK.'

'Good. Ashia! Get to work on Sherry's face. I think eyebrows, sideburns, and hairline could all do with some work.'

'Nothing drastic, Ashia, please! Subtlety is the name of the game here.' I snatch a quick look at Ashia's hands as she prepares whatever it is she's preparing. I fear they're too ham-fisted and lumbering for subtlety. 'Been doing this long, Ashia?'

'No, got sacked from my forklift driver's job last week.'

'So anyway, Sherry, you want to know about Heidi?' Chloe manoeuvres over to the other side of the chair, successfully drawing my eyeline and attention away from the one-woman pit stop crew around my face.

'Yeah, what do you – owww! Shit!'

'That's just the wax, Sherry. It'll cool down in a minute. So Heidi, have you spoken to her?'

'That's what I was going to ask you.'

'You *haven't* spoken to her then?'

'No.'

'Nothing at all? She hasn't told you anything since she left?'

'No, nothing. What do you know, Chloe?'

'Nothing. I just can't believe she would've disappeared like that without telling you anything. She needs to take a long, hard look in the mirror, there's other people's lives to consider, not just hers. You wait, next time I see her I'll let her have it.'

Why did I think Heidi would be any more open to her friends and work colleagues than me? Of course she didn't let on about anything else in her life. You could trust her with any secret no matter how embarrassing or juicy. She wouldn't go around exchanging gossip for gossip, exploiting problems in her life to gain morsels of problems in the lives of others. She didn't trade in emotions; she banked them, offering interest and keeping them safe.

As the wax was being spread across specific areas around my face, I continued to probe. 'She may not have told you anything, but she must have given something away, in her reactions, phone calls, days off, moods?'

Chloe considered her answer. 'I don't think so.'

I don't know if it's a side effect of my condition, but I become totally immersed in every movement and expression on someone's face as they talk to me. I can understand a whole conversation even if the words are muted and the lips hidden. I can hear the words Chloe is saying, but I saw a lie flash across her face.

Now, the trick is to scout out what the lie was about. Is it that she *has* heard from Heidi since she left or that she didn't expect Heidi to leave? People often take a false step at this point. They can smell a lie and so they push it, they give away the very advantage they've just gained: the knowledge of the lie.

Out of the corner of my eye, I see the forklift driver extend a strip of material between her hands. She rests it gently against my cheek.

'Ashia's just going to shape your sideburns for you. It won't hurt a bit, Sherry.'

If it isn't going to hurt then why mention it?

'Owww!'

'Don't be such a baby, Sherry!' Chloe leans over me and assesses Ashia's work. 'Very good. Now I think the eyebrows could do with some work.'

I don't want to leave empty-handed, especially not after this ordeal, so I probe further as hot wax is applied around my eyebrows.

'Heidi must have handed in her notice, left a forwarding address, that kind of thing?'

'You know all that stuff's private, Sherry, but she did hand in her month's notice, worked two weeks, then took the last two weeks off as holiday.'

My heart sinks.

'Oh, you didn't know she'd handed in her notice? You mean to say the Wigthorn Retail Grapevine didn't deliver you this news? Temporary zero-hour contracts have a lot to answer for.'

The realisation that at least two weeks of pre-planning had gone into her disappearance only serves to submerge my self-esteem even further. What kind of hell must I have subjected her to in order for her to have to plan her way out? I can't see what I look like, but I always thought I knew who I was. The only mirror for an internal reflection is how other people react to you, and I've always thought people reacted to me well: with respect, humour, affection and sincerity. Now, the person I was closest to, the love of my life, has had to plan an escape route from me.

Perhaps the most surprising fact is not that Heidi left, but that she stayed for so long.

I continue the questions. 'So you've heard nothing from her since the day she left work for the last time?'

'Nothing, I'm afraid, not a dicky bird.'

As I deliver the question, I focus on Chloe completely but there's no deception, only truth. Chloe must be hiding something about the reason *why* Heidi left.

'Did she mention me at all? You know, in a negative way or anything?'

'Not really. Nothing out of the ordinary anyway. Just stuff like *"Meeting up with Sheridan to have dinner"* – that sort of thing.' Chloe changes her stance and tone. 'Look, are you sure you were straight with her? My friend wouldn't have just disappeared for no reason.'

'What's the reason, then?'

'Flipping heck, you two are as bad as each other at avoiding answering bloody questions.'

I feel a strip go across my whole eyebrow. I shut my eyes and prepare for the reaction I'm going to get from my mates and work colleagues when they see my eyebrows have been 'shaped'.

'Owwww! Shiiiiiiiit!'

'Jesus! You all right, Sherry?' Chloe is bending over me, assessing my eyebrow. Her expression doesn't fill me with confidence. 'Move your hand away.'

I reluctantly allow her a quick look. 'Everything OK?'

'Err . . . yeah. Your eye is still in there.' A nervous smile unnerves me. 'Here, have a look. It's not too bad. Streamlined. It gives you a more aerodynamic look, doesn't it, guys? Ashia, get a tissue.' I can see she's fishing for a few supportive compliments from the other staff as she lifts up a hand mirror in front of me.

I move my hand to feign looking in the mirror before noticing there's spots of blood on my palm. I feel the eyebrow with my fingertips. It's too smooth. Like, *way* too smooth. Just like hairless skin. My fingertips now have blood on them too. 'Jesus! Is my eyebrow completely gone?'

'It's fine, Sherry, it'll grow back soon. It looks worse than it is.'

'That's not the point. "*Shape it*" you said, not completely remove it!'

'Do you want me to remove the other one?' asks Ashia.

'No, I think you better stick to forklifts.'

I'm going. This lot aren't helping me. In fact, they've made me look a complete idiot. One missing eyebrow isn't a good look, even I know that.

'Sherry! Don't go. We can thin the other one out, add some eyeliner . . .'

'Eyeliner? At no point in my life is *eyeliner* gonna be a viable solution. You've done enough, Chloe. Just let me know if Heidi gets in touch. Goodbye.'

Was the sacrifice of one eyebrow worth the information I gathered? I don't know her whereabouts, but I do know this wasn't a spontaneous act. She planned it. Why? She seems to have acted as though she was caged under an oppressive regime, and yet I'm 99%

34

sure I wasn't like that. If I were so tyrannical, surely people wouldn't speak to me, let alone express a level of sympathy. If I were a wife beater with amnesia, I'd sense it in other people's reactions, wouldn't I? People don't keep quiet about that, do they? Heidi's sister does hate me, but that's it. I'm pretty sure she hates most people and probably life itself. My friends would say something to me, wouldn't they? What if they wouldn't? No, no, no, I'd know. I'd know if I were a wife-beating twat, wouldn't I?!

Although, twats and dickheads seem to sail through life oblivious to their own twattishness and dickheadedness, don't they.

No, I'm a good guy. I don't need a mirror to see that.

Oh shit. Mike is approaching.

'Shezza!'

I hate it when he calls me Shezza, especially in public. Of course, that's why he does it. And I can never mention it because . . . you know the score . . . we've all been kids . . .

I keep my face directed towards a shop window. 'All right?'

'Yeah. Why are you looking at women's clothes? You got another bird already?'

'No.' I overcook my forthrightness and turn my head.

'Holy shit! What happened to you? You looked in a mirror lately?'

'No.'

'Good, don't bother.'

I straighten my jacket. 'Are you ready?'

'Yeah, let's do this shit.'

'Well, holy fucking shit! If it isn't the optician nerd and his homosexual girlfriend!'

My back's against the wall. I've exhausted all options except one. I *have* to step into the lion's den, and it isn't going to be pretty. I'm probably going to get nothing except a torrent of abuse, but I *have* to tick this box. I have to explore every possible avenue. I have to visit Heidi's ex-boyfriend, Gary.

Mike insisted on coming along with me and, to be honest, I could do with some backup. '"Homosexual girlfriend"? How does that even work? I'm a girl who's a lesbian, or I'm gay but I'm transgendered, or . . .'

When talking with someone like Gary, you have to adopt playground rules, and Mike loves going back to the playground just as much as Gary loves living there.

I play teacher. 'Mike, go and look for a new flat. Gary, I just want a word.'

Mike puts in a cheeky offer as he passes Gary's desk towards a display of properties. 'Fucking bellend.'

Gary is an estate agent. I've no idea where he lives, so visiting his work is the only option. Anywhere outside the relative civility of work and he may not want to just talk, although the way he's suddenly risen to his feet, arms spread, inviting the whole office to watch on (and they do), it may not be that kind of office where physical violence is strictly an off-limits activity.

'Sheryl, sit yourself down here. What are you and your boyfriend after? A one-bedroom flat, large bath, mirrored ceilings, uphill garden, dungeon?'

'It's Sheridan.' I remain standing. 'Have you heard anything from Heidi?'

'What? You lost her?'

I'm nervous. Not because of what he might do to me, but what I might do to him. I may not emerge from any scuffle or fight with any self-respect or anything approaching a moral victory but the opening and shutting of his mouth is stirring up something deep. I'm talking the ancestral, Neanderthal survival instincts required when cornered by a sabre-toothed tiger. As a kid, I sometimes got my lunch money stolen in the playground. Fighting back never seemed worth it; this does.

Gary playfully opens some drawers and looks behind a plant. 'I ain't got her here, mate. What have you done with her, Sheryl?'

I remain silent, locking eyes with my aggressor, flint tool readied behind my back. Chemicals begin to mix within my stomach, adrenaline surges throughout my body and something long forgotten reminds me of itself, slamming the door as it steps into the forefront of my memories. I want to welcome it like a long-lost angry friend, someone I used to trust, someone I used to stand side-by-side with in those dark, unforgiving corners. I want to give in to them, throw myself into their more powerful arms, let them take control.

'Come on, Sheryl! You need an eye test or something?'

It's amazing what you can accept when you don't have to look yourself in the mirror. When a faceless entity stares back at you without emotion or understanding, who knows what message they're trying to get across that mirrored divide? Are they frowning? Do they have a soft, forgiving, empathetic aura? Are they silently mouthing foul, hate-filled words your way? Are they even looking? Are they watching your back by looking over your shoulder, or are they beckoning the wrath of the world onto your doorstep?

'Have you heard from her, Gary?' I'm robotic, monotonous, restrained.

'Yeah.' He looks down, his face sullen. He's playing with me; I've been here before. 'She phoned last week complaining about your maggot cock and the fact it was stuck up your boyfriend's arse all the time. She couldn't take it anymore and said she had no choice but to leave and find a real man.'

'She left last week?'

'Yeah.'

It was a million to one shot and it didn't pay off, but that's the last box ticked. I've tried every avenue I can possibly think of to find Heidi. This last box has played out exactly how I thought it would: I'd be humiliated, I'd get no closer to finding Heidi and any hope of finding Heidi on my own would be extinguished. My pessimism has become predictably reliable.

This is the tipping point I needed to reach in order to let go. I've tried everything I can. I've tried my best. I can look back on this period of my life and say I tried everything humanly possible to find my love, but failed. Or, she succeeded in keeping me away from her. Either way, it's obvious she wants nothing to do with me, so the best

I can do is let her be. The tipping point is not only about me exhausting every avenue; it's also about me not turning into a stalker.

She knows where I am. I haven't moved. I haven't changed. The ball's in her court, but I have to move on.

'Come on, Mike, we're leaving.'

Mike has other ideas. 'Hang on, I've seen a nice flat here . . .'

Of course, Gary can't let us just walk out of here without sending us on our way in front of his work colleagues. 'Fuck off, mincers!'

'Wait up, Sherry.' Mike gets his phone out and takes a photo of an advertisement for a flat. 'Excuse me, sweetheart, you got details for this place?'

The agent sitting nearby flashes a look at Gary before sweeping some hair behind her ear. 'I'm afraid not, sir.'

'I bet you haven't.' Mike turns his attention to Gary. 'Oi! Gazza! This flat you're flogging for well under market price, got any offers yet?'

'Fuck off out of it, ladyboy.'

'Yeah, I didn't think so, considering a crappy photo and poor description is sitting right at the bottom of this display in a dark and dusty corner of the office. Strange that, innit? I wonder why this ex-grace-and-favour apartment in the centre of town, recently refurbished to a very high spec at the taxpayer's expense, and due to be sold off as part of the council's budget cuts, is being sold off so cheaply? Might it be because the mayor has no plans to move out and wishes to buy it for himself? You getting a tasty commission for this? I hope so, sweetheart, because I'm all over this shit like a bloodhound on heat. I'll be in touch.'

Gary's on the back foot. Everyone in the office silently turns to look at him. I feel emboldened. 'That pimp ever catch up with you, Gary?' I address one of Gary's colleagues on the way out with a supplementary note, 'He's absolutely riddled, mate.'

With that, we leave with a little more dignity than when we entered. I hadn't expected that.

'*Bloodhound on heat?*' I ask Mike.

'Yeah. I sniff stories out so I can shaft someone; metaphorically, not literally.'

'Fleet Street's loss is the *Wigthorn Herald's* gain.'

As Mike regales me with his plans on taking down Gary and his employer, spit-balling a few headlines, I get a text.

Sorry bout last txt. Heidi is OK. I can't tell you anymore so please don't ask..

Gemma, Heidi's sister, has just peered around the iron curtain.

Chapter Four

NINE MONTHS BEFORE TODAY

I should have told Heidi about my condition, I should've trusted her to understand it and deal with it – after all, it's not that bad. It only affects me, no one else can react to it or judge it. The condition itself is not really a problem, an errand crumb or hair aside, so why keep it a secret? Maybe it's my secretiveness eating away at me and not the condition itself? The secret looks back at me every morning in the mirror as clear as day, clouding my reason.

Heidi may have gone but the blur in the mirror remains. If there's anything I should be reflecting on, it's that.

And that's why I'm here with Alkin Schofield (Al for short), adding to my collection of self-portraits in all their various forms, searching for that one representation which will shine through the fog and guide me to . . . myself?

'OK, mate, this is going to be a little cold.'

'Oh, bloody hell! You ain't wrong.' Al could be a little gentler too, he's kneading my face like it's clay. 'This stuff stinks.'

'Don't talk, keep your face still.'

'Oihh! Hitz gon hup mi noze!'

'What did you say?'

I said '*Oi! It's going up my nose*' but I don't think Al is too concerned about my wellbeing as he slathers my face in Algi-Safe Alginate. The fact it has the word 'safe' in it makes me even more nervous, I mean, that should be a given with any consumer product, right? Anyway, it's used to make a face mould, or any kind of body mould for that matter. Al here is one of the top special effects designers in the country which is why I've come up to his West London studio and forked out over a month's wages for the privilege. All around his workshop, a unit on an industrial estate, lying on paint-splattered trestle tables and hanging from whitewashed brick walls are various heads, arms, bodies, hands and fully formed beings from all ethnic backgrounds and beyond; aliens, witches, zombies, vampires, elves, trolls, dragons, monsters, the cast goes on. I recognise some of them too, the menace from the eyeless masks following you around the room. If it has lived and breathed in reality or on the screenwriter's page, then Al can recreate it.

That's what I'm hoping anyway.

'OK, that's most of the gunk on.' I like a man who dispenses with technicalities when speaking to lay-folk, formality only serves to elevate fear in the uninformed. Just look at politicians. 'Take a deep breath in through your nose . . . that's it. Now I'm going to cover your nose and nostrils . . . right, now I want you to breathe out through your nose to make an air hole so you don't die on me.' I force the alginate out, I don't care how safe it is, I need to breathe. 'That's it, now sit tight for five minutes and let it set. Don't move your face!'

I stick a thumb up, I think it's going to be a better form of communication at this point. Now I just sit here and wait with my fingers crossed hoping that Algi-Safe Alginate is special – maybe the chemicals rendering it 'safe' also allow it to render me?

In the darkness, in the silence, I focus on my dilemma.

My condition has no name.

There are plenty of related conditions, all shrouded within the comforting blanket of a label, but mine has yet to be embraced. The related physical conditions include:

Prosopagnosia: or face blindness, not recognising friends you've known for years, celebrities, your own children, or even your own face – I remember everyone.

Hemispatial Neglect: the inability to observe one side of your spatial awareness, usually as a result of damage to one hemisphere of the brain. My spatial awareness is excellent, I don't need my car's collision avoidance sensors to park.

41

Hemianopia: a trauma causing decreased vision or blindness in one or both eyes. I have 20/20 vision.

Then there are the related physiological conditions:

Aphantasia: the inability to produce mental images, a blind 'mind's eye' – I can imagine anything I want.

Autophobia: a fear of oneself – I sometimes hate myself but fear is stretching the point.

Catoptrophia: a fear of mirrors – I don't fear them, I use them to assess my fashion choices; maybe they fear me?

Eisoptrophobia: the fear of seeing yourself in the mirror – I probably have the opposite of this, there's nothing I'd like more than to see my face in the mirror.

Ommatophobia: a fear of eyes. I'm an optometrist, for God's sake.

The nearest I've ever come to defining my problem is *Scotomaphobia*, the fear of blindness in your visual field. Sounds perfect, right? Wrong. Excluding viewing my own face, my visual field is 100% 20/20, like an owl with infra-red goggles trained by Nostradamus. Yet stick a mirror, a photo, or a tree bark etching containing my image in the way and I have a glaring blind spot in my visual field.

I've never met anyone else with what I've got, not that I've looked too hard. I don't want to stand out as a medical oddity, to be experimented on by scientists or toured around the world's chat shows as some kind of circus freak. *'Roll up! Roll up! Come see the man who can't see his own face! Young boy, why not chuck a doughnut at his face and watch as he struggles to clean the jam and sugar off, but first, Coldplay with their new single.'*

Maybe I'm the first? Maybe my condition could be named after me? Sheridan's Disease, Maddox Syndrome, Sherry's Disorder. It's a bit of a double-edged sword, having a medical condition named after you. It satisfies our desire to be remembered and leave our mark on the world but to be remembered as an ailment can't be at the top of many people's lists. Motor Neurone Disease is also popularly known in the USA as Lou Gehrig's disease, after a famous baseball player from the same era as Babe Ruth. The soul of Lou Gehrig must want to strike out every time a visitor to the Baseball

Hall of Fame comments on his contribution to the neurological sciences rather than baseball. 'The Iron Horse' won six World Series titles, he shouldn't be let down by his nervous system *and* sports fans; that's a double no one wants.

Should a discussion you're involved in ever find its way on to the subject of 'Sheridan Maddox Syndrome', please, for the sake of my legacy, please reply, 'Oh, you mean Auto-Scotomaphobia?'.

I hear Al's footsteps approach across the wooden floor. 'I think that'll do you, let's get those bandages on now.'

Al starts wrapping the bandages around my face to support the alginate once it's set, allowing it to come off in one solid piece. Currently, I look like a mummy. Obviously I can't see myself because I'm covered in gunk . . . well, I can't see myself anyway, but I know what I look like because Al took me through the different steps with some photos and called this the 'Mummy Stage', straight after the 'Gunk Stage'. I think Al is pandering to me.

'So what's the reason for getting a mould of your own face then? You ain't no movie star, no offence, mate.'

'Hmmph.' Hang on, why's he asking me a question when I can't speak? I throw out a questioning arm gesture.

'Oh, sorry, mate, I always do that.' Al carries on organising things for the next stage which I hope is the removal of this mask. 'I'll give you ten minutes to come up with a passable story.'

It's all right, Al, I did that on the drive up here. My story goes like this: I'm experimenting with a 3D rendering of my own head to place myself in the position of a potential customer who could see themselves wearing a pair of glasses from all angles, not just a head-on view in the mirror. Now, I know what you're thinking, 'Surely a computer could do this faster, cheaper, and better?' Yes, but I got a computerised 3D image of my head done two weeks ago (complete failure, by the way), so I'm going to say I'm getting this as a comparison to prove a computer model is just as good as seeing yourself. If he has any other questions I'll just whip out my business card, offer him a free eye test at a local branch of Twenty20, and hopefully that'll shut him up.

You may detect a slight cynicism in my tone, a lack of excitement regarding this procedure, and you'd be correct. Not that I doubt Al's abilities: on the contrary, I can see from the work all around me, and the invoice, he's truly an excellent special effects designer. No, my negativity stems from a paradox stalking me from the very first moment I was exposed to a photograph of myself; the worse the image of myself, the better I can see it. This results in my favourite representation of my own face being one drawn by an impoverished and imperfect street artist in Wigthorn about a year ago. It sits proudly, framed on the wall of my toilet at home, as an ironic joke to the rest of the world but to me, the closest thing I have to an image of myself I can actually see. Everyone who sees it asks who the caricature is of, and when I say me, they comment on the total ineptitude of the artist – but to me he is Da Vinci. A Special Brew-fuelled Da Vinci and I'm his Mona Lisa. His gift to me is worth more than the tenner it cost or the five minutes it took for the sitting, he has done more for me than a couple of therapists, hundreds of photographs, and thousands of mirrors. He has helped me more than anyone to find my place in the world.

Until I met Heidi, that is.

Heidi, the girl who left me for no real reason that I can discern, and a street artist's ham-fisted caricature are all I have to establish any sense of self. Maybe it's all I deserve. Maybe I have to face up to the fact that it's all I'm worth.

I have a couple of photos of my parents, when they were young, about my age now, they never made old bones. I can see their faces beaming back from the past, during happier times. I have one photo of them with me, my mother cradling me in her arms, swaddled in a yellow knitted blanket, whilst my father stands behind her with both hands on her shoulders. Looking sullen, their smiles gone. I've never shown anyone that picture.

It must be so easy for people to see themselves so clearly, nothing hidden from view, no fog or mist obscuring their most important side. Yes! The most important side. Don't try and bullshit me with inner beauty, soul, heart, intentions, no one can see those abstract,

44

subjective view points of our personality as people walk past; they only see our faces.

Life is etched on our faces; experience carved those lines, nurture coloured that expression, and a combination of both fills our eyes. Some of us may not have been graced with beauty but at least everyone else knows what they're working with. I have no idea.

I'm not shallow. Anyone talking about looks is shallow, right? The model confessing how she can feel ugly too, the handsome film star insisting looks haven't helped him get where he is even though he can't act for toffee, those with God-given gifts dismissing them as millstones. If these people had any idea about the whole philosophy of aesthetics they wouldn't be so quick to dismiss their own blind luck. I've never heard of a mathematician cursing his innate skill with numbers, it would be absurd! Isn't art about beauty? What, then, can be more important than art?

Of course, a conceited beauty is ugly, but it's the conceit that offends us, not the beauty. Have I been tricked into thinking I'm one thing when really the blank canvas of my face projects something completely different? Am I choosing only to see what I want to see? Could I see my own face if I really wanted to but something deep within me is preventing it? A past trauma?

Both my parents died in a fire when I was two. Apparently, that's traumatic, but I was two, I have no memory of them. I have no siblings, I have no grandparents and no uncles or aunties. I was brought up by a very nice elderly foster couple, who are now dead, and then a handful of 'guardians' supervising my time through boarding school and university. I left with an MSc in Optometry and the healthy remains of my trust fund enabling me to buy a very nice two-bedroomed flat with cash. I've never thought of myself as living with trauma. Maybe that's what's etched all over my face?

'Time's up . . . hang on, what's this? What do you girls want? Oh my God, Sheridan, if only you could see this, about twelve naked lingerie models have just walked into the studio. How can I help you, girls? What was that? You want to do a quick dance and then leave? Go for it! If only you could see this, Sheridan!'

Al, you're cracking me up, probably literally.

'Only joking, Sheridan, let's get this thing off.'

No shit. How could you tell someone was a lingerie model if they're naked? I feel my sense of humour going the same way as my reflection.

I can feel his hands on my head, a tool digging in behind the hardened Algi-Safe Alginate to separate it from my skin. It finally comes off, a slight coldness in the air welcoming me back to life.

'Look, Sheridan. Check out the inside of your head.'

Al holds the face mask up for me to see the inside, clearly proud of his latest creation. I never considered this view, Al missed this stage out from his briefing and it never occurred to me. Maybe this alternate perspective might allow me . . .

No.

'Look at the detailing, always surprises me. Your eyelids, all the lines around the eyes . . .'

I can't see it, Al.

'The lines on the lips . . .'

Nope. Nothing there Al.

'Even the hair, your eyebrows, a few eyelashes there too.'

I can't see any of it, Al. You may as well be holding open a sliced pumpkin!

'I'll just go over it and fill in a few air holes before pouring in the casting solution but that's you all done, Sheridan. Over there is a sink and some face wash. Clean yourself up whilst I get started on the next stage.'

The skin on my face feels warm, a little tight, and slightly sticky to the touch. It doesn't feel like I'm having a face mould done, it feels like I've just had a new face put on.

I approach the sink with my eyes lowered, as I normally do because seeing a faceless person walk towards you is a little off-putting, even to me, even after all these years. The sink is obviously used for washing out pots, pans, and cleaning paint brushes and tools, as it's splattered with all manner of colours and gunk, but the water is warm and the face wash smells . . . homely?

It smells like Candleina. I rinse my face and examine the bottle closer.

'My wife bought that, a bit poncy, innit? She says it smells how women want their man to smell, not how men think women want them to smell, or something along those lines.'

Yeah, that's what Heidi said too. 'It's . . . nostalgic.'

'As long as it washes the smell of that gunk off then I ain't going to argue. Hang on, you've still got a bit on your face. Is my mirror really that dirty?'

I rub my face all over, ensuring no stray dollops of gunk are left behind. It's not until I see Al look at me without further comment that I'm completely confident it's all gone. Using other people as mirrors may not have the immediacy of an actual mirror but they do have the ability to reflect more than just the features lying on the surface. I've noticed that not many people come to accept this as readily as myself; 20/20 vision can be an affliction. A distraction.

I'm a better listener than most.

'It could do with a bit of clean, to be honest.'

'OK. You go out and get some lunch whilst this mask sets and I'll start doing some undercoat painting. When you get back you can sit down and admire all my handiwork on the walls whilst I finish off the detailing and touching up. Should be done by four, how's that sound?'

'Top notch, Al. Where do you recommend for lunch?'

'The Songbird, a pub about a mile down the road, the landlord looks like one of my horror masks but he's a great cook.'

When you've got a mask made of your own face, what's one of the first things you do? Of course you do. I ring the doorbell.

'All right, Sherry . . . whoa! Holy shit, what's that?!'

I peer round the door, planting my head next to my mask. 'All right, Mike?'

'Urgh, Sheridan, that's just too creepy.'

'What do you reckon?'

'Your narcissism is becoming a real problem, mate.'

'What do you think of the likeness though, does it look like me?'

'Yeah, in a dead-eyed zombie kinda way. So, yeah, you on a good day.' Mike leads the three of us into the kitchen. I'm pleased in a strange way. I can't see the mask at all but my oldest mate thinks it's a good likeness so I guess it's money well spent. I'm not sure how much closer I am or if this is a step backwards or a complete waste of time and money but it's a scratch itched, at least. 'Oh, Jesus! You're not going to kill me then have sex with my corpse whilst that mask is over my face, are you?'

'Go fuck yourself.'

'That's what I'm insinuating!'

'Bloody hell, Mike. Just get me a beer out the fridge, will you.'

Chapter Five

EIGHT MONTHS BEFORE TODAY

Waves of regret wash over me, relentlessly pounding the inside of my head, eroding the very foundations I stand on. This past month I've been living an exhausting single life as Mike has taken it upon himself to ensure I'm out every weekend on the pull. Of course, we never pull. It's the only reason I'm still agreeing to go out with him.

With Heidi gone I'm rejoining my tribe, my band of blokes, brothers from other mothers, losers in boozers, dead-end bellends. This new path may not launch me into an elevated state of self-actualisation (no, me neither) or introduce me to the next great love of my life, but at least it'll stop me feeling so down on myself. When I'm with my simpleton mates, it makes me feel better. No longer do I stand, dumbstruck, in the shadows of the amazing, beautiful, talented, serene Heidi, but I step into the light and become someone in my own right. Cast my own shadow. These boys actually look up to me. I'm a small-town success. Status, expendable cash, an address on the posh side of town, new German car, designer clothes, letters after my name, all a valid contribution to the facade we project. Even I can see that.

First I need to manage the hangover which is currently welcoming me, violently, into this Saturday morning. My brain is rattling around in my skull like a steel toe-capped work boot inside a washing machine. It feels like a diseased man has been cremated and the ashes spread inside my mouth. I think I might have smoked last night . . . *cough, cough* . . . Oh Christ, yes I did. I'm going to throw up . . . hang on . . .

. . . so, anyway. Let's see what drinks Mike has in the fridge, I could murder an orange juice.

'Was that you throwing up, Sherry?'

Mike is still in bed, alone. 'Yeah, no one else came back last night, did they?'

'Nearly, old son. Nearly.'

About as nearly as 'not at all'. 'You got any juice?'

'No idea.'

Yes, he has, I've got to down the lot to inject some life back into my mouth. 'You got any aspirin or paracetamol?'

'Yeah, in that drawer.' Mike enters the kitchen, 'I've also got all the required food groups for a full English breakfast too, so you sit yourself down and let Uncle Mike resurrect your fragile soul so we can start all over again tonight, cash in on some of those seeds we sowed last night.'

'Knock yourself out, I could eat a horse.'

'I got this lot cheap down the market, so you might well be.' Mike throws down a packet of bacon onto the kitchen worktop, the lack of branding a glaring omission.

'I'm not going out again tonight, Mike. I'm having an early one, give my liver the night off.'

'Oh, do be quiet, princess, it's Saturday night!' The letterbox comes to my rescue with a rattle. 'The postman!' It never fails to awaken the young birthday boy in Mike as he rushes over to pick up the delivery from the floor. 'More bloody junk mail but check this out, a reply to a competition I entered.'

As Mike opens up his reply to find out if he's won a discount on something useless costing a fortune, I aimlessly flick through the junk mail he's dumped on the table: a curry house menu, pizza offers, and a freebie paper with absolutely no news in it whatsoever. Amongst the advertisements on the front page is one for the 'Wigthorn Open House Art Event' featuring a previously exhibited photo of Heidi's; two old ladies sitting on a bench, laughing hysterically. The universe is conspiring against me. 'You want me to give you a hand with breakfast?'

'Don't worry, Shezza, it's all in hand.'

An advertisement in the paper catches my eye, 'Want To Find Out What Your Customers Are Thinking?', promoting the benefits of advertising in that very paper, using market research to find out more about your customers and their desires. It's similar to what I need. I want to find out what other people think of me, but anonymously, secretly, from behind a curtain, not to my face. I need their honest answer, not with a metaphorical gun pointed to their head. My face reflects me but I can't see it, so if I ask friends of mine what they see maybe I can get an approximation of the face I show to the world?

There's logic in there somewhere. I tear out the ad, I'll call them later on at work.

Fuck! Work!

'Mike, I gotta go to work!'

'Relax, Sherry! You're the boss, ain't ya? You can be late.'

'Assistant manager, Mike. One of the assistant managers, I can't be late, what's the time?' I search the kitchen for a digital clock somewhere on one of the machines. I get the time in about five different time zones. 'Mike, which one of these clocks is correct?'

'None of them.' He checks his phone, 'It's only eight thirty a.m., relax, Shezzarino. Let Mikey-boy set you up for the day with a fry up.'

He's right, I can be late. I don't have an appointment until 10 a.m. It's time I took advantage of my position. 'You're not the Saturday boy, Sheridan!' was always Heidi's refrain as she snuggled up closer to me on a Saturday morning. How did I leave that warm embrace so willingly?

'You're right, Mike.' My God, those words don't sit comfortably, my hangover is worse than I thought. 'I'm not the Saturday boy, I can be late.'

'Hark, the optician has finally seen the light.'

'I'll just make a phone call.'

I get to work at 10 on the dot, not ideal as I need to sort a few things out before I see my first customer, Mrs Lancaster, who is already sitting down in the waiting area, but I give her a smile and a warm hello as I walk swiftly through the shop. 'I'll send someone down to you in five minutes, Mrs Lancaster, just got to get the old steam generator going.'

Not sure she appreciated that one. Actually, I'm not sure she heard it, she should go to the hearing shop too. Never understood why we don't do both. Maybe there's an audiologist out there who can't hear himself think? A right pair we'd make.

Daisy, one of the sales assistants, speeds up her walk to escort me to the back of the shop, 'Sheridan, just to let you know . . .'

'Not now, Daisy, I'll catch up with you later.'

'But, Sheridan . . .' I cut her off by shutting the staff door behind me.

Bollocks. The area manager is lurking round the back. I need to start listening to Daisy more. 'Hi, Steve, didn't know you were in today.'

'It wouldn't be a surprise visit if I told you.'

'Indeed not, how's things?'

'Hungover?'

'Me? Course not, taken a vow of sobriety.'

'Ill?'

'Picture of health, fighting fit, me.'

'Cutting down your hours to concentrate on helping the kids down the orphanage?'

'No, no, no, I see what you mean, I've been up and about, researching . . .'

'I'm only playing with you, Sheridan, you're one of my top boys, you don't need to explain yourself to me. Do they even still have orphanages?'

Sort of. 'So, what's up, Steve?'

'Nothing, just a surprise visit, see how things are ticking over. Everything looks fine, your staff are working well, the shop's clean and tidy, profits are good, you've got the whole place running like clockwork.'

'It's not just me, Steve.' I dilute his praise with some humility, I can't be seen to be too good at my job.

'Most of it is, Sheridan. Barry has been managing this place too long but I daren't move him sideways or upwards as he'd crack. He's in a routine that's working. At the moment.'

Steve and I have always seen eye to eye.

'I've also come here to dip my toes in the water.'

'How so?'

'Giving you your own shop.'

'Oh?' I don't want the responsibility, I don't want to lose the customer contact. I need it. I'm 99% certain I'm not going to see my reflection in any profit and loss spreadsheets. 'Thanks, but you must have better candidates?'

'No, I haven't. Look I'm just sowing a seed, let me know how it's grown next time I'm down.'

There's a lot of seed-sowing going on lately.

'OK.' It'll still be a no. My ambitions lie elsewhere. 'Oh yeah, there is something you could help me with though. How do Twenty20 advertise themselves most successfully, you know, to get into the mind of their customers?'

'Not really my bag, all down to those marketing slimebags up at HQ but I know the focus is quickly moving online. That's where the big advertising dollars are being spent nowadays; Groupon, Facebook, Instagram, Snapchat. If it's true about what they say about wanking causing blindness then we should be advertising on porn sites too but I don't think that *synergises with our brand identity*" or some bollocks. Why? Oh, I see . . . Jesus! You're good, Sherry. Not many branches take advantage of their allocated local advertising spend but if anyone would, I should've known it would be you. So what are you thinking?'

You know why I've always liked Steve? I can never do any wrong with this guy. 'Just dipping my toes in the water.'

'Good man. Look, I'll get in contact with a friend in marketing up at HQ. I'll ask her what cutting-edge shit they're doing online and that there's a willing branch manager down in sunny Wigthorn wanting to join the ride.'

'Sure, thanks.'

53

'Right, I better be off, got to see that branch down the road. Mostly bloody idiots. I'll surprise you again, soon.' Steve taps his nose and marches off.

Without even trying, I've recruited a marketing consultant to bounce ideas off . . . for what exactly? I'd better get thinking how I can weave shop advertising in with my own goal of contacting friends and family with a questionnaire. What questions will be the most effective at discerning their thoughts when they see me or think of me? I'm not sure I want to dip my toes into this water anymore.

'Sheridan, Mrs Lancaster is still waiting.'

'Yeah, send her in, Daisy, thanks.'

Focus on testing people's eyesight, that's what you're good at.

'Hello, Mrs Lancaster, sorry for the delay, just needed to tidy a few things up. So how are you?'

She shuffles over to the chair, squinting. Places her handbag on the floor before retrieving her glasses from it. If she had her glasses on when entering the room then she wouldn't have to squint to see the chair. Yes, I know she wants me to see her squinting to emphasise her troubles but I don't have a £2,000 slit lamp (that thing you rest your chin on) sitting here for decoration. I'm making my professional diagnosis via specialised digital equipment, not by how much you squint, Mrs Lancaster.

'I think my eyes are getting worse.'

'I see. Have you been wearing your glasses as much as possible?'

'Oh yes, Doctor, all the time.'

Except when you walk into rooms. 'That's great. We better take a look then. If you can just pull up your chair and rest your chin here, I'll beam these death rays into your eyes.'

That brought the room sharply into focus.

'Ha, ha, ha, of course I'm only joking, Mrs Lancaster.'

I begin the exam, which consists of 'Better, worse or the same?' and 'Read the top line', etc, etc.

'So, Mrs Lancaster, I'm just freestyling here as you're one of my regulars, but what would you think of an additional service enabling you to see how others see you? I know it sounds radical and a little out of left-field, but let me explain . . .'

'Would it affect my prescription?'

'Good question. No. So, anyway, it's all about perception, right? I can keep examining you every year, changing your prescription, but what does that give you?'

'Good eyesight?'

'If you can now look through here with your left eye. Yes, you get good eyesight with our existing services, but what I'm talking about is perception. What is the world's perception of you? How do others see you, Mrs Lancaster?'

'I'm not sure I see what you mean?'

'Very profound, Mrs Lancaster. Now your right eye. Thanks. What I'm talking about is something that cannot be examined through the lens of specialist equipment and definitely not through rose-tinted glasses but requires the hard focus of a critical eye only found behind the veil of anonymity.'

'I've got a coffee morning at the Salvation Army soon.'

'Yes, all those people you see at the Salvation Army, at work, at home, family, friends, friends of friends, even those who have had the briefest of interactions with you all have a valuable opinion of you, one that's worth knowing. What if it was possible to mix all these opinions up to gain an accurate portrait of how you're perceived in the world?'

'I'll be meeting my sister so I really don't want to be late.'

'Yes, yes, I see, good thinking. If you could look up to the right. Yes, the opinions of those you're closest to should bear more weight than relative strangers', of course, you're right. And now to the left. You may be having a bad day, late, nothing going your way and then you run into someone who's blocking your every move, adding to your worries, raising your blood pressure, wasting time you don't have . . .'

'I can relate to that.'

'So even though that person is a relative stranger and their opinion should not carry as much weight as a close friend or partner, their opinion should indeed carry some weight. All of our thousands of tiny, fleeting interactions with people will all contribute to the overall person we present to the world.'

'You know what? I think my eyes are getting better. My current prescription will be fine for another year, Doctor, don't worry yourself.'

'No, no, we're nearly done, Mrs Lancaster. If you could sit back and tilt your head, I just need to take a closer look with my retinoscope. So, which questions would be most pertinent? What is key to understanding the perception others have of you? Asking them what you look like, how you come across, your manners and politeness, intelligence? Would you ask the same questions to a close friend as you would the sales assistant who just served you? I guess not.'

'Are you seeing a therapist?'

'No I'm not, you think taking a therapeutic approach would help? Yes, yes it would, of course. This would be like a psychological assessment via hundreds of therapists, psychiatrists, laymen, strangers, all giving their verdict as you lie on a couch protected only by a curtain, which is actually there to protect them. So you're saying I should consult with a therapist or two, maybe read some books to help construct a questionnaire with the most probing and rewarding questions? I suspect questioning people online with brevity and conciseness would be the key attributes to ensure the widest possible participation. I'll check that with the marketing person up at HQ.'

'I think you should visit a psychiatrist, yes.'

'Probably expensive, especially if I wish to consult with them about creating a new questionnaire, but how serious am I, right? How much do I really want this? Money should be no object.'

'I can go now?'

'Mrs Lancaster, your eyes show no sign of deterioration so your current prescription should be fine for another year. If you have any problems please don't hesitate to see me. Let me show you out. Thanks again for all your feedback and I hope you don't mind me using you to bounce ideas off, you've been most helpful.'

'I hope you get the help you need. Goodbye.'

Well, that went much better than I expected. I never meant to discuss my idea with her but it just seemed to happen. Who would've thought little old Mrs Lancaster with her over-developed sense of hypochondria, the only customer who insists on a new pair of glasses every year, would be so enthusiastic about my idea? And so perceptive too! I really need to open my mind up more to different people. I'm not only blind to my own face but also to the opinions of others, it seems. And I always thought I was an excellent listener. I wonder if that point of view will be a recurring theme in the results from this questionnaire? If so, how much have I missed from the mouths of others? Is that why Heidi left? Have I been so blind that my biggest problem is deafness?

Chapter Six

'I think these Dolce & Gabbana ones in silver are the best fit for your face.'

'You think? They're a bit *architecty* aren't they?' I mean *poncy*.

'What's wrong with being seen as an intelligent, aesthetically astute professional with a well-paid job?'

She's got a point. 'Yeah, better than looking like an optometrist, right? We don't have that aesthetically astute thing going for us.'

'Some of my best friends are optometrists, sir.'

I'm at the annual Conference of Eyewear Retailers in London. An extravaganza of designer frames, technological advances in optical testing equipment, lens-crafting, professional services, and bullshit. A lot of bullshit.

I make the most of this annual conference by getting my eyes tested a few times by different people using different equipment just to keep up to date on how the equipment works, how they carry out the test and most importantly, what they say. Not so much the technical stuff, just a few one liners, some humour to make the customer feel at ease. All these providers of high-end equipment and cutting-edge services send their most personable people, not socially inept nitwits like me.

The other thing I always do is get fitted for new frames. I don't wear glasses, that would be like having a mechanic with a broken car or a brain surgeon with a lobotomy . . . kind of . . . anyway, I don't need to wear glasses is the point I'm getting at. I get fitted not to keep up to date with the latest brands and fashions but because someone talks about my face.

'The Paul Smith ones with the red trim are good too. They accentuate your jaw and contrast nicely with your hair.'

'Remind me, these are the ones that cost four hundred and ninety-nine pounds?'

'Do you know the first thing a woman notices about a man?'

'The price tag of his glasses?'

'His eyes.'

'What about his shoes?'

'Rubbish. If any woman you first meet looks directly down at your shoes, run away. You want to frame the windows into your soul with mass-produced Far Eastern crap or fine European haute couture?'

'You've gone mildly off script here.'

'Mildly. You know the second thing a woman notices about a man?'

'No.'

'If he has jam on the side of his nose.'

Bollocks. I normally stay away from jam doughnuts, pastries, anything with icing sugar, loose crusts, or a liquid centre unless I'm going to the toilet straight after so I can wash my face. These tiny specks get lost in the blur. That'll teach me for skipping breakfast on the way here. 'Thanks.'

'I was wondering when you were going to spot it after looking at yourself in the mirror all this time.'

'Ha, ha, ha, yeah.' What the hell am I laughing at? 'My eyesight is terrible. The shoemaker's children and all that. I left my glasses in the hotel this morning, can you believe that?'

'You should go back to the hotel and get your glasses, no point buying frames if you can't see what they look like.'

'Exactly what I was going to do.'

'Have you spoken to any of the laser eye surgery providers?'

'Not here but yes, I'm getting them done next month.'

Not true. Although I have thought about it and have spoken to someone about it. Maybe the lasers could burn out my blind spot, allowing me to see myself, but unfortunately the laser eye surgeons suffer from an affliction called 'ethics'. They won't operate on someone with healthy eyes. I spent a whole year about six years ago trying to worsen my eyesight. Do you know how hard that is? Worsening your eyesight without making yourself go blind, I mean. For one year I sat too close to the TV, worked on the computer in the dark for hours, excessively masturbated, stared into the middle distance, virtually gave up vitamin A, all in the name of damaging my eyesight. I'm a bloody professional optometrist with all the scientific knowledge that entails and I went without carrots for a year. I tried everything, even rebelling against bloody myths. Nothing. Twenty20's top optometrist, if I may be so bold, still has 20/20 vision. We're all a slave to our genes.

'So why are you looking at frames?'

The problem with this conference and being around fellow eye professionals is that I can't blind them with bullshit. 'Just wanted one last fitting, I suppose. You know, before defecting to the other side.'

'I understand. Well, don't tell my boss, but I think you look better without glasses.'

Heidi used to look at me like that; a reflex half-squint after opening herself up, a coy retreat then slowly returning to view the aftermath of the devastation she'd caused. Once I'd restarted my heart from skipping a beat, rebooted my brain, and taken a breath, I'd only manage to cobble together a word, 'Thanks.'

She takes a curious step forward, crossing that invisible border into my personal space, focusing in on my face. 'Handsome but not pretty. Intriguing but not unusual. Mysterious but not strange. Welcoming but . . .'

But what? She's moving even closer . . . she's touching the side of my face . . . don't kiss me . . . please.

Please kiss me.

'. . . but lost.'

Lost. I raise my hand to touch her hand on my face. She must know something, she must recognise my condition, see through my lies. I can't let go. 'You know?'

'I'm so sorry, you must think I'm hitting on you. I'm married, see? Happily married. I'm sorry. It's just . . . you know, sometimes strangers connect in such a way it makes you wonder if you're really strangers.'

'Yeah.' That's all I can manage, a simple yeah, because I have no idea what 'face' I'm presenting to this girl.

'What did you mean when you said I know?'

'I was just going to say thank you. It's not everyday you get more than you were expecting.'

'Are you lost?'

'Without my glasses I am. I better go, someone's doing a talk I need to get to. Nice to meet you, thanks for your . . . err . . . feedback. I feel more confident ditching the glasses now.'

'Good luck.'

Blimey, that was weird. Good weird, but weird nonetheless. It's always strange, isn't it, when you connect with someone you've never met before. You never know when it's going to happen but when it does it throws you all out of whack. You feel like you're walking away from someone you shouldn't be. You should have left more with them, taken more from them, the whole experience feels satisfying yet unfulfilling all at the same time.

I need to get to this talk, it's a blind guy talking about being blind. As I enter the room I catch the speaker in mid-flow, '. . . so when you look in the mirror every morning, what do you see?'

Nothing.

I'll skip the talky bit, I only really want to speak to this guy alone, ask a couple of questions. What better opportunity am I going to get to speak with a blind person and not look like a complete nutter?

In the meantime, I'm going to reply to the Indian web developers I've hired to build a web app for my questionnaire experiment. I spoke with the marketing person Steve put me in touch with and after some digging and some measured questioning she suggested getting an app up and running on Facebook would be the most effective method of reaching people I know cheaply and anonymously. I've spent a few weeks putting together a questionnaire and, reading through this email the developers have just sent, I now need to come up with a name for the app. Something snappy, something explanatory, something catchy. A name that cleverly encapsulates the basic premise of a Facebook app anonymously asking a series of multiple-choice questions about someone on Facebook (a friend, a friend of a friend, someone in your town/work/college), the answers being collated and analysed by an algorithm resulting in that particular person being given a written assessment of how they are 'seen' by others.

Every time I dip my toes into the industry of others, I'm even more satisfied with my career choice. I'm crap at all this creative marketing stuff. Just call it 'Opinion Machine' or 'What do you think of me?' They may fail on the snappy and catchy elements but they pass the explanatory test with flying colours.

I send a reply approving a couple of updates and tell them I'm still trying to think of a name. I know I'm going to have to rely on blind luck and good fortune on this one.

I re-enter the conference room towards the end of the talk and listen to the blind speaker wrap up as I take a seat at the back. Everyone is listening intensely, not one glazed over look or head teetering on the edge of Snoozeville. His voice is soothing, calm, undistracted by the faces laid out in front of him. I wonder if he pictures everyone in the room naked?

At the end, there is respectful applause. The talk was thoroughly enjoyable to merit applause but sufficiently moving to command respect. A few people go one-by-one up to him to ask another question or two, or simply to shake his hand and say thank you. I wait fifteen minutes until he is alone.

'Hi,' I call out as though I'm the one in the dark.

'Oh, man! I didn't know anyone else was still in here.'

'Sorry, I didn't mean to sneak up on you, sir.'

'I'm only kidding, you were like a marauding rhinoceros in clogs. I noticed you arrive late and sit at the back.'

Who needs eyes? 'Wow. You knew that was me?'

'Yeah, you stuck your head in earlier, still late by the way, and then retreated when I said something about looking in the mirror. You needed to pee?'

'I needed to respond to an email and I don't like mirrors.'

'Mirrors have no bearing on my life. I have no opinion on them, positive or negative. They're like religion, I've looked into both and see nothing.'

'I don't see much either.'

'You know, disliking mirrors is not a reflection on mirrors themselves, it's a reflection on you. A mirror doesn't just reflect an objective reality, it reflects your reality. Would you mind if I touch your face, see if I can see something the mirror can't?'

'Go for it.'

He slowly raises his hands and starts to touch my face with his fingertips, gradually increasing the surface area until the palms of his hands are lightly sweeping their way across every contour.

'Even though my other senses are heightened to levels that even astound myself, there's no substitute for vision to truly see someone. Don't let others bullshit you on that score, my friend.'

'That's kind of what I wanted to ask you. Would you mind if I ask you a question?'

'Go for it.'

It can be quite off-putting recollecting your thoughts as a stranger caresses your face. I look him in the eyes as I try to remember what I wanted to ask him. His eyes look normal, no damage as far as I can see as they flounder around in their sockets looking for one point to focus on. A couple of times they pause, blindly, on me so I search for my reflection in them.

Nothing.

His blindness allows me to relax, I'm on level ground, neither of us can see my face.

'They say eyes are the windows into the soul, so do you think you're missing out on an element of "knowing" yourself when you can't see into your own eyes?'

'Yes.'

OK, I was expecting a little more than that. 'Is that it?'

'You were expecting some spiritual, hippy crap about extra-sensory perception or the eyes only see distraction or what you feel inside is how the world perceives you, right?'

63

'Something a little more profound than yes.'

'I don't want to bullshit you. Would I prefer to see? Yes. Would I like to see myself? Yes. If someone took away your sight, you'd want it back, right?'

'Yeah.'

'OK. But that's not a true analogy, everyone would like something back that's been taken. A true analogy would be having something no one has the ability to see someone's aura, for example. OK, you may not believe in that hocus-pocus, but say it was true. If someone asked you, would you like to see your own aura? Would you say yes?'

'Yes.'

'Of course you would, you'd be an idiot to say no. So asking me, would I like to see my reflection, or, would I like to have sight? Of course I'd say yes. It's one of our natural senses, not a superpower. This doesn't mean I'm a complete stranger to myself, though. Just because I can't see what I physically look like to everyone else, doesn't diminish who I am to myself. What do you actually see when you look through your windows and into your soul?'

'Well, this is why I ask. I can't.'

His blind eyes flicker for a moment as his brain wheel spins on unfamiliar ground. 'Are you blind too? I don't think you are. Bad eyesight?'

'No.' I pause a little as I tentatively head down a road I've never gone down before. 'No, twenty-twenty vision. I have a rare problem, one I've never heard anyone else having, one I've never discussed with anyone else before.' Here goes nothing . . . 'I can't see any reflection of my own face. Not in a mirror, a window, in other people's eyes, in paintings, photos, 3D computer models, nowhere.'

'Hmmm, strange. And this is just with your face?'

'Yeah, just my face. I can see my hairline, ears, bottom of my jawline, and then everything south. Just my face is blind to me. Never seen it. Ever. It's all a blur. I see a photograph of myself and the face is a blur. A painting, the same thing. I look at myself in the mirror and my face is a blur, hold something in front of my face and I can see it, remove it again and all that remains is a blurry face. It's not my eyes, it's not mirrors, got to be my brain somehow. Some bizarre blind spot, a brain cell misfiring, an errant link of genes, an ancient gypsy curse. I've no idea where the problem stems from but I can't see my own face.'

This confession comes out more thoroughly and more passionately than I'd expected. Floods out, the weight on my shoulders lightening with every word, the fear vanishing with every sentence, confiding in someone who understands fills me with a long-suppressed confidence. To be able to connect with a like-minded individual is more powerful and liberating than I could ever have dreamed of. I realise now that I have shrouded myself with a secret shame and got so good at hiding it that it's enabled me to carry on without ever having to face up to it. I've avoided confrontation for so long and built up the fear so greatly it had become this impossibly big and unbeatable monster, and now . . . it feels defeated in one simple conversation.

'So you can see everything else, just not your face?'

'Yeah.'

'Well, count your lucky stars, son, I'm blind to everything and after feeling your face, I'd be glad you can't see it. Stop wasting my time.'

'Hang on! You said I could ask anything.'

'How did I know you were going to ask such a self-absorbed, narcissistic question about a condition which has no affect on your daily life at all? Have you ever tried crossing the road without seeing your reflection? Oh yeah, of course you haven't because it has no bearing on your life. You want me to judge you? You're an idiot.'

'What?!'

'You're taking the piss, you've got to be, no one's that fucking stupid.'

'I'm serious.'

'You're seriously fucking stupid.'

'Fuck you.' I flash a screwed-up face sandwiched in a pair of crazed jazz hands. Let him echo-locate that.

Just then, a conference organiser enters the room. Typical. 'Excuse me, sir! You all right there, Mr Flannigan?'

'I think so. Is he still here? I feel vulnerable.'

'I'm sure you do. Do you have ID, sir?'

Great. I'm the world's biggest twat, picking on a blind man. Well, you know what, world? Dickheadery is indiscriminate, it affects people of all kinds.

I produce my ID tag, 'Here it is. You caught us having a heated discussion. I'll leave. Thank you, Mr Flannigan.'

'Who's there?' Mr Flannigan waves his arms cautiously in front of him as though he's walking through a darkened room. He could probably draw the blueprints for this room with his eyes closed.

'Give it a rest, mate.' I hand him his white stick which is leaning against the lectern.

'I'll escort you out, Mr Flannigan. You don't need this hassle.'

As the poor, sweet, defenceless Mr Flannigan is walked out the room he turns to flash me a smile and stick two fingers up. I return the gesture, then realise there's no possible way even he could see it, so I audibly return the compliment, 'Fuck you.'

The conference organiser pulls a radio from his pocket, '*Crackle* Security. There's a gentleman in conference room three who needs escorting from the premises. A Mr Sheridan Maddox.'

Bugger. Looks like that's the end of an eventful 'Conference of Eyewear Retailers'. Still, it hasn't been a complete waste of time, Mr Flannigan's outburst has given me a name for my new app: 'Judge Me!'.

Chapter Seven

SIX MONTHS BEFORE TODAY

'Come on!'

Don't people use Facebook every waking second anymore? I thought millions of hours and billions of pounds were needlessly being wiped from the economy due to workers skiving off work using social media sites. *I am* right this very minute! The latest and greatest app to hit the internet highway hasn't had a new user in over four hours. My hopes and aspirations are fading faster than the 'F5' printed on my refresh button.

Come on, Facebook, Judge Me! ©

The guys that built this app offered me a pretty sweet deal, only a small one-off payment and they keep the rights. I know what you're thinking, '*Why give up the rights?*' This is some crappy little app built to only please a narcissistic, needy, self-absorbed idiot, plus it saved me over £3,000 in development costs. They can do what they want with it, good luck to them. If it only delivers me the tiniest sliver of understanding the face I project upon the world then it's money well spent. Also, this allows me to spend the bulk of my personal budget on marketing, which involves shamelessly offering my friends a £20 Amazon voucher for signing up and judging five of their friends '*in the dock*', one of which is always me. Once they've judged five people they're eligible to be judged themselves. I might be getting the hang of this marketing lark.

Two hundred friends and £4,000 later I should have a decent pool of opinions to dive into. It won't give me that elusive picture to look at but all I need are a thousand words to paint with. Oh yeah, plus I've got access to all the judgements my friends make of the other four people 'in the dock' too, you know, for a comparison. It's amazing the liberties you can abuse in a circumlocutory terms and conditions with willing accomplices on your payroll. Now I understand how power corrupts.

There's a knock on my office door. 'Come in.'

'Err, your "friend" is downstairs.' Daisy's quotes, not mine.

'Send him up.' It's Mike, he's been 'quoted' on more than one occasion.

I hear running footsteps advancing up the stairs and feel the rush of enthusiasm before he even enters the room, the air recedes like the sea before a tsunami. Something has happened to Mike but not something bad, something worse . . . something good.

'Sherry!' Mike bounds in, slams the door shut before crouching over out of breath, 'Oh. My. God.'

You have to play along otherwise he'll just get more annoying. 'What's happened?'

'True love, Sherry my son. Just been on assignment at Perry's Shoes down the road here, I heard a rumour they were squeezing children into ill-fitting shoes to get rid of old stock.'

'That's awful.'

'Turns out it was total bullshit, Jerry and Freya at the paper were having me on. Anyway!' Mike takes a breath, it elevates him so much he's almost levitating. 'The manager, a certain Nicola Winters, turns out . . . she's smoking hot and can't resist your local hot-shot, journalistic talent.'

'And you want me to give her an emergency eye test, ASAP?'

'I managed to calm her down after those hacks explained it was a wind-up, she was scared of the potential PR disaster since she's only been in the job two weeks. So the soothing tones of this investigative reporter sweet-talked her down from the metaphorical window ledge, into her office, and into a world of laughter and flirtatious arm-touching.'

'Metaphorically?' Genuinely, I'm glad for the guy. Even though he can write and talk for England, charming local newsworthy residents and councillors, teasing morsels of information from school fayres and injecting the most boring local meeting with a modicum of interest . . . he can't talk to girls. Or rather, they don't respond to him. 'You asked her out then?'

'What?' Mike looks around, 'Are you talking to a rank amateur? We've already been out, Sherry my son! Just taken her to lunch at The Evening Star, and not the five-pound lunch menu either.'

'Ooooh! Look at you pulling out the big guns.'

'That's what she said. No, but at one point she was holding a kid's shoe saying how could anyone squeeze a kid's foot into an ill-fitting shoe without hurting the child? The parents would step in, they'd never come back, it was bad business, she'd never do that, she'd never allow her staff to do that. I said, "You know what they say about men with big feet, don't you?"'

'Don't tell me she operates on the same level as you!'

'No, she was in tears at this point, but what I'm saying is, I was cool.'

'She was crying?'

'Yeah because of the lies my gutter-press colleagues were spreading, but I apologised on their behalf and soon had her appreciating her new position in this fair town of ours.'

'How'd lunch go then?'

'Like a dream.'

'She fell asleep?'

'We talked about life, family, work, hopes, fears, the whole gamut.'

'So next time there'll be less talking and more . . .'

'Sherry, please! That's my lady you're talking about.'

'Your lady? Christ! You have got it bad, haven't you?' I've never seen him like this or heard him like this. So, I don't know, it sounds weird but he's being . . . respectful. 'Did you make any kind of move on her?'

'It was lunch, Sheridan, a non-alcoholic lunch on a Wednesday. She gave me a kiss on the cheek, fully instigated and executed of her own volition, may I add. Hang on, I just felt a vibration within my nether regions, it must be the aching in her heart compelling her to text me not one hour from our last tryst.'

69

'When has lunch with a peck on the cheek become a "tryst"?'

'Yes. She would like to meet me again. The exact word she uses is "soon".'

'Sounds good. Quick, reply before the alcohol wears off.'

'I don't want to sound desperate, though. I should wait a couple of days, right?'

'Are you fucking insane? First off, you *are* desperate. Secondly, it sounds like you really like this girl. Thirdly, we're in our thirties now with our own mobile phones and residences, what kind of excuse are you going to come up with that warrants a two-day delay in replying? You're not in some American high school movie, get stuck in there.'

'Yeah, you might be right.'

'Get out your phone and reply, you twat. Distract her from abusing the little feet of our Wigthornian children.'

'You're a fucking dick sometimes. Hang on, looks like she can't resist. Is that another message of love I feel vibrating in my pocket? No, it's Facebook. Another bloody game invite . . . how do you turn these fucking things off . . ."Judge Me! Win £20" . . . OK, sounds good.'

I put my nonchalant face on. Well, I think I do, I've no idea . . . blah, blah . . .'What's that then?'

'Oh look, you're on here, Sherry. It's got some questions about you, looks like I've got to judge you for twenty pounds. No brainer, I do it everyday for free. Right, what was that you called me just now; twat? Question one . . .'

Bugger, looks like I should interact with my friends as little as possible over the next few weeks, I don't want to skew the results too badly.

Chapter Eight

FIVE MONTHS BEFORE TODAY

'. . . so my sister has never been the sort of person to go out of her way, you know? It's always been me and my mum. Anyway, suddenly she finds it within herself to find my dad a present for his sixtieth without telling any of us until the last moment. Turns out she's bought exactly the same thing that my mum and I had bought: a track day in a Ferrari. My dad was happy, he went twice. The first time . . .'

This girl can talk. This girl being Laura, a friend of Mike's new love, Nicola. Both Nicola and Mike have been infected with life-threatening levels of 'love' and it's in danger of spreading to everyone else in their near vicinity. One of the side effects of being this close to such a sickening disease is their enthusiasm in spreading it to everyone else too. It's not enough for them to be sharing inane private little jokes with each other, inventing increasingly ludicrous pet names, or kissing in the most infuriating manner imaginable in public displays of infection; they wish others to become contaminated too. There is nothing so lonely than seeing others in love.

This, of course, means they've been pressurising me to go on a blind date with one of Nicola's friends. Any one of them will do! There's no apparent scientific or thorough research into our personalities going on here to find an ideal match, it's simply, 'Maggie's single' or 'Sarah's just split up from Joe'. OK, but what the hell are Maggie and Sarah actually like? Am I such a dead loss to womankind that I should be grateful for any female acknowledging my existence? Are their dreams so lukewarm and tepid as to only require a man to breathe, scratch his balls, and fart every now and again?

For those in love to speak of how special and rare it is, they expect others to find it so easily.

Turns out, Laura is quite nice. She can't half talk though.

I butt in. 'Are you nervous?'

'I'm talking a lot, aren't I?'

'No, no.' Yes. 'I was just wondering if you knew what you wanted to order yet before the waiter came back with our drinks.'

'Oh, yes. I'm going to have the tuna salad. What are you having?'

This is a minefield. People joke about not having spaghetti on a first date, but there's not much I can eat in the company of a stranger. I avoid any kind of sauces because the potential for splash back is so great. I can feel the drips but have to wipe my whole face with a napkin, making me look like a bit of a freak. I stay away from salads after the first date I had with Heidi; getting greenery stuck in your teeth is too much of a risk. One strategy is to eat everything in tiny mouthfuls, very slowly, ensuring every morsel reaches its intended destination; the problem with this is the girl finishes eating first which puts her on a downer, making her feel gluttonous and fat, which makes you look delicate, stripping you of any masculinity. The odds of getting any action after all that becomes so astronomical you'd have a better chance staying at home watching the news channel, alone. So, answer the question, Sheridan, what are you having?

'I'm going to go for it, you don't mind, do you?'

'Of course not.'

'I'm going for the full rack of barbecue ribs.' Everyone needs a full face wash after ribs. I should've thought of this option years ago.

'You're brave!'

'I like to live life on the edge, Laura. If I delicately eat a small portion of something posh then I'd be lying to you, I think it's good to be honest and start how we mean to go on.'

'And I thought we were only getting together over dinner.'

'Oh no, Laura, it's much deeper than that!'

'So what does my tuna salad say about me?'

'I've no idea, I'm making all this up on the spot just to give me an excuse to have ribs. I really fancy ribs after the week I've had.'

'That's fair enough. I like a man who likes his food.'

'This is a good start, then. I like a girl who likes her man to like his food.'

'"*Her man*"?'

Bollocks. I smile in an exaggerated fashion. This girl's all right, she's on the ball. She's not Heidi; and just as I think this impossible, unthinkable thought, I realise this has to be a positive thought. Laura hasn't run away. Yet.

'You've had a rough week then?' asks Laura.

'Not rough, just one of those, you know, nothing seems to go right, people hassle you, it drags on.'

'Tell me, we're meant to be getting to know each other, right?'

'My area manager is pestering me to take a promotion after I've repeatedly said no.'

'That's annoying, isn't it? Getting recognised for your hard work and talents. People putting their trust in you to further their business. Earning more money, gaining respect, fulfilling potential.'

'I see you're well-versed in the nuanced art of sarcasm.'

'You think?'

'It's not like that. I do appreciate the sentiment but I've said no and he still keeps on at me.'

'Why not take it?'

'If I became a branch manager it would involve a lot more sitting behind a desk doing paperwork and dealing with staff; that's not what I like. It's not what I'm good at. I enjoy what I do at the moment, having that customer contact, making sure everyone receives a thorough check-up and the best possible eyewear. I'm not saving lives or stopping wars but I'm doing something a little worthwhile. If I could improve people's hindsight and foresight too, as well as their eyesight, then maybe I *could* save lives and stop wars but that isn't going to happen. Sitting behind a desk when all I'm doing is paying invoices and sorting out staff holidays, where's the fun in that? Where's the job satisfaction in compiling weekly reports and analysing window displays?'

'I'd love to put together a window display! Anyway, have you told your area manager all this?'

'Yeah, many times, but he's adamant I'd be good at it and I'd enjoy it. He's tempting me with a good package and saying he'd be open to me splitting the job with an assistant manager so I could spend fifty per cent of my time with customers.'

'Sounds like he wants you badly. What else has been dragging you down this week?'

'I've been finding out what some friends of mine really think of me, which hasn't been too positive.'

'No way! Have you been using that Judge Me! app on Facebook too? Everyone's using that at the moment. It's like some kind of techno-voyeuristic masochism.'

'You mean that in a bad way, right?'

'Yeah. And in a good way too. Have you seen the Judge Me! Stats app?'

'No.' Is someone piggy-backing and profiting from my original idea? Welcome to the internet, sucker. How does that deal of giving away the rights for £3,000 sound now?

'Oh man! It brings you down into another level of masochism. You can drill down into your results and get stats such as what do all women think versus men, close friends versus work colleagues, older people versus younger, etc. I checked it this afternoon, people think I'm generally happy but if you divide up the responses: men think I'm flirty-happy and women think I'm scatty-happy.'

'Do you have to pay for it?'

'If this date fails, I'd think about it.'

'I meant the app.'

'I know you did.'

'Are you flirting with me?'

'Statistically, probably!'

I need to get back in contact with those app developers and my old lawyer mate from university even if he does think I'm *arrogant and narcissistic*'. The developers gave me a password to peek behind the curtain so there's no anonymous answers; I kind of regret it now. I walk around in a state of permanent paranoia with the inability to talk or look anyone in the eye who gave me anything less than a ringing endorsement, which in turn, will make their opinion of me sink even further.

'Laura, can I be bold and ask you a very upfront, unsubtle question?'

'I don't sleep with anyone until at least the fourth date.'

'Thanks, I'll make a note of that, but that wasn't what I was going to ask.'

'OK, go for it.'

'Can I ask you what you think of me, looks-wise? What's your first impression of me after only meeting me fifteen minutes ago?'

'Wow! You're right, that is bold . . . or is it needy? I'm not sure. Interesting though. You want me to judge you immediately, to your face, no holds barred?'

'Exactly. Yes.'

'Can't we just friend each other on Facebook and allow ourselves to judge each other anonymously?'

'No. Laura, I trust you to talk to me honestly. We may never see each other again . . .'

'. . . we may get married?'

'Either way, let's begin by being brutally honest from the get-go.'

'"Brutally"? That's a loaded term.'

'OK, just honest.'

'OK.'

I sit back in my chair. I don't quite know what's come over me but it feels right, she feels like someone who'll give me a fair assessment. She sits forward in her chair, elbows on the table, hands clasped together, her eyes scanning me completely. I'm the total centre of her attention, every part of me she looks at feels alive. Slowly my whole face feels rebuilt, fully projecting itself onto the world. I still may not be able to see it, but being noticed means it's there. It exists. I exist.

'You're a good-looking man, Sheridan. You have a calmness about you, I feel at ease with you. You're not panicked or skittish, you listen, your thoughts appear collected. Your appearance is somewhat *irregular*.'

'What do you mean? I'm all wonky or something?'

'It's like the opposite of *rough around the edges*; your eyebrows could do with a slight trim yet your hair is immaculately styled. You're very clean-shaven and your sideburns are straight as a ruler yet there's a couple of errant hairs just under your nose. You smell good, your clothes are crisp and well colour-coordinated and yet there's a stray spot on your forehead. There's close attention to detail in some areas and in others there are not.'

'What about my face?'

'You have lovely brown eyes peeking through a manly but not a Neanderthal brow, your long dark eyelashes help to soften it. Most women would die for your cheekbones. Faces light up with a smile but your smile hides worry, as though you have to twist your face into a smile, forcing it to do something it doesn't believe in. It looks better relaxed, maybe you need to let go of whatever is tensing you up inside. Don't worry about it though, women love that vulnerable look, we want to mother you, make you feel better. Nicola said you were good-looking and she was right. I am attracted to you if that was what you were after.'

It wasn't but I'll take that too. 'Thanks, Laura, that was very good of you to open up and be honest with me, I really appreciate it. It means more than you'll ever know.'

'I was too nice, I'll do it again when I start to see some negative things. And don't ask me if you can return the favour, I'm neither bold enough nor masochistic enough to receive such personal judgement face-to-face.'

'You're good-looking and lovely, Laura.'

'Thanks, Romeo. Saved by the bell, here comes the waiter with our drinks.'

Just as the waiter places our drinks on the table and asks us what we wish to order, both of our phones buzz and beep with a text message. We both order and then excuse each other as we silently read our respective texts.

She's dumped me, Sherry! That fucking bitch! I need to get paralytic! A truly unhealthy, toxic amount of alcohol is on me . . . until we collapse.

Great timing, Mike. I look up at Laura, who returns it with added solemnity.

'Was yours from Nicola?'

'Yes.'

'She dumped Mike?'

'Mike dumped her.'

'Oh.'

In unison, both our phones start ringing. We peer back down at them before returning to look at each other again.

'Nicola?'

'Yes. Mike?'

'Yes.' I should be there for him, I really should but I don't want to be rude to Laura, plus . . . well, plus . . . 'The ribs are meant to be amazing here.'

'Yeah, I heard that.'

'Their tuna salad is meant to be a corker too.'

'Yeah, I heard that too, I'm really looking forward to it.'

I press the ignore button on my phone, sending Mike straight to voicemail. It's not a life or death situation. Laura does the same.

'Let's eat, Sheridan, I think we're going to need to keep our strength up.'

'Good thinking.'

'G7.' I can see Mike's eyelids trying to shut out the light as he speaks but the sheer will and drunken determination to win forces them open. 'No, no, no! G . . . fucking . . . err . . . fucking, yeah, G7'

'Miss!' He's already said that but I keep schtum, it's up to him to record what squares he has and hasn't guessed at.

We discovered *Battleshots* online a few years ago and after playing it only once you quickly realise it's a serious game with serious consequences; war is hell. Very similar to Battleships, but played with shots instead of little toy ships. To play requires you to order two large pizzas plus the acquisition of a marker pen and a ruler. Eat said pizzas then draw out an 8 x 8 grid on the pizza box base and on the inside of the lid. Open pizza box and place the ships, or rows of shots, anywhere on the grid. As with the non-alcoholic Battleships, recording your previous shots is vital as to not waste your turns shooting at the same square twice, or, as with G7, three times. Bureaucracy and bravery go hand in hand in war. Mike's losing on both fronts.

I return fire. 'OK, I'm going to go for A1.'

'Fuck! You fucking lucky fuck! Are you fucking cheating?'

'A1 is so obvious, every novice with no imagination goes for that thinking it's a clever double-bluff. Anyway, it's your favourite band.'

'Fuck off!'

Mike picks up the shot glass with its dark red liquid. It's the disgusting crap we got on a lads' skiing holiday eight years ago in Austria. To call it the out-of-date dregs of the foulest mountain moonshine would be overselling it.

'Oh fuck! Eurrghhhhhh!'

'You've got another one to go after that, Mikey.'

'Fuck off! I'm going to chunder . . .' Mike's dedication to forgetting his break-up is second to none, it's admirable in its execution. He picks up the second shot glass filled with the unholiest of waters, 'Oh dear fucking God . . . eurghhhh . . . Oh shit! That one had fucking skin on it . . . seriously, I'm going to chunder . . .'

I rush over to his side to protect my carpet and grab his arm.

'Don't look at my . . .' Mike stops an errand hiccup from turning into actual vomit, 'don't look at my fucking board.'

'Just get to the bog!'

As Mike kneels there in front of the toilet bowl, praying to the Austrian mountain gods to spare his soul, I reflect on the sight of a heartbroken man. Not so long ago that was me.

I look in the mirror and stare at the blurry mess propped upon my shoulders. Even though everything else around me is slowly swaying and shimmering due to my inebriated vision, my face remains the same. My reflection is not only unseeable but also unchangeable.

Maybe I should've just got absolutely hammered instead of searching in vain for some version of self-realisation. Maybe gaining closure like this would've allowed me to move on unhindered and carefree.

'Mike? You feel any better now?'

'No . . .' *Spit, cough, spit.*

'I mean about breaking up with Nicola.'

'Nicola who? Fucking bitch . . . Oh, shit . . .'

A second avalanche gets an express cable car up from the depths of Mike's stomach to the summit, so I leave him to it and get him a glass of water.

Is my unwillingness to let go of Heidi due to my inability to change, or is it because I like to cling on to higher ideals and believe the more I hang on to the belief we'll be reunited makes it seem nobler and more meaningful than most relationships out there? Like Mike's. If it was true love she wouldn't have left. But if it is actually true love then I have to keep loving her until she comes back.

Am I only seeing what I want to see? I have a history of not being able to see the plainly obvious so am I missing something fundamental about Heidi and our relationship that defies all rational explanation? If I can't see it for myself then no one else is going to be able to explain it to me.

Mike's still on all fours as he looks up. 'That better be fucking water in that glass.'.

I offer him the glass. 'Feeling any better, mate?'

Mike gingerly gets up. 'Oh yes, I'm ready to continue this game and then get a taxi into town, which nightclub do you fancy?'

'None of them.'

'Whoa, what the fuck is this . . . 1994 or something?'

Mike fronts up to the framed picture opposite the toilet door, as his outstretched hand steadies himself up against the wall next to it. My latest quest to search out my reflection, one of those magic eye pictures that were so popular in the early 90s. I could never see them then and this one is no different, it's another box ticked though.

'I used to love these . . . is it a boat . . . or a horse . . . no . . . fucking hell, Sherry! As if you haven't got enough self-portraits you go and get a magic eye done of yourself. Ha, ha, ha! Cool. I want one. Hang on . . . it's making me feel a little queasy again, must be your ugly mug coming out at me in 3D. Quick, lets get playing again . . . err . . . C3.'

Shit. 'Hit.'

'Yes! Drink up, Shezza!'

Chapter Nine

FOUR MONTHS BEFORE TODAY

This Tuesday morning isn't going well, a day filled with appointments and by 10.30am I want to go home. Just had a 'glaucy' in, third of the morning already, sounds awful doesn't it? Putting customers into boxes and labelling them with a term you'd never say to their face, but we do it anyway. Amazing how much of ourselves we choose not to see.

Glaucies always get me down. I peer into the distorted pupil trying to find some semblance of a reflection but the imperfect circle invariably gives nothing away. Glaucoma is caused by a lack of drainage from the anterior chamber, causing pressure against the eyeball and eventually affecting the vision. Looking through my slit lamp, I thought I could feel my own eyes swelling and contracting as I peered into the fog. One theory I played with for a while was, maybe I could mirror the symptoms of my patients to better understand them, feel some kind of 'sympathy pains', but after some rudimentary testing this proved to be false; I don't become near-sighted when I'm examining a near-sighted patient, nor develop glaucoma with a glaucy. That was one theory I was glad to dismiss; being able to mirror eye diseases but not my own image. That would be one crap superpower.

I have thought along those lines though; am I sacrificing one aspect of normality in exchange for stepping into the realm of the Übermensch? It makes no sense though, how would not seeing the reflection of your face in the mirror be an advantage or something you'd be willing to forgo for a greater gift? Even Superman wouldn't give it up, how would he style his little curl?

In thirty-six years (it was my birthday last week, whatever) I haven't found what this sacrifice has given me, if anything at all. I can neither fly nor walk through walls, look through walls, or even build a wall. I'm quite good at Battleshots but, really, I'd be disappointed if that was the sacrifice I'd somehow unwittingly made.

So here I find myself, in my office at work with no cape or superpower but with a secret identity to protect and a unique difference setting me apart from the rest of the human race.

My office is located on the first floor, at the front, overlooking the pedestrianised high street with Candleina opposite and our bench in between. It's still 'our' bench. A few months ago this was the perfect view anyone could ever want from their office window. Now I want to place bars in front of it. I almost dread looking out of this window more than looking into a mirror, yet every day, every spare moment in between patients, I can't help but peer out, expecting to see Heidi waltz serenely into Candleina as though she'd never left.

Christ knows what I'd do if she ever did.

'Sheridan . . . Sheridan!'

Daisy carefully ensures her body remains outside of the room to avoid technically interrupting me, even though she's opened the door and is calling my name with excessive enthusiasm.

'All right, Daisy?'

'Sheridan, I've been knocking for about ten minutes here.'

'Mrs Longlands only left a couple of minutes ago.'

Daisy walks in, closing the door quietly behind her, a sure sign she's investigating for the office gossip lunchtime edition. 'You've got Mrs Grimshaw in five minutes.'

'OK.' I double-check Heidi hasn't slipped into Candleina.

'So, you heard about Martin?'

'No.' I think he's been seeing Hannah downstairs, I know he definitely slept with her after the last work's night out, he wouldn't shut up about it.

'He's off sick.'

'And?'

'So's Hannah.'

'And?'

'Don't you think that's a coincidence?'

'Yeah. They both got sick on the same day, so what?'

'Sam said he saw them both last Saturday after work, down the seafront. You know . . . down that dark road between the fields.'

'Sam needs to keep his mouth shut. Anyway, did you ask Sam what he was doing down there at that time?'

I can almost see the two brain cells colliding inside her head, a story forming, the headline piece she was looking for. 'Hmmm, yes. Good point.'

'Look, I should get ready for Mrs Grimshaw . . .'

'Are you OK, Sheridan?'

'I'm fine, Daisy.'

'You're not your usual self, you used to like a good bit of goss."

It's true, I'm not immune to the power of tittle-tattle or unappreciative of its superior communicative efficiency. 'I just had a crap night, that's all.'

'Looking out that window ain't going to bring Heidi back, you know.'

Looks like I'll be getting a small byline in the lunchtime edition. 'I'm not, can't I just stare out the window like any other corporate drone?'

'No one from downstairs has seen her. She hasn't updated Facebook, even Chloe hasn't heard from her. You haven't had any luck getting hold of her then?'

I continue preparing for the next customer, I'm not going to get involved.

'It's OK, we'll keep an eye out for you downstairs, let you know if we see her. Come here . . .'

She's looking at me funny. 'What?'

'You've got a bit of fluff stuck to the stubble on your chin, let me get it off for you. You're not going to impress Mrs Grimshaw like that. God knows what Mrs Longlands thought.'

After Daisy removes it, I see the offending object as she flicks it into the bin. I then look into the mirror pretending to sharpen myself up as Daisy heads out. I'm well versed in such charades.

'Daisy.' She turns around as she half closes the door. 'Thanks.'

'Any time, Sheridan.'

There's a moment in between Daisy leaving and Mrs Grimshaw entering when I take another chance to search the high street outside for Heidi. Occasionally there's a false alarm; a girl with a similar hairstyle, the same walk, matching coat, but never the real McCoy. Just now a brunette strolled into Candleina with the same handbag I bought Heidi for her birthday. The initial shock of my heart and lungs getting sucked into another dimension, rendering me unable to breathe or even contemplate one last heartbeat, soon vanished when I realised it wasn't Heidi and then worsened when I remembered that I don't think she even liked that handbag. I never saw her with it, never sensed genuine thanks after she'd unwrapped it and slung it over her shoulder, and don't remember her even broaching the more general subject of 'feminine storage vessels' ever again. She was kind and I was thankful.

The reminders don't just appear in the gait, hairstyles, and clothing of near doppelgängers but also in missed opportunities to share a private joke, exchange a look, pass comment, or discovering funny videos online, information she'd appreciate, stories she'd love, *Schadenfreude* she'd adore. All of these tiny trinkets I can't gift to anyone else keep my mind richly decorated . . . and weighed down. Now I'm compelled to share observations and judgements with an imaginary substitute perched upon my shoulder. I don't, of course. Not out loud, anyway. I may not be able to see myself but I damn well know other people can see me.

Forlorn love defaces my world with the Baader-Meinhof effect; now she's gone, I see her everywhere.

There's a knock on the door. 'Come in.'

Mrs Grimshaw enters. Now, I don't know about you but some names immediately give you a heads-up on what type of person to expect. To me a *Mrs Grimshaw* could only ever be used by a portly old woman whose social upstanding is maintained by an extreme bosom and a counter-balancing posterior, with the addition of rollers in her purple hair, a faded, flowery apron, and a constant desire to devour and discharge gossip over the back fence in a grey, rainy northern city whilst hanging up her washing.

However, this is 'Sunny Wigthorn', sitting proudly upon the South Coast. An ancient ancestor of the Grimshaw clan from up north must have had a son who, through chance and circumstance, found himself all the way *dahn sarf*. Generations later, with the name hanging around the neck like a millstone, there is a Mr Grimshaw walking around Wigthorn with a wife like a gemstone. Mrs Grimshaw is a very attractive girl with eyes so beautiful an optometrist should have no business examining them; only an artist.

'Mrs Grimshaw?'

'Yes.'

'Please sit down. It says you're only in for a routine check-up, is that right?'

'Yes, I got this leaflet through the door saying you're doing a deal and I haven't had my eyes checked . . . well, ever, I don't think.'

I put down my notes and go over to prepare the slit lamp, making doubly sure the lenses are clean and crossing my fingers that the beautiful eyes in this beautiful girl's head might be a mirror into my soul as I could look into them for all eternity. Even if they weren't the mirror I was looking for, I could still look into them for an unhealthily long period of time.

'Eyes aren't the sort of thing you check up on unless something goes wrong, really. Have you experienced any headaches, blurred vision, have trouble reading, anything like that?'

'No, I'm pretty sure my eyes are in great condition, it's the rest of me.'

'Ha, ha, ha.' Did that sound forced? Yeah, I thought so. There's nothing wrong with the rest of you, love. Nothing at all.

Now, I'm not sure if girls appreciate it or not, I still haven't figured it out yet, but the first thing I look at on a beautiful girl, any girl, any person actually, are the eyes. Even girls with low-cut tops struggling to contain a heaving bosom, or a 'great rack' as Mike says. I'm not sure if they find it a refreshing change or a little disconcerting. I mention this now because I only remember it when I find myself doing it; as I sit in front of her and slide the slit lamp into position, asking her to rest her chin and look through the lens, do I then take a cheeky look down.

I'm a normal bloke, I'm not going to pretend any different, it's just that my condition has shifted my priorities ever so slightly. We let women think we can't multitask; that's multitasking in itself. I can be in total and utter grief for my lost love and yet still be a slave to my genomic evolution and check out a 'great rack'.

I go through the examination and there's absolutely nothing wrong with her, any of her, at all. I'll have to check out her Judge Me! results.

Her eyes are even more beautiful magnified one hundred times but they're no mirror into my soul. I suppose it's for the best, I mean, what if they were a mirror for me? How would I get close to her so I could look into them again, more than once? I could misdiagnose a problem or end up stalking her like a madman, *Please, Mrs Grimshaw, I just want to look into your eyes!* Yeah, I'd be locked up for sure.

'Well, that's you all done, Mrs Grimshaw. It is with my deepest regret that your eyes are in perfect twenty-twenty condition and there's no need for me to see you again for at least another two years.'

'Thank you, Doctor.' I rarely correct people who call me Doctor, it seems to be a patient reflex. 'My husband's next, I think, hopefully you can give him the same good news.'

Smile, Sheridan. 'Yes, hopefully I can.' I show her out. 'Nice to meet you.'

Mrs Grimshaw exits as serenely as she entered, her perfect behind, tightly outlined in denim, completing this whole wonderful experience.

'Holy Christ, Sheridan! D'ya see the pair of eyes on that?!' Steve, the area manager, has been waiting outside. He does this every month after his meeting with our branch manager, poised like a hunter with his silver tongue ready to deliver his stinging pitch. We both watch her get enveloped by her husband, squeezing the life out of any fantasies that may have been conjured . . . which were definitely conjured.

'So Sheridan, you thought more about stepping up the ladder? Getting your own branch and becoming lord of the manor? I got a nice little number just come up in Guildford, prime spot in the town, very profitable, great team, don't tell anyone else but probably the most friendly, knowledgeable branch I've got, you'd fit right in. I'll make sure you get the full branch manager pay packet, all the extra benefits, what more do you want?'

I think about it for – 'No, thanks Steve. I'm all right here, cheers.'

'Sheridan! You're killing me here. You're forcing me to promote inferior people, you're upsetting the natural order of things. You're single-handedly destroying capitalism, my friend.'

'I'm happy here by the seaside.'

'The sea? OK, OK, there might be a branch in Portsmouth coming up next month or one in Eastbourne a bit later on, let me have a word. To be honest, I could sack the Eastbourne guy tomorrow, bloody liability that bloke—'

'Steve, I'm happy here in Wigthorn. I'm not looking for a promotion, I know my limits and I know what I want, and I want to stay here.'

'Sheridan, I can't be asking this of you every month but I don't want you to miss out. I don't want to miss out on having you as part of my team, you'd be fantastic. Listen, let me ask you a question, where do you see yourself in five years?'

'Yeah, that's an . . . interesting question, Steve.'

'Doctor?' Mr Grimshaw looms large behind Steve. The guy is a full-on unit.

'Yes, yes, Mr Grimshaw, please go straight in, I'll be with you shortly.'

'Was that your wife back there?' Steve butts in.

'Yeah.'

'Don't worry about your eyes, mate, they're perfectly fine. You don't need glasses, you deserve a medal or something.'

Mr Grimshaw smiles awkwardly, as he sidesteps past Steve and into my office.

'I've got to go now, Steve.'

'Yeah, sure. Good man, always on the job. Think about it, I'll be back down next month, we'll talk more, I'll buy you lunch.'

'OK.'

He's never offered to buy lunch before, he must be desperate. I get back to work, 'Mr Grimshaw. Hi. Sorry about that, our area manager is a little over enthusiastic when he's around customers, he's usually stuck in his car all day.'

'That's all right, Doctor. Don't worry about it, it's one of the crosses you have to bear when you have a hot wife; compliments from other guys. There's worse crosses to bear, I suppose.'

'Yeah, yeah. I'm sure there are.' Like being born with a ridiculously old-fashioned family name and then having to convince your ridiculously hot wife to bear the burden too. 'Let's get started then, hopefully your eyes are as good as your wife's.'

I sit him down in front of the slit lamp, ask some questions, take some notes, and think about Steve's offer. More money, more benefits; always a tempting offer. Where *do* I see myself in five years? How about next year? I'm in the same place I was in last year but the journey in between, falling in love with Heidi and then losing Heidi, means it feels like a different world.

Am I tied to Wigthorn? Why? Why not move on, go somewhere else? Start afresh in a new town, a locality without familiarity, somewhere incapable of agitating any memories or mixing nostalgia with regret. Somewhere with a fresh batch of customers to examine because Wigthorn hasn't produced any mirrors with which to view my soul.

'Mr Grimshaw, can you read the top line . . . now the next . . .'

Yeah, maybe a move would be good. Meet new people, new colleagues, more responsibility, live in a new place, a new route to and from work, a new start.

'That's all fine. Now if I slide over the slit lamp here . . . if you just rest your chin here and look through here with your right eye first . . .'

Who's going to miss me? Mike? Maybe, a little.

A handful of friends will be glad to be freed from the melancholy

I hang around their necks, the desolation in my soul sucking the life out of them like a black hole going down a plughole.

'OK, just keep your eye open while I take a look at your cornea . . .'

Anyway, it's not like you're moving abroad, you can always go home at the weekends to see people or maybe people might even deem a trip to me a viable option if they've got absolutely nothing else on. Moving abroad? Hmmm . . . that's another option. Is there a shortage of optometrists in Bondi Beach? No, maybe just stay with Twenty20, at least they know me . . .

. . .

'. . .'

. . .

'. . . Doctor?'

I don't believe it. Is that? It can't be . . .

'Is everything OK?'

I've never seen anything like this in someone's eye before.

'You've gone all quiet, Doctor.'

'Yes, yes everything's fine, sorry.'

Holy shit. I think I just saw my reflection. I look up over the slit lamp at Mr Grimshaw, who's still sitting there with his chin on the rest.

He looks up at me. 'All right?'

'Yeah, fine. Can you line up your left eye now?'

He does. I rub my eyes before settling back into position to see if this was just a fluke or a mirage. I focus.

And there it is.

My reflection.

Chapter Ten

THREE MONTHS BEFORE TODAY

'Daisy, has my ten o'clock cancelled?'

'No, I haven't heard anything.'

Good. I've constructed a little lie to see Mr Grimshaw again, a white lie, for my benefit, not his. Have you seen his wife? It's about time he paid back what he owes. He must owe something.

A small bureaucratic oversight; mislaid paperwork requiring a retest. Of course, it's a freebie whenever you're available, sir, along with a discount on any subsequent frames, if required, for the inconvenience this has caused you. We're terribly sorry.

I've never broken the rules at work before. I mean, this could be filed under professional negligence, purposely deleting someone's test results. Every part of me says I'm taking this a step too far but . . .

It was me in the reflection of his eye.

It was me. I'm sure it was.

Spoken descriptions by others, familial similarities, touching your own face, obsessing over a dodgy caricature can only paint a picture of such a limited representation that it becomes meaningless; none of them a substitute for seeing your actual reflection, mano-a-mano. I can see why people say I look like my dad. The familiarity I felt when I saw my own reflection stemmed from the photographs I've seen of him as a young man.

This means there is another aspect of my condition: I can see images of relatives that have more than a passing resemblance to myself. Genealogy is a mirror, ancestors construct us in their own image.

Life must be so easy when you're able to see yourself whenever you want, nothing hidden from view, no haze, no blur, no hurdles, no masks. To see yourself how others see you, not having to rely on interpretation or translation, a pure and unbiased perspective. The window into your soul permanently open and available, your soul always ready to speak to you, just a mirror away.

In the blinding shock of seeing the light emanating from my soul in the darkness of Mr Grimshaw's pupil, I forgot to take a moment for self-reflection, to look into my own eyes. Like a deer caught in the headlights, I froze. I was so busy consuming my own vanity I forgot to forge deeper. I'm as shallow as a puddle and foolish enough to drown in one.

So I told a little lie. So what.

Daisy peers around the door. 'Psst, Sheridan. Your ten o'clock's just arrived.'

'Thanks.'

I give my equipment one final check, ensuring the added extras are in place, plugged in, and working, giving the lenses another clean, giving myself some eye drops and a pep talk. This time I will be ready.

This time I won't let answers slip through my fingers as they did with Heidi, leaving myself treading water in an aftermath drenched in her memory. She was my mirror into the world, I could gauge what I looked like from people's reactions and interactions with her and with us. What I saw was good. People were happy to be with us and we were happy to be with each other. I couldn't have misread all this, could I?

'Mr Grimshaw, please come in.'

'Hi, thanks. I'm not quite sure why you wanted me back, I thought you said everything was fine?'

'It is, Mr Grimshaw.' *Elevated fake laughter, act natural.* 'It's totally our fault, there's nothing to worry about physically, your eyes are fine, the paperwork has been mislaid and so I need to go through the test again. I can't simply fill in the form at a later date from memory, I have so many patients all their results tend to blend into one.' *More fake laughter, shrug shoulders, open palms, what can I do?*

91

'OK, it's just that I've got to get off to the football soon.'

'Of course, as I said, totally my fault. This test is free and I'll be refunding your original test so hopefully you'll stay with us in future. This will just take two minutes, literally. Please, sit, place your chin here and we'll get this over with. It's just a formality.'

Mr Grimshaw is sitting down, peering into the slit lamp unaware of the extra mirrors and cameras I have fitted. You may never have had to think of such a contraption but let me pose you this question, how would you take a photograph of your own reflection in another person's eye?

Your first problem is the actual camera itself, it's always going to get in the way. I'm resigned to the fact I'm never going to get the perfect picture of me looking straight into the camera via the reflection of Mr Grimshaw's eye. The next best picture I can think of is to get multiple images taken from slight angles around my face and then somehow merge these into one. I haven't looked into the mechanics of how you'd merge these images into one but I went out and bought five mini cameras. These are hooked up around the slit lamp my side and I've changed the slit lamp lenses so all I see from my side is Mr Grimshaw's eye magnified until it's the size of a saucer; he's looking pretty bloody weird at the moment. So all I have to do is position myself in front of his eye until I see myself in his pupil and take a photo.

'OK, I'm just going to take a quick look at your pupil.'

I've also got mirrors positioned around the slit lamp so the image from his pupil is then deflected through a couple more mirrors to another camera for a second image. For the best image, I need to increase the size of his pupil, I want to get my best side.

'I'm just going to turn the lights out so I can get a better view of your pupil and measure its response.'

I flick the switch so the room is in darkness, I can see his pupil slowly grow to let in more light, my reflection increasing in size, my self-confidence growing with it.

'The one test I forgot last time is the "flash test", which involves flashing a bright light briefly to examine the eyes' response reflex.'

I feel for the master switch I've wired up, controlling all five cameras and a flash bulb. I line my reflection up in his eye so I'm looming large and central like the target of an assassin sitting in the cross-hairs. My finger on the trigger, I pause. I smile. I look at my smile. So that's what I look like smiling. I've always smiled for photos without realising why. It's too exaggerated, I know what a good smile looks like, I see it on other people, but without seeing the results you don't know how your face muscles manifest themselves. The smile I've been using for years is ridiculous. I tone it down, more subtle use of my mouth, that's better. I squeeze the trigger . . .

FLASH!

'Bloody hell!' Mr Grimshaw curls away, rubbing his eye. More industrial language finds its way into the room as his pupil reacts much like it should; shrinking in blind terror and panic.

'Sorry, Mr Grimshaw! Keep your eyes closed for the moment, let them relax without any light. Slowly open them when you're ready. I think the maintenance guy must have put the wrong bulb in.' Another lie, I'm getting too comfortable with this.

'I'm seeing bloody stars here!'

'Mr Grimshaw. Kevin. Can I call you Kevin?'

'You'll have to call me a lawyer if I'm not seeing properly after this.'

'Kevin, it'll be fine, just keep them closed and remain seated for a while, I'll just check the computerised image to make sure everything is tickety-boo.'

So far, so good. The flash worked perfectly, all five cameras took a photo and they've all downloaded onto the computer. Now to see what they look like . . .

Bugger.

Crap.

Arse.

Fuck.

Why did I think these photos would be any different? They're all a blur, like every other photo anyone has ever taken of me.

93

Somehow I thought Kevin Grimshaw's eye may counteract any adverse affects because I could see my own reflection in them, but no. All five photos have turned out as all photos of me turn out: a hazy blur where my face should be.

'Kevin, how's your eye?'

'OK, the stars are fading and I can see.'

'Shall I turn the lights back on?'

'Yeah, go for it.'

'Let me take a look. The digital images are all fine, I can't see any irregularities.' I bend down and take one last look into his eyes, a mental photograph of myself to deposit into my memory bank. Maybe linger a little longer to see whether my soul will provide me with any clues as to why I'm acting so irrationally.

There I am. I quickly scan his eyes to make sure they are actually OK; they are. I then spend a few seconds looking at myself, no longer though. I can't freak him out or scare him off because how will I ever get another look?

How will I get another look?

He's not due back for another two years, that's if he's that bothered about getting a regular eye test, and who is? And why would he come back here?

I can't wait two years. I've got to befriend him. Fuck! How do you make friends with another guy you don't work with or play sport with, without it looking like you're hitting on him?! The guy is clearly straight. So am I, but at this stage, all bets are off.

Act natural, Sheridan!

Mention Heidi, maybe if I underline my heterosexuality by mentioning my ex he'll be less inclined to be scared off. In what context? I don't know! OK, OK, how am I going to connect with this guy, what do we have in common? I've nearly blinded him, how can I become mates with him to a point where I can stare into his eyes . . . in a straight, platonic, non-optometrist way?

Fucking hell, this is never going to work!

Maybe I should just decapitate him and put his head in a jar of formaldehyde or remove his eyes and preserve them so I can pull

them out of my pocket anytime I want to bask in my own reflection.
A morbid pocket mirror.

Yeah, that would probably be easier.

'So, that's it, right?'

I'm going to need drugs to knock him out, he's twice my size.

'Yeah, if you could just sign here, please.'

I can't let him go yet, surely? My reflection's in there!

'There you go. Get that bulb sorted.'

'Yeah, sorry about that.'

And he's gone. Walked out the door with my reflection stuck in
his head.

Chapter Eleven

TWO MONTHS BEFORE TODAY

Ding, dong!

Kevin Grimshaw is here. This is going to be painful.

No, no, no, it's not what you think, I haven't lost my mind in the last month. I'm not painting the walls of my flat with my own faeces and there's no voices in my head commanding me to commit acts of depravity; I tend to ignore most of what Mike tells me anyway. No, I 'accidentally-on-purpose' bumped into Kevin last week down the pub, somehow managed to cross the delicate line of initiating conversation and we had a few beers. I ended up inviting him over to watch the big game today. Apparently it's a big game, anyway, I have no idea. I hate football. As I said, this is going to be painful.

'Kev, all right, mate?' Drop your 'T's', evict that middle-class southern accent on to a council estate and say 'mate' a lot. That's how football fans speak, right?

'Yeah, all right? Brought a couple of beers over and the wife, she's a big Wigs fan too, her dad used to play for them.'

Kevin's looking at me, waiting for something. I've no idea what.

He continues. '*Trevor Brown*, legendary Wigs captain who took them all the way from non-league obscurity to the championship and didn't miss one game in ten years?'

'Oh, *that* Trevor Brown! *Brownie!* Wicked.'

'Yeah, anyway, she's just parking the car, takes her a bloody age and refuses to let me do it for her. Let's crack on, I don't want to miss a second of this.'

'Sweet. I'll leave the door open for her.'

I've got to wing this. I went online this morning and read up on the game today, looks like I should've done some research on the club history too. Wigthorn FC against Brighton & Hove Albion, a local derby in the FA Cup. I mean, I hear bits and bobs from people at work but I let it waft through me and I tune out. Maybe there was a whole side to Heidi I just tuned out to and that's why she left? It's easily done. How many times have you found yourself staring at a pair of moving lips as you disembark from a daydream, frantically grappling for the subject and the context before the conversation swings your way?

I'm doing it now! Get in the game, Sherry!

'Get this beast of technology on then, Sheridan, my son!'

One of the carrots that tempted Kevin over, my huge 52-inch, curved screen, ultra HD 5K TV with kick-ass sound system. I told him all about it down the pub when nothing resembling such a set-up existed anywhere in my flat. As a result, I had to hunt around for a TV that could live up to my exaggerated, over-the-top bravado. Such boasting has set me back about £3,000 in total; an expensive lesson in humility but a massive step up from my ten-year-old 28-inch generic piece of crap TV from before. The news has never been more scary.

I stare at the new remote. Everything I learnt from last night's practice session has slipped through a hole in my memory; I'm currently scrolling through the language options. 'Fucking thing.' That's right, a few swear words will ingratiate you to your new football tribe brethren.

'Come on, Sheridan, tame this fucking beast!'

Finally, a referee's whistle blows as the huge frame fills with the green grass, white lines, and the red and blue colours of the teams. 'Tamed my, son!' Thank Christ for that.

Kevin opens a can of beer and passes it to me before opening one for himself and relaxing back into the sofa with a focused satisfaction on his face. I think I'm doing all right. I relax back into the sofa too.

'Any luck with getting a signed shirt, Sheridan?'

That was the other carrot. I said I could get a Wigthorn FC shirt signed by all the players through a contact of mine at the local paper. I then had to convince Mike to demean himself and speak to the sports reporters to wangle such an item. Not easy, apparently. I'm into Mike for a lifetime of favours now.

'Yeah, no probs, mate. My mate's coming over soon with it. Easy peasy.'

I face the screen watching people run around, chasing the ball, forcing myself not to stare into Kev's eyes. I see his reflection in the screen, the picture running over it. I try to get a glimpse but suddenly our eyes meet on the screen and for a moment Kev is focused on me and not the picture, I quickly search out the ball again.

'Ohhh! That was close, unlucky!' I try to change the subject.

'That was Brighton who just clipped the post. Don't tell me you're a Seagull?'

Crap. OK, so we're the red team. 'No, no . . . nah, nah, mate. That was unlucky for them 'cause now the Wigs are gonna do 'em on the break.'

Wigthorn FC are nicknamed 'The Wigs' and the fans call themselves 'The Judges' because the majority of them wear judicial wigs in the stand and sentence the opposing fans, players, and managers via various humorous, rude and mostly offensive songs. When an opposing player gets sent off they put on black caps, some fans even have inflatable gavels; it's all very judicial. That's what it said on a Wigthorn FC fans forum anyway. I'm warming to their sense of humour though, it's more interesting than the bloody game.

I see my reflection in the centre circle of the pitch as the home fans chant in unison; I could be standing there with my Facebook app, Judge Me!, as 30,000 fans chant their judgements towards me in obscene rhyme. Thirty thousand mirrors merging into one common reflection.

I quickly search out the ball again.

'They wanna get the ball over to Palmer more . . . oh, come on, you twat! Whittingham keeps giving the bloody thing away every chance he gets.' Kevin seems to be settling into the game and warming to my hospitality, if not the players' performances.

'Yeah, don't know why they signed that idiot.'

'He came up through the academy but I know what you mean, Hitchens keeps signing bollocks . . . Oh come on, ref! No way was he offside!'

'*Offside*'. I gave it one final go last night on YouTube and watched a kids' football cartoon try to explain it. All the little boys and girls watching the video seemed to understand it by the end but I was still clueless. It's something to do with a player being in the wrong area of the pitch without the ball and the goalkeeper but Christ knows what. They used to shout 'You're offside, Sheridan!' to me at school during the rare P.E appearances I attended until the school captain said to me, 'If you stay behind this line, you'll never be offside.' So I did, I never ventured passed the halfway line again until the second half got underway when apparently the game swapped around and I was permanently offside again. At that point I did what all the great players of the modern era do; I rolled around on the grass in agony before storming off.

Experience has served me well though, I've come prepared with a pre-scripted distraction. I'm on home turf. 'No way! The referee needs glasses!'

'Ha, ha, yeah! Sheridan, you should give him an eye test.'

'Yeah! I'll go down there at half-time and give him a check-up!'

'Yeah, ha, ha!'

'I don't think my equipment is strong enough for this blind idiot though!'

Oh, you're good, Sheridan my son. You're playing a blinder.

'Hey, Sherry! I found this beauty just hanging around outside your door, she's obviously lost or seriously inebriated.' Mike walks in with Kevin's wife, she looks doubly glad to have found Kev along with opportunity to vacate the awkwardly encompassing arm of Mike. 'She must be yours, mate, no way Sheridan could compete in this league.'

'Yeah. Hi, love.' Kev quickly stands to give his wife a peck on the cheek, motioning her to sit on the chair next to the sofa, never once taking his eyes off of the game.

'I'm Mike, mate. We'll be here all day if we wait for Sherry to introduce everyone.'

'Hi, Mike, I'm Kev, this is Lynette . . .'

'Wowza, Sherry! That TV is friggin' massive! Why have you got the footer on? You hate—'

'The Seagulls, exactly! Going to see them get absolutely dicked today. You wanna beer? Come with me. Lynette, can I get you a drink too?'

'Just a water, please, Doctor.'

I grab Mike's arms and drag him into the kitchen. 'Give us a hand, Mikey boy.'

'Mikey boy?' Mike looks round at me as we enter the kitchen, 'What the hell's going on, Sherry? Since when did you watch football? And when were you going to tell me about that bloody great TV, when did you get that?'

'Shhh! I'm just being friendly to Kev because he might be able to push some serious business my way.' I still can't tell Mike the truth, especially not now.

Yes I am. He'd want to write a big investigative piece on it and try to kick-start a national journalistic career off the back of it by making a name for himself, all from the comfort of Wigthorn. Big stories don't happen here, and since he's not prepared to leave, national attention is never going to come his way, that's why I'm not sure how he'd react. He could be a good friend and keep my secret, but then again, he might not be. Not because he'd willingly want to see harm done to me but because it could be too good a story for his journalistic instincts to let go of.

'You're schmoozing? At home? Fuck off, Sherry, you haven't schmoozed a day in your life.'

'Yeah, well maybe things are changing. Maybe I've realised I've got to move on with my life, not waste it sitting around waiting for things that'll never happen and waiting on people who'll never return. Maybe I'm going to take that promotion.'

Mike opens up a can of beer. 'That's my boy! Nice one! Forget about her, move on. Yes, promotion. More money, move up, before

100

you know it you could be area manager, company car, then you'll have the birds flocking round you.'

'This ain't about birds, Mike, this is about living life.'

'Yes, of course, because birds have nothing to do with living life.'

'My eyes are open again. I'm going for a holistic life change.'

'Yeah, whatevs, bruv.' Mike opens a beer for me and starts to get Lynette's glass of water. 'Kev's missus, you seen the rack on that?'

'You can't miss it.'

'So, you trying to get in there or something?'

'No. Seriously, he might be able to push some business my way, marketing to the local business community and stuff, make me look good, then when I say I'm open to a promotion at work, it might swing me a sweeter deal.'

'Good thinking. Bloody hell, I think you're getting all corporate on us now, this is going to take some getting used to.'

'Right, you got Lynette's drink?'

'Check.'

'You got the signed Wigthorn shirt?'

'Check. Right here in this bag.'

'Good. We'll present it to him at half time.'

'What's that?'

'When the ref blows the whistle.'

'Check.'

'Let's go back in and be on my side for once.' I start to walk out and then remember one vital piece of information, 'And don't stare at Lynette's rack.'

I sit on the sofa next to Kev, Mike hands Lynette her drink with a lingering stare before sitting in the chair opposite her. I'm going to have to play a double game of keeping his eyeline away from Lynette but also try to manoeuvre mine directly into Kev's . . . all without getting my head kicked in.

'What's the score, Kev?'

'Still nil-nil. It's got it up there in the top left of the screen, you donkey.'

Bollocks, I thought that was the time or something. 'The sunlight's reflecting on it . . .'

'The curtains are closed.' Thanks, Mike. I give him a stare and he corrects himself, 'Sorry, yeah you're right, Sherry, it is a bit fuzzy.'

'Fuzzy? It's a fifty-two-inch 5K TV!' Kevin can't quite believe what he's hearing; his eyes are fine. 'Sherry, looks like your mate needs his eyes tested too.'

I try a bit of small talk. 'Anyway, Mike, Kev's a plumber, got his own business.'

Mike plays along like a really bad actor on a very poorly financed soap opera, 'A plumber, nice one. Everyone's going to need a plumber at some point.'

'That's what I'm hoping.'

Mike looks at me in a what-kind-of-business-can-a-self-employed-plumber-send-a-nationally-recognised-brand-of-opticians? Not a common look but instantly recognisable.

'Foul!' Kev shouts. The ref blows his whistle.

Mike stands up in front of the TV. 'So I managed to get a signed shirt for you.' Kev and Lynette struggle to see through Mike, 'Let me tell you, the shit I had to—'

'Nice one, yeah, cheers.' Kev takes the shirt, ushering Mike to one side. 'Really appreciate it, mate.'

I take this opportunity to change the subject. 'How do you think Wigthorn are going to get on in their final games, Kev?'

Kev is too engrossed in the present game to answer, then there's a goal. Kev goes nuts. 'Goal! What a sweet strike by Nunez!'

'Yes!' I turn to give Mike a high five, I'm guessing it's an approved method of celebrating a goal. Mike just stares at me, unmoved and very non-celebratory. I turn back to Kev, 'What a goal!'

'Quality goal, mate, always liked him playing on the wing, allows him to cut in and skin the right back.'

'Yeah, skin him.' What the hell is *skinning* someone?

I get orders for the next round of drinks and go into the kitchen. I get three beers out the fridge and top up Lynette's glass of water. In the drawer next to the sink is where I've stored a small pot of pentobarbitone pills, a recently acquired sedative. I don't want this to be any more painful for Kev or Lynette than it has to be. I open the drawer slightly to check it's still there. It is.

I said I hadn't gone mad earlier, I haven't. I like to be prepared for any eventuality. Anyway, who's to say that planning to steal someone's eyes to see your reflection, is mad? Makes total logical sense to me.

'Penalty, ref!!!'

I can hear Kev jumping up in the lounge, I rush in. 'What?!'

'Check out the replay, blatant!'

Something happens on the screen, I've no idea what but I agree with Kev, 'That's blatant!'

'Yes! He's given it.' Kev pauses for something else to happen. 'It's gotta be a red, ref!'

Mike looks at me as though we're strangers.

'He's off! Yes!' Kev agrees with the ref. The fans put on their black caps.

A player places the ball, shoots, scores, and Kev does a little dance. I feign excitement whilst Mike is transfixed by Lynette as she jumps for joy too, as though he's watching a tennis match on the vertical axis. I go back into the kitchen to fetch more drinks.

'Here we are, boys and girls. This game looks as good as over.'

'It's in the bag, mate.' Kev finishes his can as he sees me walk in with replenishments.

Lynette lifts her head at the slightest inkling of an escape. I think Mike is unsettling her, even during this assured victory over our local rivals. 'So we can leave soon?'

'No love, we gotta watch the whole game. Anything can change.'

'This game's on a knife-edge.' I back up my new mate. I heard this line in a film once.

'Kev,' Lynette switches on her eyelashes, 'Kev, my mum needs you to look at her pipework.'

I quickly spot a euphemism. 'I bet she does.'

The 'awkward klaxon' alarms inaudibly, deafening everyone. Lynette gives me a stare that would weld her mum's dodgy plumbing in a heartbeat. Kev looks at me in a way that suggests I may have taken it a step too far. Is this the true meaning of offside?

'Kevin.' Lynette holds up the metaphorical offside flag, or whatever it is they do. 'My mother has a leak.'

'OK, OK, love. Look, it's half time in five minutes, we'll go then.' Kev turns to me with a my-balls-are-in-a-vice expression. An all too familiar look.

He's going. My mirror is leaving and I only have the vaguest impression of what I look like. I need more time.

I scramble.

'Staring competition!'

What the hell are you doing?!

'What?' Kev says.

'What?' Mike enters the fray.

'Yeah . . .' Explain yourself, idiot! I need an accomplice on my side. Mike. 'Yeah, a staring competition, Mike and I do it all the time at half time, the loser gets the beers.'

'You've just got us beers.' Mike raises his own beer in reiteration.

'Drink up, you lightweight!' It's not working. 'Mike, you look into Lynette's eyes and I'll look at Kev's.'

'OK!' Mike immediately validates the whole idea.

'You what?! I think the beer's gone to your head, mate. Anyway, Lynette and I are leaving at half time.'

'No, no, it's fun, let's do it now.' I grab both of Kev's arms and hold him in position, he struggles lightly at first. I glimpse a flash of a reflection. The rest of the world disappears into a tunnel, I grip on to Kev's arms more firmly, he immediately turns his head.

'This is fucking weird, mate.'

'Errr, it's kinda fun.' Mike tilts himself forward from the chair onto his knees and waddles towards Lynette so both their heads are at the same level.

I try to direct Kev's head towards me again. I release one of his arms, tilting his chin with my hand. 'Just stare, Kev.'

My reflection returns. I see myself wide-eyed, manically grinning.

'OK, mate, this is too fucking weird.' Wigthorn score another goal. 'Right, Lynette we're off. Three-nil, game's over.'

Lynette stands up so Mike is now getting a crotch-eye view. He's still staring.

'No, no, sorry! It's just a stupid game, forget about it. I'll get some more drinks.' I rush into the kitchen to get Kev and Lynette another drink each. I grab the pot of pills from the drawer, putting one in each of their drinks.

I'm not going to go through with this, am I? Seriously? Knock someone out and remove his eyeballs? It would never fucking work. Would it?

I'm never going to see Kev again after this, so it's now or never. Knock him out then decide. Do some research online and see if it's even possible to keep eyeballs in a jar. I could always say he just passed out, both of them, even Lynette after her glass of water.

What the fuck am I doing?!

'Kev. Lynette. Here you are, new drinks.'

Kev helps Lynette with her jacket. 'We're off. Thank you for the shirt but I think we'll be looking for a new optician.'

'He's an optometrist!' Mike's still on his knees.

I put the drinks down on the coffee table. 'But . . .'

Kev takes one step towards me. Threateningly. I'm glad he does, it brings me back into the real world. It's then I see that not all understanding comes from reflection; sometimes wisdom is presented to oneself on a plate.

I correct my stance. 'I'm sorry, of course. Thanks for coming, it was nice to see you both.'

They both walk out without another word. I shut the door and see Mike downing the beer I'd just got for Kev. 'No, Mike!'

He finishes the last of it by lifting the can up to reveal only a few drops left, 'Is there something else on?'

The colour empties from his face as quickly as his drink. 'Mike? You OK?'

'Yeah, I'm fine . . .' Still on his knees, Mike's head tilts forward, dragging down the rest of his body first onto the chair Lynette was sitting on before bouncing slightly then falling sideways onto the floor.

'Own goal!' The commentator exclaims from the state-of-the-art, Dolby 7.1, surround sound speakers.

Fuck.

Chapter Twelve

ONE MONTH BEFORE TODAY

I don't need any help, I can get through this myself.

The flames are getting higher, the smoke drifts away up over the trees, I warm my out-stretched hands against the fire.

I don't need any help.

That time last month, I didn't seriously consider removing Kev's eyeballs, not for long, anyway. I just got a little flustered; I panicked. I thought I'd exhausted every conceivable option to escape this darkness and find sanity within the hidden void of my own pupils like everyone else, but there is one option I haven't considered; completely ignore the problem. Seems like a cop-out, right? I know, that's what I thought but how many of us 'ignore' things we can't control, compromise the dreams we'll never realise, lower the summits we'll never conquer?

Many things could make us happy but only a few of them actually will.

This futile slog to see the mask I portray to the rest of the world, to fool the face that fools me, and to see the soul eclipsed by the facade, must be reflecting a face no one else wants to see. I must look like a right old miserable sod, even I can see that.

This obsessive ambition I've allowed to lead me for the past year would've pulled me too close to the flame, if I'd let it. I was entertaining the idea of seriously and permanently hurting someone just to see my own mug. If my life up to now had consisted of multiple approaches from model scouts and artists all falling over themselves to profit from my beauty, then maybe there'd be some value in my chase, but the brief images reflected in Kevin's eyes confirm why I've never been feted by artiste nor aesthetician. I'm nothing special. I may be unique, we may all be unique, but I'm not worth writing about.

What if I'd been more successful by being even less moral? What if I'd left behind the humanity driving me forward? Would I even want to look at myself in the mirror if I could? There's no sanity to be found in the infinite blackness of a black hole, you only end up staring into a black hole and that's going to suck the life out of you.

I've re-considered my reluctance to seek professional advice. I've been to see three different therapists over the past three weeks.

I didn't gain much. The therapists all thought it was a metaphor for not wanting to confront a deeper issue, mainly the death of my parents; who I never knew and bequeathed me a private education and mortgage-free life. They'd never heard of such a problem, thinking it must be psychosomatic, diagnosing the reflection I saw in Kevin Grimshaw's eyes as not being my true reflection but a manifestation of the impossibility of reconciling with Heidi. I was seeing myself in the eyes of an alpha male whom I had nothing in common with, therefore so out-of-reach as to be impossible. Maybe I wanted to be that person, maybe I thought Kevin was the sort of man Heidi wanted, so I strived to become closer to that person by letting them be my mirror. If I could see myself in that person's eyes then I could imagine myself being in that person's body looking out, being the person I thought Heidi wanted me to be.

I don't buy it. I don't want to be Kev. I've tested the eyes of other alpha males before: good-looking guys, rich guys, well-dressed guys, successful guys, confident guys, even a couple of minor celebrities performing at the local theatres, and I've never seen my reflection in their eyes. Not a dickie bird.

All three therapists were very interested in my predicament, wanting to see me again at reduced rates but I didn't want to waste my own time being a springboard for their careers. I've wasted enough time as it is.

Where do I go from here? What have I found out? The reflection

I saw may not be my true self but one created by my subconscious to fill a void I'd been desperate to fill. The only information I've found out about Heidi is that she's alive and her sister, Gemma, confirms she has moved out of town but won't tell me any more.

My love has well and truly gone, and my reflection has only offered the briefest of glimpses. I've tried to find both of them this year but unsuccessfully. What now? Give up? Yes. Why not? I've tried everything, I've given it my best. Should I spend the rest of my life banging my head against a brick wall or move on? How can you live in a state of permanent lament?

Love lets people down all the time. Why not me? Why not now?

Love is a fragile hope; a fragmented phoenix fuelling its own future.

Do people really see themselves? Does everyone see each other in the same way? What good is your reflection other than to pluck the hairs from your eyebrow or find an errant bit of pastry? I shave without a mirror. I have friends, I fell in love, I have a job, I know myself as much as the next person does, maybe it's humanity as a whole that needs the ability of self-reflection, not me.

What does seeing your own reflection really give you, anyway? Murderers, rapists, abusers, corrupt politicians can all see themselves in the mirror but it doesn't stop them carrying out despicable acts. I can't see myself but I've never hurt anyone .... removing Kev's eyeballs was a mere thought-crime.

Self-reflection is over-rated. It's a subjective delusion. You see what you want to see which is purely dependent on your state of mind. If you're feeling like shit, you'll see a piece of shit. If you're feeling over-the-moon, you'll radically over-estimate yourself. The irony isn't that you are not the best person to reflect on yourself, the irony is that no one else is. You're too close, everyone else isn't close enough.

I'll tell you what doesn't help in all this: having loads of portraits and artefacts of yourself in your flat. Visitors think you're slightly self-absorbed, and rightly so. That's why I've got a bonfire going in my back garden; a crematorium of my dalliances into self-discovery.

First to go are the portraits; the oil on canvas (£450), the 3D magic eye print (£80), the mosaic print (£68), the cubist which, like all cubism, looks nothing like the subject (Freebie from art class sitting), the watercolour (a kindly old lady from evening art class sitting), line sketch (a fashion student friend), black and white photo (£80), colour photo (£100), photo from newspaper article when Twenty20 got flooded (£30), photo fit (from police officer) and a print Heidi gave to me, her favourite photo of me. I've propped them all up along with the broken frames, doused the whole lot in lighter fluid, wafted the flames, and now they're melting into an oblivious blur like the reflection they're were representing.

The flames leap up the canvas, gnawing at the wooden frame, the chemicals in the photographic paper crackling and spitting in contempt.

It's liberating.

I have found strength in all this. I can survive heartbreak, I know my limitations, I'm tenacious, I'm willing to carry things through to the very end, and I know where the moral line is. If that isn't a good enough reflection to illuminate upon the world, then I don't know what is.

I've kept the caricature. It's not so weird to have a crappy carica-ture from a street artist in the toilet, is it? People laugh at it, it doesn't freak them out, unlike the model head moulded from Algi-Safe Alginate. That thing freaks me out and I can't even see it in any kind of detail. I reach down and pick it up, looking at the eyes, or where I think the eyes should be. It's a great bit of modelling, well worth the money. I can't see a thing.

I wonder briefly if he can see me.

I balance his head atop the pyramid of burning effigies. I watch the flames jab his chin, flick his earlobes, gradually melting him back into the primordial soup from whence he came. The eyes droop, a cheek falls, the nose drips melted Algi-Safe Alginate, the mouth snarls a final goodbye. The more grotesque and disfigured his appearance, the clearer I become.

This doesn't shake me. I don't read a macabre metaphor into this. I smile. Macabre metaphors are funny.

'What's so funny?' Mike appears behind me. 'You weren't answering the door and then I thought I heard flames, what's going on? Holy crap! Is that your model head going up in flames?'

'Yes.'

'You paid thousands for that, are you mad?'

'I think I was a little mad to get it made, so yes.'

Mike steps forward and prods a few burning items with his foot. 'These are photos of you and that 3D print? What's going on, you all right?'

'I'm fine. I'm having a bit of a clear out, all this stuff is a bit weird, right?'

'It's what you do, isn't it? Everyone's got to have a hobby. I'm not a therapist, I don't know why you do it. Some say low self-esteem, some say curiosity, some say vanity. I say you're mental.'

'People talk about me?'

'People talk about people, Sherry, in case you hadn't noticed. And yes, when someone invests thousands of pounds on portraits of themselves, then people are most definitely going to talk about that person. Your little hobby isn't exactly stamp collecting, is it?'

'Do you think I'm a head case?'

'Everyone's a head case.' Mike pulls some paper out of his back pocket. 'Here, I wrote this for you.'

'What is it?'

'It's another self-portrait to add to the collection but since you're collection is now going up in flames, you may not want it.'

I open it up and it's entitled 'Sheridan Maddox in a Thousand Words by Michael Barnstaple'.

'It's a portrait of words. I thought you might like it, a different take on all your other visual-based portraits. I thought a wordsmith might be able to carve out something you hadn't seen before, give you a new perspective.'

I start reading it.

It's . . .

. . . amazing.

His piece is purely about the person I reflect out to the world.

111

There are no stories from the past from which you could derive my morality, there are no examples of behaviour which could give you any clue about how I might react in any situation. It's all about surface; the contours, the expressions, the lines, the synergies, the light, the contrasts. There's nothing digging any further than a few microns of epidermis; moisturisers penetrate deeper. No justifications, no reasons, no postulations, no theories, just what is projected out into the world. The what without the why. A portrait of words; not a character study nor a description. You read it and know what I look like but nothing about who I am . . . and yet . . .

And yet you may feel as though you know me. Are our reflections totally divorced from who we are? People react to faces, people can be moulded by reactions, faces can change.

'Feel free to burn it too if you want, you know, if all this is some kind of cathartic act to cleanse your past.' Mike puts a hand on my shoulder. 'You mental head case.'

'I'll keep it, thanks. This and that caricature.' I look at Mike's face flicking in the light of the fire. 'Thanks. I . . . I didn't know you could write like this.'

'I used to know a thing or two before I sold my soul writing about school fetes and bypasses.'

I read through the piece one more time before folding it up and putting it in my pocket. The fire has reached its peak: the model head has completely melted, all the portraits have burned out and now just charred wooden frames are left. I pick up a box filled with smaller portraits; photos, sketches, computer-generated scans, X-rays, an ultra-violet print, a clay model, and then there's a few mirrors I thought may help during a long period of denial in my late teens when I thought the problem was to do with mirrors themselves. Mostly small handheld ones made from different materials and finishes, plus a couple of larger mirrors, one with a cropped photograph of a minor Colombian soap opera actor who, it is said, looks like me. I stuck his head on a full-length mirror then stood in front of it so his head was perfectly super-imposed upon my body. It worked well . . . if I had bright, shining white teeth, a perma-tan

112

and perfectly manicured stubble. I have none of those attributes, by the way.

'Hey, hombre! You can't chuck out Carlos!'

'Carlos is going.' I chuck the 'Carlos Mirror' onto the fire. '*Hasta la vista*, Carlos.'

'You're serious about all this?'

'You know there's that point in your childhood when you get rid of all your teddy bears? You can never remember when that point is but you look back on your childhood memories and they're split into 'Pre-Teddy Bears' and 'Post-Teddy Bears', like Before Christ and Anno Domini.'

'My mum left home the day after my ninth birthday, rapidly followed by all my teddy bears.' Mike opens up a repressed memory from his childhood.

'She took them all?'

'No. My Dad chucked them at her and Mr Stevens, from down the road, as they both left our house carrying a few suitcases. Next door's Rottweiler chewed them up as my dad and Mr Stevens were fighting in the gutter.'

'Fucking hell.'

'Yeah, that's what I said at the time, especially when I saw my mum and Mr Stevens saunter into his house just five doors down. He was a nice bloke to be fair.'

I pick up the cuddly toy version of myself I'd ordered online a few years ago. TeddyYou.com, purveyor of hand-made teddy bears based on photos sent in by the customer.

I offer it to Mike, 'Go ahead, chuck it on the fire. This thing is big enough to be cathartic for both of us.'

'I can't chuck "Sherry Bear" onto the fire.'

'If you don't, I will.'

Mike grabs the toy, straightens him out, looks him in the eye. I can see his face, whoever made it never once examined the photo of me at any point during its construction. Mike lightly tosses it into the fire. It bursts into flames, the eyes pop out, a quick flash before turning black and shrivelling up in an instant.

113

'Fucking hell.'

I nod in solidarity. 'Feel better?'

Mike sighs as his load lightens, 'I think so but I've always been a little bit of a pyro, so I'm not too sure if this is the feeling of old wounds healing or forbidden desires being reignited.'

'Shall we go inside?'

'Yeah, I could do with a drink but none of that crap your mate Kevin brought round, that kicked the shit out of me last time.'

We prop ourselves up at the kitchen bar on a stool each, I crack open a bottled beer, hand it to Mike, who examines the label forensically, then do the same for myself. I stare out of the window watching the fire slowly burning out with the sunset.

'So, have you finally made a decision about the new job, Sherry?'

'Yes. I'm going to take it. Fresh beginnings, new starts and all that. I just have one choice to make; Plymouth or Oxford.'

'Oxford.'

'Oxford? I was leaning towards Plymouth.'

'Students. Intelligent, beautiful, nubile, inexperienced, drunk students.'

'OK. I see your point of view but I've been trying to weigh up the two options based on more than the opportunity for sexual conquests.'

'That's an interesting approach, if somewhat unusual. Go on.'

'Both places give me everything I want in terms of responsibilities, pay, and allowing me to still spend fifty per cent of my time with customers, so it really is just based on location. I prefer Plymouth because it's near the sea.'

'You don't go in the sea though. You can't swim, remember?'

'No, I realise that, but it's nice knowing it's there on your doorstep.'

'What? Just in case you feel like quickly nipping out for a quick windsurf?'

'Plymouth also has one of the largest universities in the country.'

'Done!' Mike laughs at me rather than with me. 'So you checked it out, too! Your training is now complete. You have my blessing to leave.'

114

'Thank you, master.'

Mike takes a sip and joins me at the window, watching the embers flickering in the ashes. 'Hey, you remember that Facebook app that was knocking around a few months ago, the one that got your friends to answer questions about yourself?'

'Yeah, I may recall such an application.'

'I just read online today that the two blokes who invented it have just sold it for a cool ten million dollars.'

I wonder if I can squeeze this beer bottle hard enough to make it shatter in my hands? 'Really? That's about seven million pounds isn't it? Before tax, commission, etc. Yeah, so not as much as you might think. And what does seven million pounds really get you nowadays?'

'In India? Ten million dollars is probably equivalent to, like, I don't know, a billion quid. Those boys are made for life.' Mike takes a large swig of beer, toasting the entrepreneurial princes of the sub-continent, 'Imagine, it just takes one good idea.'

Imagine.

With sublime timing, my phone bleeps, a text message to hopefully sweeten the bitterness.

I hear you've got a new job. Where is it? When do you start?

It's from Heidi's sister, Gemma. This contact with her is comforting in a Stockholm Syndrome kind of way. It tortures me. It keeps all the distant memories and the hopelessness alive. It's not good for me, I know, but I want it. I text a reply.

I have a choice of Oxford or Plymouth. Have 2 weeks to choose.

I want to ask about Heidi. I REALLY, REALLY want to ask about Heidi but I refrain. She won't tell me anything, blood is thicker than water. I used to resent their closeness but now I'm witnessing their bond first hand, I've learnt to admire it, even if it does mean I gain nothing.

OMG! Plymouth!

Wow. OMG indeed. I've never seen her express emotion via text before. What has her so animated about Plymouth?

Why Plymouth? I was thinking Oxford.

Nothing like a well-placed lie to ease the truth along.

Intellectuals wear such terrible glasses, you'd be wasted up there.

Hang on a minute? How did she know I'd been offered a new job. I'd only confirmed it a day ago. Someone at Twenty20 must have spoken to someone at Candleina who then told Heidi? The Wigthorn retail grapevine still remains more efficient than the internet.

Mike can't stand to be ignored. 'Who's that? Come on, I've finished this beer, let's quickly have another then go down the boozer and make a night of it. Work out a plan of attack for getting down to Plymouth.'

'What about Oxford?'

'Fucking hell, who's that texting you?'

'Heidi's sister, Gemma.'

'She said Oxford?'

'No, she says Plymouth.'

'Good. Anyway, who cares what Heidi or her sister think?'

'You originally said Oxford.'

'That's before I knew about all the fit young fillies in bikinis frolicking upon the beaches of the South-West.' Mike gets out a coin. 'There's only one way to settle this. Flip.'

Chapter Thirteen

TODAY

'I think that bird on the ground floor likes you. Seriously, she couldn't get enough of you when we walked downstairs.' Mike nudges me as he rubber-necks past a couple of girls sitting on a bench.

'Since when does asking if a parcel had been delivered count as interest? I considered it a neighbourly question initiated through her desire to receive the contents of the aforementioned parcel.'

'Sherry, my son. You have a lot to learn.'

'Apparently.'

I hate moving but one vital part of this promotion to a new town was to get relocation costs included. I almost enjoyed just sitting back and watching as the movers packed away my stuff and loaded the van. I say almost because there was a measure of guilt getting in the way, compelling me to at least chip in a little effort. I packed my underwear. The weight of judgement I could sense from the removal men as they went through all my stuff was unbearable to the point of me almost cancelling the whole thing and doing it myself. I rationalised this speed-wobble by remembering they do this every day for hundreds of people and their memories of my belongings and the judgements they came to will eventually be crushed by the weight of more memorable customers with far more embarrassing belongings than me. Had they come a month earlier and moved my entire portrait collection, I'm sure I would've easily made the humorous highlights package briefed to all the new recruits. Anyway, once I'd made them a cuppa and presented the fresh jam doughnuts I'd bought that morning, they were all as good as gold and couldn't do enough for me.

Perception trumps reflection every time.

That was all last week. All my furniture and possessions have been delivered, unloaded and organised in my new two-bedroom flat. I'm renting at the moment just to see how I get on. My own flat back in Wigthorn is being rented out via a letting agency so I don't have to worry about anything, meaning it's going to take me a couple more months to totally relax. They say the new tenant is a professional who travels a lot for her job but they probably say that to all the landlords. She's probably organising a party as we speak. With the rent I'm earning plus the money I'm saving from not getting any more portraits of myself commissioned means I'm almost rolling in it. I'll try and save some, start an ISA or dip my toe into stocks and shares, make the effort to travel more, invest in some proper art; hang a framed image up on my wall I can actually appreciate.

Mike is visiting so he can have a nose around and check out whether further visits will help his ailing love life. At the moment, I'm grateful for an ailing love life, I'm focusing on work for the immediate future. I haven't focused on it for too long and I'm realising how much I enjoy it. Heidi and my reflection are consigned to the past. I'm going to enter into the world of being career-focused, I've even been reading management books because, you know . . . I'm a bloody manager now!

Mike and I are in an electrical store getting some new bits. Bringing my old toaster, kettle, microwave, cutlery, and all that sort of stuff made me feel a bit too much like a cheapskate. As I said before: out with the old, in with the new.

'What do you reckon about this kettle and toaster combo? They match that microwave over there.'

'Does one of them boil water and the other toast bread? Yes. Get them. Come on.' Mike doesn't have an ounce of design appreciation in his body.

'Bored?'

'Jesus, Sherry! You're worse than a bloody bird. Couldn't you order all this shit online, it would make a good opener with that bird downstairs. You could have deep discussions about the post office and courier services and how they only deliver when everyone's at work.'

'OK, OK, I get the message. I'll get these, then we'll leave and get some lunch.'

'Now you're talking my language.'

I'm in Plymouth. The coin toss went the way of Plymouth too, not that I would base a life-changing decision on Mike's coin toss but, you know, it's nice to have fate and your intuition on the same side.

'Give us a hand with these bags, Mike.' My phone rings, it's a number I don't recognise so I ignore it and let it go to answerphone.

'Oh, here it is! The money shot. You only wanted me down here to lug around your poncy new kitchenware.'

'You invited yourself down.'

'Only because you never asked me. So where are you buying me lunch?'

'No idea. Hang on, let me pop into Twenty20 and ask one of the guys where they recommend. It's just around the corner—'

'Are you mad?! They're going to think you're checking up on them, then they'll spend the rest of the day talking about their new sad, dickhead manager who pops in on his day off.'

'Don't be a twat.' Now he's got me paranoid. 'How are they going to think I'm checking up on them when I just stroll in, ask for a lunch recommendation, and then stroll out?'

'You're not going to ask how the shop is doing?'

'No.'

'Sure?'

'Definitely not.'

'Be my guest then. I'm gonna pop into this shop and have a look at the laptops while you make a fool of yourself.'

A place called 'Helsinki Port' is a new, rustic, well-priced gastropub recommended by a couple of my new colleagues. Mike was spot on, though, it was hard not to ask how things were going, even in an innocent, enquiring way. Now I'm paranoid everyone will think I'm irresponsible for not asking.

I stroll out into the high street from Twenty20 and see Mike through a shop window in deep conversation with a sales girl. She thinks she's highlighting the latest developments in laptop technology; he thinks she's talking to him because of his devilish charm.

In one breath, the high street in Plymouth momentarily transports me back to Wigthorn, there's a familiarity in the air, a smell. I turn, like a bloodhound, following my nose, memories flooding my brain, drowning in the year just gone. I walk, my nose the carrot, my hopes the stick, beating me with every step. Essential oils, exotic fruits, incense, lavender, vanilla, jasmine, tea tree, and berries all wafting over me, pulling me forward, beckoning me to the front door of the Plymouth branch of 'Candleina'. I stand outside like an ex-smoker confronted by a proffered cigarette.

I give in, like an alcoholic downing one last shot for the long road to sobriety.

The layout of the shop is different to its sister shop in Wigthorn but the branding's all the same, the look, the colours, the smells. I struggle to see any staff at first, the till area has been vacated, but very soon the sound of voices draws me to the back of the shop where a group of women have gathered, talking loudly, laughing, bending down, throwing their hands up, having a grand old time. One of them turns to look at me in mid-conversation, I smile and start to browse. Visibly relieved that I won't be requiring any assistance, she continues to talk with the others about whatever it is they're talking about. I daren't get close enough to find out; I'm here to dip my toes into an old memory, not make a new one.

Familiar with their product range, I walk over to the body treatment stand near the till and try the hand moisturiser, Heidi's favourite, Vanilla Cream. I squeeze a little out of the sample pot and rub it into my hands, savouring the thick fragrance as I cup my face in my hands, breathing it in. I turn to look at the group of women hoping none of them are looking at me thinking I'm some sort of weirdo, because now I'm self-conscious that's exactly what I look like.

That's it; the last drink, the last ciggie, the last hit, the last bet, the last indulgence. I'm in a new town, in a new job, beginning a new chapter. As much as I can, I take a long good look at myself, reiterating my commitment to a fresh start, my dedication to moving on and my acceptance of who I am and what I can achieve. How many people recognise their own limitations and accept them? I can't see myself but I'm not blind. I've been in love but I can love again. I reflect what I feel and what I do. My image does not define me, I define my image. I don't need a mirror. No one needs a mirror. We can all see ourselves in the words we speak, the relationships we have and the life we lead. I finally accept my condition.

It's me who's at an advantage, not everyone else. Mirrors are masks.

The chorus of voices fades behind me, silence filling the shop like a fresh essential oil. My position next to the till has probably caught the attention of the shop staff and now they're having a silent stand-off amongst themselves over which one of them is going to have to leave the huddle and serve me. I feel conspicuous, so I turn to leave without buying anything which results in me feeling even more conspicuous. I need a drink.

Just as I reach the door to leave, the silence is broken.

'Sheridan? Is that you?'

HEIDI

Chapter Fourteen

TWO YEARS BEFORE TODAY

I'm watching my boyfriend fuck someone else.

I don't know why I'm leaning against the door frame of my bedroom watching. I'm certainly not getting off on it. I'm letting the scene sink in, it's not everyday you catch your other half red-handed with the time to measure your reaction and fully gauge your emotions. I can't stand emotionally led halfwits who fly off the handle. Inevitably they're in the wrong, too boneheaded to admit it while continuing to rely on their 'gut instinct' even as it vomits forth putrid bile, dissolving all semblance of rational, common sense, as they wonder why their lives always end up in a fucking mess.

I'm not a seer or a visionary, I just listen.

I might feel a shred of jealousy if he was performing any better than he does with me. To me. At me. She could be anyone. It's only now I realise, I could've been anyone.

I have no idea who she is but he's being just as selfishly inept as he always is in this situation. She's the one who has my pity.

I'm watching his skinny arse thrust into her. Have I really been on the receiving end of that? No wonder I used to drift off into closely held sexual fantasies to get off. Whoever got off thinking of England? Although I don't think that was the point of that piece of advice. Oh . . . here we go, I recognise that groan . . . the final furlong. Thankfully, Gary is mercifully quick.

As he's rushing to the finish line, she clocks me. She's looking straight at me, but she hasn't bolted out of bed or made my presence known to Gary. She's holding my eye as Gary thrusts away between her legs like a little terrier digging for a bone. This girl hasn't locked herself away in a sexual fantasy and nor is she thinking of England.

This is a good test for anyone, watching your other half fuck someone else: it pulls you free from the physical act so you can watch them, and only them, in action. Do they turn you on? I realise now I've never been attracted to Gary, never. Not once have I looked at him and thought he was a bit of all right. Another test would be, do you feel any pangs of jealousy whilst watching your other half fuck someone else? No. I feel a door has opened through which I can chuck him out and never see him again. A bona fide reason.

Finally!

A euphoric relief fills me with light.

Gary's finished, a sweaty dish rag slumped upon the poor girl's body. She's still looking at me, totally nonplussed, unconcerned. Unsatisfied. Exactly how I must look after sex with Gary. She taps Gary on the shoulder.

Only then does Gary remember the person he's with may have feelings, that their wellbeing should be of concern too. 'Was that all right, love?'

'You have a visitor.'

Gary rolls off her onto his sweat-ridden hairy back. He sees me. 'Holy fuck! Heidi! What the fuck are you doing here? I didn't hear you come up.'

'Hello, Gary.' I remain poised against the door frame, arms crossed, unmoved.

'You're meant to be in fucking . . . London . . . errr, no, fucking Bristol.'

'Fucking Guildford actually. The course finished a day early so I thought it would be fun if I rushed home to my fucking flat, relax in the bath with some new products, watch a film, and get a pizza, but no. Once again, Gary fucking Kline has spoilt my plans for another day. Not anymore.' I pause, not for effect but to savour. 'Get out.'

'Babe! This girl means nothing.'

'She means more to me than you do then. She's helped me see the

126

light. Thank you, I hope you and Gary have a wonderful life together.'

The girl casually sits up in bed, naked, not covering herself up at all, no shame, no embarrassment. She pulls her hair back into a ponytail, ties it back before retrieving her clothes from a nearby chair. Slowly she dresses with no concern for me or for Gary. My surprise at seeing her in my bed gives way to a sisterly concern that she was getting fucked in more ways than one, like me, but now I have a growing respect for this girl. She doesn't give a shit and doesn't give a shit who gives a shit about whether she gives a shit or not.

She talks, I'm listening. 'Look, this guy and me are no item, sweetheart. You save your shit for him, I'm out of here.'

'Heidi! Please don't do this, I need you, I love you. Look, I can sort this out. I was weak, I admit it, you were gone for ages and I gave in to temptation, I'm sorry.'

'I went on a three-day course that turned out to be a two-day course. If that's the extent of your commitment to me then we're done. Get your skanky, skinny arse out of my bed and get out.'

The girl is dressed. A little too Friday night for a Wednesday lunchtime, but she quietly asks Gary for something whilst holding out a hand. Gary crawls across the bed to pick up his jeans and goes through the pockets in an exaggerated manner before looking up at me sheepishly.

'Have you got eighty pounds you can lend me? I'll pay you back Friday, I've made some good sales this month.'

I address the girl, I can't even look at Gary. 'Is it OK if Gary pays you Friday?'

'Not really.'

'Why the hell are you borrowing money off this girl if you—'

Oh.

You have to be fucking kidding me.

One realisation is paramount in my mind. No, it's not that I feel less jealous because the woman's a prostitute. And no, it's not that he has the front to ask me for money to pay for a prostitute he's been fucking behind my own back in my own bed. And no, it's not that

127

I'm suddenly scrolling back through our five-year relationship searching for clues on other digressions of trust.

No, it's that I saw something in this girl I respected, admired. Before knowing she was a sex worker, she was someone I aspired to be, even though I've only seen her for five minutes, half of that time consisting of her lying on her back getting fucked. I admired her confidence, her unabashed front. Shamelessly being who she wants to be without fear or reproach. And now? I still envy her confidence but I'm not going to sell my body to walk the same path she has. The rejections I'd suffer as punters drove on passed me would knock me down even further. How she maintains her self-belief after sleeping with the likes of Gary is something to behold. I never could. Maybe it's stubbornness rather than strength? I can never tell the difference.

'How the fuck were you intending to pay her if you haven't got any cash?'

Gary glances over at my dressing table. 'Your bottom drawer.'

Where I keep a few hundred in cash for emergencies. I'm waking from a nightmare. Now I know why most of my friends eventually faded from my social calendar over the past five years: Gary fucking Kline.

'Forgive me . . . *ma'am*,' I'm not familiar with the etiquette of this situation. 'I'm uneducated in the world of sexual procurement but if my film, TV and gangsta rap studies have informed me accurately, might you be working under the watchful eye of a pimp or some form of security?'

'That would be correct, ma'am.' She's humouring me.

'Excellent. Please would you inform your business partner that a non-paying client will need eighty pounds sterling of shit kicked out of him or eighty pounds worth of shit repossessed from the following address—'

'What the fuck are you doing? Stop! Fucking hell, Heidi!'

For a second, a couple of seconds, I consider giving her the £80 myself, after all, she's performed her end of the bargain quite admirably and the sisterhood part of me doesn't want to see her go out of pocket, but this isn't my problem. I'm no longer a fucking doormat.

Not anymore.

I give her Gary's full name, address, and phone number. And email address and Facebook account and place of work address and phone number. We shake hands. She leaves. I really want to get her number but I have more pressing priorities to contend with.

'Gary. Get dressed and fuck off.'

I move my suitcase into the lounge and make a cup of tea while listening to the sweet sound of Gary dressing and leaving.

I watch the kettle boil. The water matching my blood, centigrade by centigrade. I'm waiting to explode if Gary hasn't left in the two or three minutes it takes for this water to reach 100 degrees. I haven't felt this alive in years. The shackles of a constantly disapproving partner have been removed, I'm free to do or say what I want. Gary suppressed me but I have to admit, I've not been too forthcoming with my own liberation as I should've been. Tiny moments have been dripping down upon my head for years, keeping me from looking up. Weak excuses have gently been nudging me into a corner, keeping me from finding my own place. I stayed with him because it was routine. I never allowed us to live together because I knew no good could come of it. Now I have a real reason to end this charade, 'cheating'. The dumb shit would never accept I just wanted out. No matter how hard I tried to convince him I didn't want to be with him, the more he'd try to convince me he'd change, things would get better, we could have a baby! The arguments only ended when I was sick of the bullshit coming out of his lying, cowardly, bullying fucking mouth. It's been a war of attrition since I can remember, a girl's got to sleep at some point.

Now I have a reason and I have belief. I'm grabbing this with both hands.

I hope he hasn't left just yet so I have the excuse to go absolutely batshit insane in his ugly fucking face and unequivocally underline my total unwillingness to ever see him ever again. This is a very rare event, I plan to cherish it.

Steam increasingly rushes from the spout, finally the kettle switch clicks off. Thank you, Jesus.

'Gary! You gone yet?!'

'Babe, please let me . . .' He's topless, only jeans and trainers on.

'Fuck off!' I pick up his shirt and walk to the window.

'Hey, what are you doing?'

I open the window and chuck it out. 'I said, fuck off!'

'We can talk, Heidi.'

'We can talk about how you're going to fuck off!' As he looks out the window to grasp the reality of his shirt on the pavement below, I kick his skinny arse. I'm ashamed to admit it. I didn't kick him as hard as I could in case I booted him out the window. It was merely a guiding hand; a step in the right direction towards the front door.

'Ow! What the fuck are you doing? You touch me again and I'll—'

'Do it, you fucking twat! Fucking hit me! Fucking do it!' I try to kick him again but swing and miss, he's ready for it.

'Fucking hell! You've lost it.'

'Yes I have. Now fuck off!'

He quickly scans the bedroom for any of his possessions, does the same in the lounge, and then leaves with a parting shot, 'Bitch!'

I feel unclean. I need to freshen up.

I start by chucking all the bedding, pillows, and duvet out the window. Gary looks up as he puts his shirt on, he shouts something at me but I try to chuck a pillow down his throat. I go back to the bed, just the mattress remains. It doesn't have handles, it's heavy, they're expensive and no one actually, directly touched the mattress so I leave it where it is. The window's too small anyway. I flip it over as a compromise.

I stand back and look at my bedroom. I open the bottom drawer of my dressing table with the money in to double-check the cash is still there, it is, but that isn't my main concern. My digital SLR camera is in there as well. Gary didn't sell it or swap it for magic beans, the dumb arse probably didn't realise how much it was worth.

I pick it up and turn it on, the battery light flashes. I charge it.

This never left my side when I first got it seven years ago. I spent two years walking around town, the seafront, travelling up the

South Downs, out with friends, driving out of town, just taking photos. Subscribing to magazines, visiting online forums, doing a photography for beginners evening course, then the advanced one, for about three years I only saw the world through a viewing lens analysing which F-Stop, film speed and exposures would achieve the best result.

Is F8 more widely focused than F32 or is it the other way round? More light, slower speed? I don't know, I've forgotten. I go into the lounge, which is actually a large open-plan lounge/kitchen diner conversion, south-facing with big windows and a big blank wall on the opposite side; it could make a pretty good photographic studio. Give it a coat of bright white paint, move the sofa, TV and other bits into the bedroom, move my desk and computer from the bedroom into the corner of the lounge; more room for photography, less room for a man.

He's only been gone five minutes and I'm over him already. I am. This isn't some extreme reaction or a denial, I was over him years ago. It's time to focus on me. Let everything else blur into the background, now would that be F4 or F16?

I should phone a friend, that's what girls usually do after dumping their boyfriend, right? Even if he is a low-life, cheating, skinny-arsed, sack of shit.

'Chloe, hi! Yeah, the course wasn't bad, finished early, caught Gary with another girl in my flat . . . Yeah, yeah, I know . . . Anyway, I've dumped him . . . Yeah, I'd love it if you could come over . . . No, no, I'm fine. In fact I haven't felt better. Can you come over today? . . . Great, I need to move some furniture and paint some walls, it's time to make a few more changes – and bring a bottle of wine!'

Chapter Fifteen

23 MONTHS BEFORE TODAY

'You know you don't have to pose like an idiot, right, Chloe?'

'I'm not, this is my *Vogue* cover pose.'

'That's too extreme even for *Gurner's Monthly*.'

'Thanks! What about this one?'

Chloe is a good-looking girl, a great sales assistant, a colleague of mine over at Candleina, and a good friend, but she makes a lousy model. You may think modelling is easy, but you try to self-consciously not look self-conscious.

'Chloe, I'm only testing the light and the background, you don't have to do anything, just stand there like a brain-dead zombie . . . that's it.'

'Very funny.'

'Stay there a minute, I just want to move these spotlights.' I couldn't wait to test these spotlights later on this evening so I dragged Chloe back to my flat during our lunch break.

'I could try some poses on this stool.'

'Go for it.'

These two spotlights are my pride and joy. After three weeks of intensive research and astute bidding on eBay, they're finally mine. There's no chance of Gary coming back into my life to steal savings which are no longer there, but the symbolism of spending it all on photography and leaving no safety net was too strong. It was my money, but the fact I saved it while I was with Gary somehow tainted it. Not enough to chuck it out of the window, but frivolously spending it on a pair of professional grade spotlights seemed about right. Shine a light on what's important and leave everything else in the shadows.

I say 'no safety net': I haven't given up my job. I'm feeling re-energised and reborn, not intoxicated.

I've cleared out the lounge, turning it into a photographic studio. In the past month, I've painted the whole room white, cleaned the south-facing windows and swapped curtains for blinds to improve the light coming in, ripped up the carpet and polished the wooden floorboards, and bought two spotlights, a backdrop frame with assorted backgrounds, and a tripod for my camera. This room and I are now in symbiosis; Gary-free and focused on photography.

'This stool is rather . . . precarious.'

'You're ungainly, Chloe. Modelling isn't as easy as it looks, is it?' Rearranging the spotlights has improved the lighting, giving me the effect I wanted. I change a few settings and take a couple of shots before checking the results on my laptop. They're good. You know what? I may actually know what I'm doing here.

Chloe starts directing the shoot. 'Focus in and I'll start making love to the camera.'

'I'm not sure you really want to do that.'

Chloe starts to get a bit too confident on the stool; leaning forward, coyly turning away and then turning back, hair tossed aside revealing twisted pouts, various faces of surprise and ambivalence in varying intensity until her confidence overshoots her balance as she tries a flying scissor manoeuvre with her legs. The stool begins to lift up on one side, then rocks back.

I quickly switch my camera over to sport mode to enable quick, continuous shooting; my senses are awakening, instincts are reviving old connections, my 'photographer's premonition' is stepping into the foreground.

A few seconds later, a scissor move along with a head flick prove no match for gravity and Chloe topples. I press and hold the button, Chloe falls to the ground frame by frame. After she hits the floor, I click one more time before rising up from behind the camera to see my friend and not a mere subject.

133

'Chloe! Are you OK?'

Chloe rolls over gingerly holding her shoulder. 'Ahhh, shit!'

I crouch down next to her, helping her up, 'Is your shoulder OK?'

She moves it slowly. 'Yeah, it's fine.'

We stand there, both looking down at the stool and then back at each other. Her face cracks into a smile before crumbling into hysterics; relieved, I follow.

'Don't tell anyone about this, all right?'

'Oh come on, Chloe! I've got photographic evidence here.'

'You still took photos as your friend was falling to her doom?!'

'Yeah.' I do feel a little bad but also a little proud. I kept my wits, changed the settings, and kept on shooting. Maybe this is something I could do well at?

'Good girl! That's what you've got to have to succeed, Heidi. A bit of grit and determination. Good on you! Look at this place, what you've done, it's brilliant. You're like a proper little David Bailey in little old sunny Wigthorn, who'd have thought it?'

It's always embarrassing getting complimented by friends, why is that? I never know what to say, so I say what everyone else says. 'Shut up.'

'Let's have a look at the photos then. My fall from grace in all its well-framed, exquisitely lighted, and expertly focused glory.'

I scroll through each photo, zooming in on Chloe's face as the realisation of her situation dawns on her more clearly with every frame.

'Oh, shit! We better get back to work, Chloe, look at the time.'

We're out the door in a matter of minutes, still laughing about the photos and forgetting we've had absolutely no lunch at all. The walk back to work is only about ten minutes, taking us from one end of the town centre to the other, giving us a chance to catch up on any high street gossip and maybe bump into various sources on the way.

'Do you know Darren from Sports Stadium?'

I know what this piece of news is. 'The guy who was going out with Yvonne from Chandlers Electronics whilst also seeing Hanna from Briggs Bakers?'

'Err . . . yeah.'

'What about him?'

'I hear he's single.'

'That's what Hanna heard too. No, Chloe, I'm not interested in Darren from Sports Stadium and to be honest, I'm a little disappointed you would actually try to set me up with someone like Darren from Sports Stadium.'

'No, no, no, no, just wondering, you know.'

We continue on along the main pedestrianised high street, passing shops stocked with employees to gossip about: from disposable, own-brand, loss leaders to luxury brand-name items. I'm not sure where I'd place myself on the shelves of consumer desires, but obviously not in the same department as Chloe would, it seems.

Chloe spots a guy from the optician's across the road from Candleina. 'Oh look, it's Sheridan from Twenty20, what the hell is he doing?'

'Looks like he's getting a caricature drawn.'

'Come on, let's have a closer look.'

'Chloe, leave it out, we're late as it is . . .' My words fall on deaf ears as Chloe makes her way over; the smell of an exclusive shrouding her senses.

'Sherry, darling! Whatchya doing here making a spectacle of yourself?'

'What's it look like? I'm getting a caricature done.'

'I can see that. Let's have a look then.' Chloe gets behind the artist, who seems oblivious to her, me, and probably Sheridan too by the look of his illustration and from the smell of his immediate vicinity.

I take a peek over Chloe's shoulder; she looks back at me with a scared grimace. 'Sherry, love. Why would you spend your lunch break getting a caricature done?'

'Oh, you know.'

'No, not really.'

'Who's your friend?'

'This is Heidi, she works with me over at Candleina. Heidi, this is Sheridan.'

'Hi, Sheridan, I've seen you around just never had the chance to say hello as my eyes are . . . errr . . . twenty-twenty.' Bloody hell, did that sound like flirting? I've been out of the game for so long I've no longer got any idea.

Chloe raises her eyebrows at me as she mouths, 'Easy, tiger'.

Bollocks.

'Hi, Heidi, I've seen you around too. That seems to be half the problem, the only women I meet all need glasses and then when I sort them out, I never see them again.'

'I have a similar problem where I work, the only men I meet are gay or buying gifts for their other halves.'

Chloe jumps in, 'And enjoy the rest of your lunch break, Sherry, we've got to go. Come on, Heidi. See you around, Sherry.'

'See you later, Heidi.'

'Bye.' I smile at him and take another look at the caricature, it doesn't look good. I circle my index fingers and thumbs around my eyes as though I'm wearing glasses and look at Sheridan whilst nodding towards the artist. Although, in reality, I think laying off the cannabis and taking some art classes would better improve his illustrative skills than glasses.

Chloe marches swiftly away. It can't be the fact we're late for work that has sparked her into action, it's never concerned her before.

'Chloe, wait up, what's the rush?'

'We're late.'

'Give over, what's the real reason?'

'Sherry was flirting with you.'

'Yeah? See, I wasn't too sure—'

'You were flirting with him! That's what I'm worried about. I'm doing you a favour.'

'What do you mean?'

'He's a bit . . . well, strange. He never looks comfortable with his surroundings.'

'What's that meant to mean? He looks perfectly normal to me, he's got lovely eyes and don't tell me you didn't notice his lovely toned arms.'

136

'He's getting a caricature done in his lunch break by a stone-head who's looking pretty sketchy himself, let alone capable of sketching anyone else.'

'Maybe he's helping out a struggling artist?'

'Just chuck him a fiver and move on, why sit there for half an hour just to get a scraggy bit of paper with the scribblings of a pot-head? It's madness, you can do better, Heidi.'

'OK, I see what's going on here. You want control over who I go out with next, regardless of who it is, even Darren from Stadium Sports is better than Sheridan from Twenty20? Can you just ignore my love life? Let me be single. I don't need a man. I don't even want a man. Not Darren, not Sheridan, not no one.'

'Joe from Pound Pharmacy is quite the catch—'

I tut, sigh and head towards work, Chloe skipping after me with apologies. The afternoon sun sparkles in the window display of Twenty20, a multitude of glasses watching my every step. I turn into the shadow of Candleina, the smelling salts and essential oils of reality blurring any dreams of photography from my field of view.

Chapter Sixteen

22 MONTHS BEFORE TODAY

'Heidi! What are you doing on this side of the street?'

'Hi, Daisy, I've got an eye test booked.'

'Great, let me see who's available, I don't think Henry has gone for lunch yet.'

Oh. 'Errr, it was actually Sheridan—'

'Only joking! Of course you're booked with Sherry, I wouldn't put you with anyone else.' Daisy taps her nose. Did I really think I could get this done under the radar of the high street grapevine? I could back out, my eyes are fine, always have been. Why am I here really? Curiosity? Defiance? Adventure? Boredom?

Before I can fully plunge into my inner thoughts, Daisy locks arms with me, walking me to the back of the shop and up the stairs. 'Let's see if we can catch Sherry unawares. I caught him staring into a mirror for ages last week, God knows what he was doing because when he turned round he still had a bit of cress on his top lip from a sandwich. Men, eh?'

I can't argue with that.

We approach Sheridan's office, his name embossed on the metal plate adds some much needed gravitas to the image I have of him sitting in front of a stoned street artist. Daisy looks at me briefly before opening the office door without any forewarning. I hang back in case she has chosen a truly inopportune moment.

'Sherry, your next appointment is here!'

Thankfully, Sheridan is sitting at his desk, fully clothed, and the computer screen is filled with a wonderfully boring spreadsheet. I breathe out and take a step forward. 'Hi, Sheridan.'

'It's Heidi!' Daisy announces.

'I know! I can see her!' Sheridan looks at me with mock surprise in his voice.

'I'm glad you can see me, otherwise this whole appointment would be a waste of time.'

'Indeed it would. Please come in, Heidi. Thank you, Daisy.'

'Do you want me to get you anything, Sherry? Heidi?'

'No thanks, thank you, Daisy.' Sheridan gives me another look as he waits to hear the door close. It doesn't, I can see Daisy agonisingly dragging herself out of the room in conflict with every instinct in her body. 'Close the door on your way out, please, Daisy.'

The door clicks shut, the awkwardness in the room evaporates. Sheridan really looks the part in his office: sleeves rolled up, clean shaven, styled hair, a technical thingamajig in his hand, ID tag clipped to his shirt pocket. Removing the junkie street artist from view has really done him the world of good. Relieved, I break the silence. 'Here's the free test card if you need it.'

'Thanks, but we give these out like sweets. They're a carrot to tempt you in for a test so we can hopefully find a problem and then sell you a very expensive pair of designer glasses.'

'And if you find no problem?'

'I create one – please, if you could sit in front of the "Death Lasers" here, then we'll get this show on the road.'

I sit down. 'Seriously, what is this thing?'

'It's a slit lamp. It allows us to get a closer look at your eyes, determine their health and assess that everything is where it should be. First though, we need to do the chart. If you could read out the top line in a funny voice.'

I dispense with the funny voice. 'P. O. O. P . . . hang on—'

'Sorry, that's the kids' one, they love it. Let me get the adult one, it's got filthy swear words.'

Being in Sheridan's company is refreshingly reassuring. He's professional and friendly, calming and confident. A complete contrast to when I saw him in the high street last month. This is his office, his profession, his domain. I wonder if every time he steps out of here he crumbles a little, the further he gets from it the more withered he becomes.

I read the letters on the *normal* chart. 'B. G. J. E. Do these letters have any meaning or are they an abbreviation for anything? I've always imagined optometrists having a little laugh when people read them out.'

'No. I don't find this amusing in the slightest. Maybe it's a therapist you need and not an optometrist.'

'So they're just random?'

'As far as I'm aware. Yes. OK, that's all fine, you can see very well in fact. Now let's make sure your eyes are healthy; to the Death Lasers. Sit down there and rest your chin here, but first let me show you something.'

He goes to his desk, opens a drawer, pulls out a picture frame and hands it to me. 'Do you remember when you saw me in town and I was getting a caricature done? This is it.'

I take the frame, expecting something more than what I imagined, I mean, the frame's made from a decent wood, oak or teak or something, I'm no expert. Anyway, I look at it, questioning the effectiveness of my eyes. 'It's . . . errr . . . you want the truth?'

'Always.'

'It's terrible. I can't believe you got it framed, it looks nothing like you.'

'Nothing?'

'Well . . .' He's visibly hurt, I need to redeem some goodwill, especially as I'm about to sit in front of the death lasers. 'It's not totally without a likeness of yourself.' Did that sentence even make sense? 'He's captured your . . . humanity?' Yes, it looks like a human, that'll do.

'Well, anyway. I love it.'

He must be heavily into irony or something. 'Good for you.'

Sheridan puts the framed drawing back into his drawer, then scoots his chair back over to the other side of the slit lamp. 'OK, rest your chin just here and then look through the binocular bit here.'

'And what do you do?'

'I use it to read your mind.'

'Ohh, be careful now, Dr Sheridan. You might see something you don't want to see.'

'Maybe. OK, look to the left.'

I look to the left.

'No, your left.'

'I am!'

'Nothing wrong with your sense of direction.'

'Very funny, Dr Funny.'

'OK, look to the left.'

I look to the left.

'You've got a great pair . . .'

'Sherry, I'm disappointed in you . . .'

'. . . of eyes! What?!'

'You're going to give me the full optometrist repertoire here?'

'You're damn right.'

After a few quiet seconds I get a little paranoid, he's looking straight into my eyes and I can't see him, maybe this thing *can* read minds or at least gives him a little hint into what I'm thinking. I feel exposed.

'Now to the right.'

Maybe he's being quiet because he's found something hideous behind my eyes. Not a physical disease but something on my mind that's been eating away at me, twisting me and turning my life upside down and inside out. Something so ugly it's a mystery to medical science, something so intriguing he can sense a medical breakthrough, publish a paper, maybe get a disease named after him. Is that even a good thing? Sheridanitis? My God, what if he names it after me; Heiditis?

'And look up.'

'Everything OK?'

'Yeah, fine.'

Strangely, this feels more intimate than the one time I went to a gynaecologist. Gynaecologists, optometrists, and boyfriends all want to get in where they're not wanted, you have to pay two of

141

them for the privilege whilst the other one drains you of a lot more than just money. This is just an eye test. I don't need a boyfriend or a gynaecologist, and after today, not an optometrist either. There's only one way my life's going to go if I complicate it –

'Down.'

'Exactly . . . oops.'

'Look down, please.'

'Sorry.' I look down.

This is just an eye test. That's all. I've built this up to be some kind of crazy date. Who goes on an eye test date? Actually, it wasn't me, it was Chloe. She's hooked me up with quite a few employment-based dates over the last month. Carl the mechanic gave my car an MOT, Dave the decorator gave me a quote on doing the rest of my flat, Liam the gardener came round as a surprise – the biggest surprise he got was the one garden box on the balcony of my second-floor flat. Ollie from the electronics store came over to give me a quote on a £3,000 sound system I was never going to buy.

I don't want Carl to handle my carburettor, Liam isn't going to be planting any seeds near me and Ollie is never going to tweak my tweeters.

'All done.'

'Thank God for that. It's strange looking through a lens and not being able to see much. I started to get a little freaked out for some bizarre reason. I'm used to taking photos, not being stared at.'

'You're a photographer?'

'Easy, Sherry, that's a little strong. I have a camera.'

'And you take photos with this camera? Ergo, you're a photographer.'

'I cook beans on toast but that doesn't make me a chef. Anyway, I'm struggling for inspiration at the moment to be honest with you. I've set up a studio in my flat, so hopefully—'

'Whoa! Hang on. You're not serious but you've set up a bloody studio? That's great!' He scoots his chair around the slit lamp to sit closer. 'You're going for it then? You're actually, properly going for it. You know how many people don't go for it? Too many.'

OK. I have no idea what to read between the lines there because the only way that made any sense was between the lines. 'Anyway, as I was saying, I'm struggling. I want to start taking portraits to make use of my studio but I don't really want to take those traditional family portraits, you know? I want to go for something more arty, if that doesn't sound too high-minded.'

'Hmmm . . .' Sheridan gets up, completes his notes, files it, does something on the computer and then perches himself on the edge of his desk. 'First, the good news, your eyes are in pretty good nick and wonderfully healthy. The right eye is very, very slightly weaker than the left but nothing to worry about. It would be remiss of me to even try to sell you the weakest of reading glasses. As a customer, you're dead to me.'

Is he flirting? I have no idea, so I say nothing and keep my face parked in neutral.

'Secondly, I may have a solution to your lack of a muse: a party.'

'A party?'

'A party. A "Prop Party" to be more accurate. An old university friend of mine was a film student; great with the technology, editing, and all that stuff but lacked in the story-writing department. So he thought he'd have a Prop Party where everyone would bring one prop along and then he'd figure out a story using all the props. Not quite the same situation as yours but it's an excuse to have a party where you can take loads of photos of people plus you never know what kind of props you'll get and the crazy inspiration they'll spark.'

'Wow, that's actually a good idea, Sheridan.'

'You doubted me?'

'Of course. I'd have to host a party at my place, which is a whole world of problems in itself but—'

'No pain, no gain.'

'Exactly.'

'You've come this far, why not go a bit further?'

'What was your friend's film like?'

'A crock of pretentious shit, but the props were amazing.'

Chapter Seventeen

21 MONTHS BEFORE TODAY

'Hi, Daisy!' I lever the door open with my foot as I have a glass of wine in one hand and, in the other, a plate with a cheese and pineapple hedgehog. Don't mess with the classics.

'Heidi!' She leans in to give me a peck on the cheek, I swing the cheesy hedgehog out of her way. 'Wow! Listen to that! It's a *prop-er* party you got going on here.'

'Nice, I like what you did there, Daisy.' Fifth time I've heard that tonight. 'I would say there's been no expense spared for this little social gathering but Chloe's boyfriend is cheap and DJs for as long as there's free booze. Come in.'

I notice the big bag she's keeping behind her back. She notices me noticing. 'I've come bearing props!'

'There's no entry without props, Daisy!'

She presents the bag. I have a dilemma: both my hands are full, I offer Daisy the hedgehog in exchange. 'Look at the size of that bag. Interesting.' I lie. It's too light to be anything of any use. I open the bag trying to keep up my high-energy, over-the-top enthusiasm in the hope of disguising the disappointment soon to befall me. 'Oh look, wigs!' I down the rest of my wine to drown the grimace spreading across my face. 'A whole load of different coloured wigs!' What does she think I'm going to do, start photographing children's parties?

'Seven to be exact. I thought they'd be fun.'

'Brilliant, thanks so much, Daisy. The kitchen is just through there, take the hedgehog with you, then follow the music to find everyone else, not that you can get lost in my flat.' I swiftly open the nearby closet and chuck the bag of wigs onto the floor. 'Have you seen Sheridan?'

'Yeah, I bumped into him in the off-licence, he should be up here in a minute with his friend.'

Sheridan's bringing a 'friend'?

Off she walks as I see Darren from Stadium Sports head down the communal hallway towards my front door, closely entwined with a date. 'Darren! Hi, and . . .' Is this Yvonne from the hairdressers round the corner or Maggie from the hairdressers up the other end? I'm neither a loyal nor a fussy salon customer, I'm a slave to late cancellations.

'Hi, Heidi, you know Maggie, right?'

'Yeah, she's turned my bad hair days around on many an occasion. Hi, Maggie.'

'Hiya.' Maggie's exquisitely crafted nails lightly stroke the back of Darren's finely moisturised neck as they stand in my doorway in perfect harmony. He better be careful, I've heard this girl openly reveal her many tales of scorn. She uses an industrial grade shellac and she's not afraid to use them.

Darren quickly proffers his gift, a brand new but unpackaged football, obviously a Stadium Sports returned purchase or a damaged delivery. Not bad, better than wigs, I'll give him that. I see Sheridan enter the corridor over Maggie's shoulder, with the mystery 'friend' hidden but audible behind him, so I quickly move Darren and Maggie inside.

'Sherry!' I hug him around the neck, up on tip-toes, purely as a strategy to see who's behind him.

A bloke. Good.

Why *good*? Why am I relieved? Where's my glass of wine? Release your grip on the poor man!

Sherry points an ear into the flat. 'Listen to that! I hear a kicking party going on.'

'A *Prop Party* is going on and it's all thanks to you.'

'Me?! I just told you about a party an old mate of mine had,

145

you've actually gone and organised one. So . . .' Sherry steps forward, inviting me up into a conspiracy, 'you got any good props yet?'

'I have. It's been great, so many people have gone out of their way and been super generous.'

'Feeling inspired?'

'I think so, yeah.' He looks at me as though he can read my mind, which would be far too revealing. Inviting him into my home is already about twenty steps too fast for my liking. Darren from Stadium Sports can think what he likes about my flat, Sherry on the other hand. 'So what have you got me, Mr Optician? A big bag of bloody glasses to go with my big bag of bloody wigs I suppose.'

Sherry gazes at his shoes as he passes over a plastic bag . . . I open it . . . a plastic bag full of cheap plastic bloody glasses. Shit!

'I'm sorry! This is great. Look at them all, loads of different styles, colours, and . . .' I put a pair on. 'Look at me.' I try to extinguish my faux pas with a pair of jazz hands, this only fans my embarrassment.

Yeah, look at you with your funny bloody glasses and big smelly feet in your mouth.

Sherry cools me down with a smile. 'It's OK, Heidi, chill out. They were actually meant to be a joke. This is for you as well.'

He gives me a small dark blue suitcase; a hardwood construction, leather-bound, a metal plaque by the handle embossed with a German name and 'Frankfurt' underneath. It's heavy. I look at him: it feels expensive, important, inspiring.

'Open it.'

I place it on the floor and kneel down, looking up at him, he nods me onwards. I unclip the fastenings and lift up the lid; the breath from an old oak tree sobers me up. Inside there are eight lenses, the top row of four arranged in order of length, the bottom row in alphabetical order of function: fisheye, soft-focus, stereoscopic, and tilt-shift. I suddenly feel a little 'tilt-shifty' myself. 'Sherry, I can't—' I shut the lid. 'It's too much.'

Sheridan bends down, placing a hand on mine, both our hands against the closed case. 'Listen. I'd love to tell you this cost me two thousand pounds or something but it didn't, it was free. Zilch. Gratis. I had a word with a few suppliers, companies that make all kinds of optical equipment, from contact lenses to photographic lenses. This German company, don't even ask me to pronounce their name, are looking to export over here so they sent out a few samples to head office, who then distributed them to some area managers, mine being one of them. The guy loves me, it's unhealthy. Anyway, he mentioned them, I asked for a favour, and here they are. Take out a lens and have a look.'

I pull out the soft-focus lens, hoping it will soften the hard light of generosity currently blinding me. 'Hmmm . . . it looks OK, feels all right.'

'Read down the side.'

'*Porno Lens* . . . blimey!'

'Exactly, they had a slight potty-mouthed translation issue in pre-production which wasn't spotted until it was too late, luckily only a few sets were made but obviously these can't be sold.'

'I wonder what the others have got written on them?'

'As long as your delicate, innocent faculties can ignore such vulgarity, these lenses might be useful for you.'

'Sherry, it's the best gift ever. It's amazing.' I shut the case and give him another hug. 'It's inspiring.'

'You two gonna get a room or something, some of us are gasping for some beers and seeing the talent on offer round here. Come on, let the dog see the rabbit.'

'Heidi, this is my mate, Mike. Mike, this is your host, Heidi.'

'All right , love. Here's your present, life size, if you know what I mean.'

Sheridan's enlightened acquaintance hands me a package wrapped in a plastic bag before taking off into the kitchen with a box of beers.

'Please note, I had absolutely no input into this present. He's one of those friends whom you don't realise how embarrassing they are until you introduce them to someone new.'

I weigh it up: it's light, not a good indicator of robustness. I open up the poorly taped plastic bag. 'Oh, wow.' I look at Sheridan. 'A giant inflatable penis.'

'You won't be needing the zoom lens for that bad boy. Let's get a drink.'

Most people arrive during the next hour, a who's who of Wigthorn high street employees working at the retail establishments with the potential to provide the most interesting gifts. The guys over at Gadgets Plus all chipped in to get a smoke machine which is currently turning my studio into a pretty good dance floor. Of all my gifts, the stand-out ones are a vintage wooden step ladder from Olivia's Furniture, some old crates from the boys at J.J.'s Grocers, a great looking floor lamp that was sitting in storage from Henry's Shoes, a crazy mirror from Jeff and Reg at MirrorssrorriM and an ex-display window frame from whatever that double-glazing place is called down the road. I didn't even invite anyone from there, one of the hairdressers is going out with a guy there and hey presto! Angela from Holidays Plus gave me a collection of her old jewellery which will come in handy if I'm ever involved in a 'Chavs vs. Pirates' photoshoot. All in all, everyone has come through for me and I couldn't be happier. Even those without the stock or size to have spare, interesting props lying around were more than willing to help in other ways: the girls at Harry's Sandwich Bar helped with a little light buffet and Pavel from my local off-licence brought round an impressive amount of beer with the request, 'I just ask you dump empty bottle out of town, yes?' No problem, Pav, thanks!

There's also a cross-section of the high street whom I didn't invite, somewhat on purpose. Banks, building societies, mobile phone shops and, of course, estate agents. Those establishments had neither the props I might find inspiring nor the characters I wished to party with e.g., mainly, Gary. Whereas, on the other hand, I invited every single charity shop worker and their almost endless supply of interesting props. These mostly older women were flattered but ultimately declined my invitation yet every shop seems to have one token 'youngster' whom was glad of the invite. I say mostly, I've just noticed Edith and Gladys talking to the DJ. Not sure if he's got a remixed version of 'Jerusalem'.

Employees from those vicariously seasonal, generically named shops that spring up from time to time in empty retail spaces selling every-thing cheap from clocks and party balloons to carpets, doormats, furniture, mirrors, and Christmas items also make good invitees. I'm just gutted I never got the number of Gary's prostitute. Technic-ally, she works in Wigthorn and I'd be intrigued to see what work-related prop she would've brought along.

Time to start becoming a part of the party. I join Sheridan in the kitchen, his head further in the refrigerator than is natural. 'Sherry, what are you doing?'

Sheridan replies without removing his head from inside. 'We gotta start off with a shot of something, a little lubrication before we move onto the beer. What the hell is this stuff?'

'Beer. Just black market, under-the-counter, don't-ask-any-questions, beer.'

'It's got "safe" in the title, that can't be good.'

I reach up into a cupboard. 'I've got a secret bottle of vodka here, how about a couple of shots of this?'

'Nice one.'

The next hour goes by in an unexpected hurry, leaving behind it the unimaginable realisation: I don't want my own party to end. This eclectic group of people, mixed with alcohol, fuelled by cheese and pineapple sticks, all find a shared brotherhood in the one thing we have in common: Wigthorn high street. Sales assis-tants, charity shop workers, managers, cleaners, a pharmacist, a dentist, a journalist, multiple hairdressers, baristas, chefs, the highly skilled and professional, the plodders, the grafters, the underpaid, the overworked, and an optometrist, of course. They're all here in my flat: getting on, laughing, dancing, drinking, nibbling, chat-ting up, taking the piss, looking relaxed without the pressure of sales and customers. All human life is here, I have to get my camera.

For the next half hour I prowl the savannah of my one-bedroom flat glued behind multiple lenses, testing out Sherry's gift and taking advantage of having so many faces to capture in a moment. Using the shadows, smoke, and guests to hide myself, I search for subjects unaware of my presence. As soon as self-consciousness washes over their face, the moment's gone and I'm off.

I find Sheridan sitting on the floor in front of the crazy mirror, staring into it like he's been hypnotised or given some psychedelic drugs. Don't tell me he's into drugs! I had enough of Gary getting wasted on ecstasy when he was without me or stoned when he was with me. I shouldn't complain, really, Gary without drugs was much poorer company. Maybe Sherry's drink has been spiked?

I take a couple of photos before I disturb him; the documenter in me is really coming to the fore tonight. 'Sherry? Are you OK?'

'Oh yeah, yeah, just checking out this mirror, funny isn't it?'

'Yeah.' Has he got the mental age of a six-year-old? 'So, you want another drink? I'm going to make an announcement in a minute.'

'Exciting, what about?'

'A little game we can all play.' I make my way to Steve the DJ, who's being carefully guarded by his girlfriend. I can see Chloe's menacing face slowly appear through the smoke and disco lights, blocking access to Steve who's standing behind the dining table in the corner of the photo studio/lounge. 'Chloe! You all right? Why don't you dance or get another drink?'

'I'm fine right here, thank you. Do you know these hairdressing floozies?'

'Floozies? My flat isn't a saloon bar in the wild west.'

'They're all over Steve like flies round shit.'

'That's a bit harsh on Steve, isn't it?' She gives me the same warning face she's being projecting on to the entire room like a pissed-off lighthouse. 'Lighten up, will you, they're probably requesting songs.'

'That's what Steve says.'

'There you go then.'

'He would say that though, wouldn't he.'

'Look, I need to get through and use Steve's mic, I've got an announcement to make.' Chloe, somewhat reluctantly, lets me through. Steve gives me the mic and lets me know he's got his pre-arranged playlist at the ready.

I take to the 'stage' and down the rest of my drink. I hate public

150

speaking, even in my own flat in front of a load of merry partygoers. 'Hello, party!'

Everyone cheers, looks round, laughs, whoops, whistles, shouts my name. That wasn't so bad. 'Hi, everyone, thanks for coming!' More cheering, Steve fades the music out. 'And thanks for not breaking anything . . . yet!'

After the inevitable *waheys*, I continue, 'First of all, thank you to everyone for all the fantastic props you got me! There are so many great props to inspire me, I can't thank you all enough. So, as this is a Prop Party I thought it might be fun if you all became my models and took part in a photo shoot with all your props! I've set up my camera on the tripod just over there, the backdrop is set up just in front,' I point, over-dramatically. 'So if you all queue up behind Chloe here . . .' She looks at me in horror. 'Individually, in pairs, in groups, whatever you want, grab a prop from over here, decide on a pose, pose in front of the camera, then join the back of the queue and start again. Comprendez?!'

'Yeah! Si! Ja!' More cheering, people dive for their favourite props and partners.

'Can we go naked?!' shouts Darren, lapping up the laughter.

'If you want, but I don't have a telephoto zoom lens for something that small!' The pain and worry of organising this party in my own flat suddenly pays off in a second as Darren shrinks back under his stone, the laughter he initiated backfiring. 'OK, Steve, hit it!'

The unkempt chords of David Bowie's 'Fashion' breaks the silence, Chloe stiffly walks in front of the backdrop, ironically poses, and then walks off. The rest of the party soon loosen up and start posing, especially with the wigs and inflatable penis. The two props I instantly took a dislike to become an instant hit with the whole party. I notice the men growing ever more uncomfortable with the poses the girls think of to incorporate the inflatable penis, and with the ease and familiarity of the banter regarding the size of it. I chuck a group of guys the football and they soon forget their shortcomings.

Madonna's 'Vogue' kicks in next and I slightly change the spotlights and get a new backdrop. I tell everyone to relax and chuck the inflatable penis away. I can't imagine Annie Leibovitz ever having this issue. I begin to relax more as well. Everyone knows what I'm doing, why they're there, why I'm behind the camera, no surprises or intrusions, which is always my biggest hang-up when photographing people 'out in the wild'. It's so much easier and unobtrusive to find inspiration in architecture and nature rather than people when walking the streets with camera in hand. But people are so much more interesting subjects. I admire the paparazzi their heartless, merciless stalking of celebrities. It may be ethically repugnant but their sheer audacity and front is something I'd love to possess, which, in turn, I find ethically repugnant about myself.

I even envy these street fashion bloggers taking photos of the public in fashionable or, at least, unusual, clothing. How stupid though! I'm too shy to even stop someone in the street and say, '*Hi, I really like your fashion sense and would love to take a photo of you.*' If someone came up to me and said that, I'd be so happy!

Those great photo-journalist portraits showing war-torn, hungry, oppressed subjects looking directly into the camera: no hiding, no creeping, no secrets. The subject, fully conscious and aware of the photographer, naked, exposed, eye-to-eye via a lens, a moment frozen for all time. The woman and her children in the dustbowl of the American depression or the intense green eyes of the National Geographic Afghan girl. Were these shots only possible by the simple question, '*Can I take your photo?*' How many people do you have to ask before you get a good one? A great one? An iconic one?

I'm not going to get rejected tonight, so with that certainty I feel a whole lot more confident in taking shots, directing people a little and even moving around more. The camera shutters start snapping at the beginning of Duran Duran's 'Girls on Film' and I decide to go mobile. I leave one camera on the tripod and get Chloe to take photos by simply clicking the remote button but this is a distraction, drawing the eye of the subjects away from me. I pick up my secondary camera and slowly gain confidence in moving around, crouching down, getting in people's faces, taking photos of people queuing up, getting dressed up, finding new partners, practising new poses, trying out new props; peeling back the curtain of this photo shoot and finding something a lot more interesting. It also reveals that maybe fortune favours the brave.

By the time the next tune, Taylor Swift's 'Style' comes on, the party's enthusiasm for posing dies out and only a few die-hard models survive. I signal Steve to carry on with his normal dance tracks after this one whilst I put away the tripod, spotlights, and cameras, and change the backdrop to a plain white one. I download all the photos I've taken to my laptop, then hook it up to a projector and play a slideshow of all the photos onto the backdrop. I retreat back into the kitchen and watch the smoke machine pour out, the guests dancing on cloud nine. This is a pretty good party if I do say so myself. I deserve a drink.

I turn around and Sheridan's standing with a drink for me, a colourful concoction.

'Do you always host such great parties?'

'This is the first.'

'You're a natural. The slideshow is a great idea. Did you get any good ones of me?'

'Of course, you're very photogenic.'

'Am I?'

Chloe comes in and whispers in my ear, 'There's someone at the front door.'

'Just let them in.'

'No, you better go. It's Gary.'

Fuck. Why tonight, why now? How did he know I was having a party?

'Are you OK, Heidi?' Sheridan takes my drink, placing a hand on my waist to steady me.

'Yeah, fine, I'll be back in a minute.'

I pause slightly by the front door to regain some composure. I don't know why I'm so nervous. It's not like I hold any kind of candle for this lowlife, in fact the complete opposite, I'd like to drown him in hot wax. I want nothing more to do with him, why is he here?

I open the door and stare at him in silence. He hasn't changed; stubble, combed-back hair with a slight mullet, wrapped in cheap sportswear to cover his skinny arse. I try to discover one redeeming feature, a reason why I stayed with him for so long, what attracted me to him in the first place. He used to be quite funny, sometimes charming, but mainly I think it was because I was lonely. He filled a space in my life, his physical mass attracted me, like the sun, and I got burned.

'Hiya, babe, I guess my invite got lost in the post.'

'What are you doing here?'

'I've bought along a prop for you.' His smile is a crack in the facade, revealing a decayed interior. He hands me a gift.

'I don't want it. You're not invited, go away.' I hold on to the frame of the door.

'That's not very nice of you.'

'Gary. Just fuck off.'

'You fucking ungrateful little bitch.' The facade crumbles, here comes the decay. 'I come here to let bygones be bygones, give you space to get over me so we can carry on as friends, and this is how you treat me. Does everyone in there know what a fucking slag you are?'

'So you came here to make friends and you speak to me like that? Are you mental? I don't welcome you with open arms, begging to be a part of your life again, so you react with this hatred? Do you really wonder why I want nothing to do with you? Understand this. I never want to see or hear from you ever again. Never. Do you understand?'

'What the fuck are you looking at, mate?'

I feel Sheridan's presence behind me, his gravity grounding me. I let go of the door frame, turning to look at Sheridan. His gentle smile reassures me.

'Is this guy causing you a problem, Heidi?'

'Fuck off back to the party, this has nothing to do with the likes of you, sunshine.'

I want to wind up Gary and I want to hold on to Sheridan. I can achieve both easily but I don't want Sheridan to think I'm using him. I want to hold him regardless of who's standing by the front door. I want to shut the door on Gary without a word but he's too stupid to accept reality, I have to spell it out for him.

I hold out my mobile phone. 'Go away, Gary, or I'll phone the police.'

Gary looks at the phone, tries to intimidate me with that stare of his that used to work so effectively but with Sheridan behind me, it means nothing. I dial 999 and show it to him, my finger hovering over the ring button.

'You ain't got the guts.'

I hit ring, putting the phone on speaker.

'Hello, nine-nine-nine, which service do you require?'

'Police. I'm being harassed and he won't leave. His name is Gary Kline, he lives at—'

'Fuck you.' Gary walks off: fuming at my self-esteem, angered by my self-belief, frustrated by my independence, furious at my self-confidence, hating my hopefulness, resenting his loss of control.

'Cancel that, he's just left. I'll phone back if he comes back. Thank you.'

I shut the door, feeling both of Sheridan's hands on my waist. I look down as his fingers creep round from behind me, around my hips. I place my hands on his, encouraging them on further until they're wrapped around my stomach, drawing us together.

'Well done, Heidi, that was amazing.'

I spin around, wrapping my arms around his waist and resting my head against his chest as one of his arms goes behind my back, the other holds the back of my head. I allow myself to relax; breathing out the stress, inhaling Sherry's comforting warmth. 'Stay.'

'Are you worried he might come back?'

'No.'

Chapter Eighteen

20 MONTHS BEFORE TODAY

'What number was it, love?'

'Number forty-three.' I squint through the window of the taxi to get a better view of the house numbers, 88, 86. 'Further down, just by that blue van, I think.'

Sherry's been to my place a few times now but this is my first time at his. Mine is more convenient, being in town, but Sherry's place isn't deep in the sticks or anything like that so, yes, I am a little nervous about what I may find there. You never know with boys, do you? Especially those who have been single for quite a while. Without the guiding hand of an ex or the watchful eye of a flatmate, anything could be possible within those four walls.

I trust Sherry. I don't think he's been putting this visit off on purpose, it's just the way things have worked out. Believe me, I've met some dickheads and Sherry is not a dickhead but you can never be too sure, can you? I mean, neighbours always testify on the evening news that the serial killer next door was 'as nice as pie, always said good morning and took his bins out on time'. Statistically, I could be struck down by a leopard on a meteorite wearing a monocle as I walk up Sherry's drive. The problem with probability is that nothing is impossible.

I'm nervous and I don't deal with nerves well. It gets exhausting but I'm nervous because I care and I haven't cared in a long time. Sherry has a calming influence on me and I like that about him, he allows me to express myself without putting me down. He gives me confidence by giving me freedom. Sherry's greatest gift is his support. Someone believes in me. Like a long-forgotten god from a long-forgotten religion receiving his first prayer from a newly discovered believer, I wish I could perform a miracle for them as a sign of my thanks. For what are gods and humans without someone believing in them?

I don't want to push my new-found confidence into over-exuberance though, I've caught him a couple of times looking at me a little strangely, as though he's looking through me or examining my mental state. I need to find a balance. It's just that I'm so glad to finally be happy with someone who I respect and like, and fancy.

I've brought along a bottle of red wine as Sherry is cooking dinner. Some of my nervousness may come from that. I've never had a meal cooked for me by a boyfriend. I know, I've known some real dickheads. I'm nervous that he's a terrible cook and I'll end up getting smashed on wine and an empty stomach. Sherry's a sensible, educated professional though, surely he hasn't got through single life on a diet of toasted cheese sandwiches and takeaway? He's got abs, for God's sake!

Another thing I like about him.

Just ring the bloody doorbell, you stupid cow.

Ring, ring!

'Heidi, hi!' I've actually heard this before, it may be shocking to hear. 'And you say . . .'

'Ho-De-Ho.'

'Come in!'

At least things can't go downhill from here. 'I've heard that a million times, Sherry.'

'You bought wine, great. Let's have a look.'

I walk into Sherry's flat, passing him the wine along with a confession. 'It's red, that's all I know about it. I'm the opposite of a connoisseur; a wine dunce.'

'Hmmm, interesting.' Sherry examines the label. 'A cheeky little Aussie Shiraz.'

'Ozzie Shiraz plays for Spurs, doesn't he?' The joke is lost on Sherry; he thinks David Beckham is just an underwear model.

'Brewed upon the fair hills of Erinsborough by the esteemed Margaret Ramsey . . .'

'Erinsborough?' I look at Sherry. 'You haven't got a clue about wine either, have you?'

'Not a dickie bird. Let's get this thing open, though, before I start humming the theme tune. Come through into the lounge and I'll pour us a couple of glasses.'

I follow Sherry into the lounge from the hall, full of alertness, my eyes like those of a hawk transplanted into the head of a meerkat; surveying the foreign environment, following every hunch and assumption to a highly illogical conclusion.

'Sit yourself down and I'll get the drinks.'

No chance, I want to have a nose in your kitchen. I follow Sherry into the kitchen, sneaking up on him as he reaches for a couple of glasses. 'So, Sherry, nice flat you've got. How long have you been here?'

'About five years now.'

'You own it?'

'Yeah.'

'Did you do all the decoration and DIY stuff yourself?'

'No chance, I pay professionals to do all that stuff. I'd only screw it up.'

'Nice.' I'm not listening, I'm trying to make conversation to cover my tracks, analysing his living conditions.

Clean and tidy kitchen, shiny even, top marks. The glasses he's pouring the wine into look very clean, good-quality too. All the cupboards and white goods look new, and all the accessories match. Hmmm, maybe a little too OCD. Oh well, you can't have everything.

I have to look in his fridge. When you're out of your twenties it's not about checking out the music or film collection, it gets more fundamental; what kind of shit is this person putting into their body? The fridge, and the bathroom cabinet, containing both secrets and truths.

A distraction. 'You're not going to let that breathe for a bit?' Two steps over to fridge.

'I think it's dead already.'

And open the fridge. 'You know I'm not driving, right? Don't be shy.' Damn, that sounded like he's got a cast-iron shag tonight. You gotta make a boy work for that. Anyway, a quick scan of the contents of the fridge: some vegetables, milk, orange juice, only a couple of bottled beers, cheese, various condiments. Not bad. Not bad at all, young man.

'A full glass of the finest Australian wine, my lady?'

And stand, and turn, and close. 'Thank you very much.' No chocolate. A little OCD with the kitchen accessories and no chocolate in the fridge. I make a mental note.

'Would you like a tour?'

'Is this place like the Tardis or something?'

'No, I just—'

'Just kidding, Sherry.' I kiss him, then grab his hand and walk him out of the kitchen into the lounge. 'I'd love a tour of your flat, it looks fantastic. So, when you hired professionals to decorate and all that stuff, did you also hire an interior designer?'

'No, I've chosen all the colours and furniture myself.'

'You've got a really good eye.'

We both look at each other, acknowledge the unintended irony with a slight pause, raising an eyebrow at each other and chinking our wine glasses before continuing.

'Did you run out of money when it came to getting a new TV?'

'What do you mean? There's nothing wrong with that one.'

'Is it colour?'

'Give it a rest.'

'Seriously, though. Does it get ITV and Channel Four?'

'That's a classic piece of British engineering!'

'Yeah, I know, the problem is, Britain stopped making TVs in the sixties.' I sip some wine, give Sherry a sloppy kiss on the cheek, and lead him on into the hallway.

'And this is where the magic happens.' Sherry opens a door.

It's the toilet.

Like I said, he's got a good eye for design and optometry. Humour, not so much.

I stick a cursory head into the toilet – not down the toilet but

159

inside the room containing the toilet – you know what I mean. Plain, simple, clean. Gets a tick and a smiley face. 'OK, where next?'

'Next door is the bathroom, just your standard—'

'Well, let's have a look.' Fridge: check. Bathroom cabinet: in progress. 'Nice, Sherry, very nice. Love what you've done here, very clean and modern. Are there lights on this mirror?'

'Yeah, I'll turn it on. Look in the bottom right-hand corner, it's also got the time and date.'

'Ooh!' Tone it down a bit, Heidi. 'Very flash. Boys and their toys, right?'

'I admit, the time and date function swung it for me.'

'And there's storage behind this mirror?' I slip my hand around the edge of the mirror, feeling for a handle or catch.

'Yeah, just here.'

The trick is to take a mental photograph immediately and then analyse the image later. We've all done it, someone hasn't minimised their email program or text messages quick enough, giving us an unexpected peek into their innermost secrets. Or their lack of spam control.

I open the mirrored door, take my panoramic mental photograph, comment on the spaciousness, and then close it again. All perfectly innocent, all perfectly nonchalant.

Sherry shows me his bedroom as I analyse the contents of the bathroom cabinet in the background of my mind. This multi-tasking allowing me not to feel too nervous or try to make any stupid jokes whilst in his bedroom for the first time, plus giving me a chance to assess what I've just seen.

Thankfully, not much. No STD creams or an excessive amount of pills nor a narcissistic amount of grooming products. I tune back into what Sherry's saying as we walk around the bed and I notice the bedside table. No, some areas are just too sacrosanct for a first visit. That crosses the line from curious to a violation.

Sherry leads me out of the bedroom and turns right, back to the lounge, which is strange because a full tour of the flat would surely include the door to the left, at the end of the hallway.

'And what about that door, Mr Maddox?'

'That's just the spare room.'

'And? Is this a full tour or just a semi-tour?'

'There's not much in there, just storage and crap.'

I look Sherry straight in the eye as I take one step towards the mystery spare room.

A flicker.

'Come on, Sherry. I'm not going to go in there without your permission but do you really want me not to go in there now? Do you want me to leave here tonight – 'Or tomorrow morning, I'm still open to any further developments at this stage. '– with a nagging feeling that one room in my boyfriend's flat is off limits?'

'I'm your boyfriend now?'

'Well, not if we have rooms that are off limits to each other, no.'

Sherry looks at his feet, scratches his face and attempts to begin a war of attrition. It's cute when boys try this. You think the Russians defending Moscow in 1941 put up a stubborn resistance? Sherry's no Barbarossa, I can freeze him out with an icy stare all day if I have to.

'You want another glass of—'

'We are only a few seconds away from the moment when this turns into something a little weird.'

'OK, OK.' Sherry passes me, eyeing me suspiciously. 'You promise you won't laugh?'

'How can I promise that after all this? You haven't got your dead mum in there or something, have you?' I drink the rest of my wine in one gulp in case I need to use the glass in a frantic escape.

'Do behave. See for yourself.'

I walk through into the spare room.

Holy shit.

I look up at Sherry, the seriousness of my face contrasting with his sheepishness.

There's a few framed photographs of Sherry, an oil painting, a . . . what is that? A bloody X-ray, an illustration, a watercolour, and other bits. All of them portraits of Sherry. Except one which

161

looks like a Mexican actor from the seventies or something, and one of those bendy circus mirrors.

Oh yeah, and a spare bed, but that's the least interesting thing in this whole room.

'Sheridan, an explanation, if you please. And please, let me stand by the door.'

Sherry steps aside and picks up a framed photo leaning against the bed. 'It's just a little side project, like a hobby, everyone's got to have a hobby, right? There was a photographer who went around the world getting local portrait photographers to take his photo, resulting in him being able to see himself as the rest of the world saw him. I just really liked that idea, so I copied it a little but also added more portraiture options than just photographs – like this courtroom style sketch I commissioned a couple of years ago.' Sherry holds it up against his own face. 'What do you think?'

'It's very good.'

'No, no. Does it look like me?'

'Yeah, I could tell it was you straight away.'

Sherry lowers it, stares almost forlornly at it before placing it back on the floor.

'Just a hobby then?'

'Yes.'

'Why this?'

'Why not? I don't like sport, I'm not musical or artistic. Collecting stamps or train spotting really doesn't do it for me. This is interesting, it's kind of fun, stupid, bizarre. It's unique, right?'

'It's definitely unique.'

'Which is why I hide it all in here and don't have it on display throughout the flat. You think you know yourself but it's not until others tell you what you reflect that you truly know yourself. There are aspects of yourself which only others can see. To see yourself as someone else would see you is an insight not many people ever get to see.'

'Is that important?'

'Maybe. I'll let you know when I know.'

162

It's sort of cool in its own way. Strange, granted. But these are just normal portraits, Sherry isn't dressing up as a king or trying to be a model or super-cool in these images, he's just himself. He wants to see his true self; who really wants to see that? It's interesting. I'm interested.

'Would you like me to take your photograph?'

Sherry smiles, he relaxes into his surroundings. 'Yeah, yeah I would.' He finishes his drink. 'That means we'd have to see each other again.'

'I know.'

Chapter Nineteen

19 MONTHS BEFORE TODAY

I'm pretending to reorganise the front window display. In reality, I'm hiding behind a pillar, losing myself in the aroma of caramel-scented oil, staring at the bench in the middle of the pedestrianised street. This is to be our first lunch date after a few weeks of secretly seeing each other. We've tried hiding our relationship from our respective workmates and the all-knowing eye of the Wigthorn high street grapevine but recently we've been failing to the point where denial is becoming a bare-faced, embarrassing lie. Today we're giving up completely on discretion.

I'm glad. Sneaking around puts me on edge and I hate being the subject of gossip. I can already feel the CCTV cameras on Wigthorn High Street twitching every time I walk by. Lunch on that bench though, maybe that's a bit too much to begin with. Why couldn't we have walked along the seafront or sat inside a coffee shop?

Sherry told me not to bring lunch, just my camera. I'm curious as to what he has in store, obviously something to do with taking pictures but I'm not exactly sure what, he wouldn't say. He woke me up this morning lightly stroking my hair, our cheeks gently meeting, our lips lazily kissing. We're in that second wind of a relationship when all the big 'firsts' have been hurdled: first kiss, first time at a restaurant together (out of town), first time making a cup of tea for each other, first time seeing each other naked, first orgasm, first time going down on each other, first time waking up next to each other, first conversation after sex, first conversation about sex.. We're no longer strangers but not yet committed.

164

I don't know what I'm doing or what I want, I'm having fun though, he's lovely. I enjoy being with him, now all I have to do is not analyse this relationship to death. Which is like *not* breathing.

The bench is innocuous, as all benches are, but now it's been given the task of becoming a benchmark (pun intended) in the very early stages of our relationship, it is now escalating itself to the status of a throne, a foundation to seat the future.

I look out of the window of Candleina and see an old lady sitting on it. Doesn't she know? Can't she feel the immensity of today? I look across the road at the Twenty20 shop, their window display doesn't change as much as ours, should I mention that or not? I look up at Sherry's office window . . . he's looking straight back at me!

I avert my eyes. What am I doing? We're meeting in ten minutes. I look back and smile. Walk to the front of the window display, wave, then make a funny face while holding two candles so it looks like they're sticking out of my ears. Sherry laughs. As do three kids standing just to the left of me, looking into the shop window. I give them the funny face too. I look back at Sherry and he's gone.

'What are you doing, Heidi?'

Thankfully, it's only Chloe. 'Just entertaining the kids.'

'You ready for lunch then?'

I've told Chloe all about it, obviously, I'm not a robot. It was probably her that let on about it to someone who then elaborated to someone else, but I don't care. I want people to know. I got cheated on by an idiot estate agent who treated everything like property, and me like a fixer-upper, but now I've upgraded to a professional, educated gentleman. I took a step up in the world, who wouldn't want others to know about that?

Maybe Sheridan.

'Not much to get ready for, just meeting Sherry over there.'

'On that bench?'

'Yeah.'

'I thought he'd want to get back to your place and have his wicked way; stick his little scented candle into your slit lamp.'

165

I know. I've had numerous optician/candle/pot pourri euphemisms all week now.

'Yeah, well, maybe he's a gentleman who'd prefer to court his lady properly. Don't compare everyone else to your own sordid little hook-ups.'

My face is granite, or so I think.

'Don't give me that, Heidi. Yeah, yeah, I can read you like a book! He got some this morning, that's why he's taking it easy at lunch. Sherry's pacing himself!'

'Shut up! I'm saying nothing.'

'You don't have to, you harlot!'

Our laughing and jibes are interrupted by the manageress. 'Heidi, are you going to lunch soon?'

'Yes.'

'Good, then go. We'll go through the delivery when you get back.' Oh, joy.

I grab my coat and camera bag from the back and head out to the bench, five minutes early. The old lady is still sitting there. I look up at Sherry's window, he's not there. I approach the bench willing the present occupant to leave.

As I sit, she gets up and walks off, maybe she's finally realised, left the stage for us. I remove my coat, fold it and lay it over my lap with my camera bag to one side. I look up at the sun with my eyes closed and wait. The sun warms my face, the brightness creating a kaleidoscope of colours inside my eyelids, allowing me to create and play with fanciful ideas of the future; is this the end? Will he propose? Will he ask me to move in? Will he say he wants to see other people, or does he just want some head shots in the sunlight outside the Twenty20 shop for their new website? Sherry's hard to read; I can't quite get a handle on his expressions or mannerisms. Chloe was right before when she said his face never appears to be completely relaxed. It's not showing signs of being permanently strained but his eyes always search your face, digging into your pupils to excavate the mystery linking you both.

It does make him look kind of cute though. Like a couple of well-placed dimples or a signature mole or a small flock of wrinkles, those imperfections creating a unique natural beauty because they clash against our manmade ideals; beautiful little accidents.

He's got a nice bum and muscles. I'm not that deep.

Oh crap, he's coming! I jostle my coat, sweep my hair back, and give him a little wave. 'Hi, Sherry.'

He walks over with a confidence I've never seen before, a bag swinging with his cadence. I'm not going to get dumped. Please don't let him propose, please, please, pleasepleaseplease.

'Hi, Heidi, how you feeling?' He sits down quickly throwing his arm up to rest on the back of the bench, slightly turning himself towards me.

'Good.' I correct myself. 'Curious. Why are we meeting here in front of the whole high street and why bring my camera?'

'You have a problem. I may have an answer.'

OK, he's not going to propose, thank God, because if he was this is the most bizarre start to a proposal I've ever heard. 'What's my problem?'

'Shyness.'

'I'm not that shy.'

'OK. Take a photo of this old guy coming towards us.'

'I don't want to.'

'Don't or can't?'

I don't say anything; I don't admit defeat without a battle.

'This is the challenge I bring to you, Miss Heidi. In this bag is lunch.' He holds open the bag for me. 'I have carefully selected your favourites from specially crafted questions I have been asking you over the past few days. We have a small but freshly made lasagne, blackcurrant cheesecake, a dark chocolate Bounty bar, bottled water, and even a packet of pickled onion Monster Munch, which I regretfully purchased as I'll be unable to kiss you until you've thoroughly decontaminated your mouth. The challenge is this: you earn your lunch via the accumulation of photographs. One rule: the photos have to be of strangers on Wigthorn high street. A mouthful or sip per photo.'

I smile through gritted teeth.

'Are you serious?' A weak refrain, like sticking a flower into the barrel of a gun.

'Oh, I'm Robert Capa and I'm going to sit at the back of this big battleship taking photos of the cooks peeling potatoes, I'll leave the D-Day landing photos to someone else!'

He's started doing this recently, a little whiney voice drilling into my self-doubts. The accompanying little flappy hands don't help either. 'How do you know about Capa?'

'Know thy enemy.' He finishes this with a smile; it charms no one.

'I'm hungry, Sherry, we can do this another day when I'm prepared.'

'No.'

Gary never showed the vaguest interest in my photography: he never pushed me, he never challenged me. I wonder if he really showed any interest in me other than what was between my legs and the cash in my sock drawer.

'If you could see yourself now, Sherry.'

'Why, what do you see?'

'Cruelty.' A little overboard, but that lasagne does smell good.

'Just a simple photo. Look,' He motions to the camera bag. I get the camera out, turn it on, take the cap off, change the settings, and pass it to him. 'I'm an ignorant jackass who quickly looked up famous photographers on Wikipedia before I came out and now look at me . . .'

Without a second thought, he brazenly walks up to a man in his fifties. 'Excuse me, sir, I've got a fashion blog where I take photos of people who are really rocking a unique look and I love your coat and shoes. Would you mind if I take a photo of you?'

The man quickly lifts his head above the flattery, taking a gulp of air. 'Yeah, sure.' He poses, Sherry takes the photo.

'Thank you very much, sir.'

'What's the website address?'

Sherry looks at me. I smile back at him. Genius hasn't thought that far ahead.

'Err, search for "Fashion on the streets" and I'm number one. Thanks, see you.'

Sherry walks back to me, mock wiping sweat from his brow but sporting a big, victorious smile. 'That wasn't so hard was it? I think flattery and confidence is the key to this malarkey.'

'But not everyone is going to be so accommodating.'

'So what, move on! How many portraits of interesting strangers do you have so far? None. Sitting on that bench doing nothing means you're always going to have a big fat none.'

Sherry looks around and sees a group of four college girls walking along, all of them annoyingly pretty, curvy, and carefree. Sherry winks at me and approaches them. Where the hell is he getting all this confidence from? He's like a different person.

'Ladies, my only wish is to attempt to catch your beauty on film. That's all. I'm not up to the task, I am but a mere man trying not to become consumed by your natural effervescence. I have one of those street fashion blogs and you, my love, are rocking that scarf and coat combo like it's on stage at Wembley. Can I take your photo?'

'What about me?' Sherry's complete focus on one girl has put another's nose out of joint.

'And you, my love. All of you, a group shot would be great! OK, If I start with you, then you, then you, and then you, then a group one.'

Sherry directs them quite well actually, organising them quickly so as not to interrupt their day too much. The posing is awful, the sun is behind their heads, and I know Sherry isn't focusing in enough, but that's not the point of this exercise is it? Reluctantly, I have to hand it to him.

'Remember, girls, check out Facebook: "Fashion Highs on the High Street".'

I sit on the bench watching him return like a caveman with a sabre tooth tiger swung over his shoulder.

'You're getting too much background in.' I am just a spoilt, hungry cavewoman who prefers mammoth to sabre-toothed tiger, her stubbornness more acute than her hunger.

'So what you're saying is, "If you're not good enough, you're not close enough."'

Damn him and his new best friend, Robert Capa. 'Go on then, let's have a look.' I scroll through the photos, not great.

'Not impressed?'

'Hmmm.' Hell is critiquing the artistic endeavours of friends.

'Well, doesn't matter, I'm about to tuck in to some freshly baked lasagne. So let me think; one guy, four girls, one group shot, I believe that's six succulent spoonfuls of sizzling supper for Sheridan.' At this moment I feel more like his little sister than his girlfriend as he makes a big show of slowly enjoying the lasagne, one careful mouthful after the other. 'Oh, that's good pasta, mamma!'

I look at the camera, make a few changes, check the sun and the shadows, and sit on the bench like a surfer, bobbing up and down in the sea of humans waiting for the best wave.

'Heidi, we're not after quality, today is all about crossing that threshold of fear. I'm here for you but you don't want me around every time you're out taking photos. We've got thirty minutes left of lunch, the lasagne's getting cold, so just get out there and take a few shots. I'm just as shy as you, I only managed to get out there because I don't care what people think or say about me, plus I'm showing off to you. Don't be so precious. Yes, you'll get some rejections but it's those gems you should be thinking of. Also, you don't want to be taking photos of flowers for ever, do you?'

'No.' I close my eyes, no more waiting for the best wave, just take any wave. I stand up, eyes still closed. I walk out amongst the people, get cold feet and walk back to the bench.

'What are you doing?'

'I can't just take a photo of anyone! There has to be something about them I can focus on.'

'Lie. OK, the next person to walk past in a green top, say green is in fashion this season and you like their top. Go!'

'I can't!'

'You look beautiful.'

'What?'

'Your hair looks great, your body is sexy as hell, and I really like that top you're wearing.'

'OK.' I smell a change of tack here. 'Thanks.'

'See? Flip it around, imagine if a stranger came up to you saying you looked so good they stopped you out of everyone else just to take one simple photo, how would you feel?'

We look at each other; him waiting for an answer, me determined not to give one.

Sherry breaks the silence. 'One photo and you can have the rest of this lasagne. Flatter them, specify what you like, ask them if you can take their photo then immediately ask where they bought that item of clothing. Be confident, direct them and before they can say no, you've taken their photo. Just like being with Gary, it'll be over in seconds. Now go! Please!'

OK, OK. A part of me is lamenting the time before an attentive boyfriend, when they ignored you to the point where you could just get on with your life.

Fuck it. Do it!

I step out into the human traffic, spy a young man in a green cardigan and white T-shirt – he looks quite photogenic actually. 'Excuse me, sir. Hi, I've got a fashion blog and I take photos of fashionable people and I'd love to take your photo. I love your green cardigan. Where did you get it?'

As he answers, I slowly pivot around him so the sun lights up his face, I direct him to place his hands in his pockets and look into the camera as I crouch down. Snap!

I say thanks, he smiles and walks off.

That was it.

'You did it.'

'I did it.'

'You deserve lasagne.'

'I do.' We sit on the bench, Sherry getting out another fork and

171

passing over the lasagne, me checking out the photo. It's good. Very good, in fact. 'I need to get a website and give these people a card so they can see what happens to their photo.'

'Great idea. Now eat, maestro.'

I take one mouthful, then I get back out there. We've only got fifteen minutes of our lunch break left.

Chapter Twenty

18 MONTHS BEFORE TODAY

'Are you sure you want to do this?' I pull Sherry closer to me, giving him a squeeze as I peer up at him and give him a kiss. The front door to my mother's house standing before us like a vertical trapdoor.

Sherry smiles and goes ahead with pressing the doorbell. As the bell goes through its ding-dong routine, Sherry gives me a mock, cross-eyed face of shock as he chews his fingernails. Meeting my mum and sister for the first time is a breeze for this sophisticated charmer; so this self-styled sophisticated charmer thinks.

My chain-smoking, widowed mother whiles away her time spending my father's life insurance on keeping up appearances; it's an expensive business. My younger sister stares through the imaginary bars on her open window and bangs against the open door of her room; too afraid to leave. My dead father neither mourned nor remembered. I try to visit as little as possible.

'Heidi!' My mother enthusiastically wraps me in her arms, a fog of fragrance soon following. She's always been taller than me, even as she advances into old age. I'm forever her little girl.

'Hi, Mum.'

'So lovely to see you, come in, come in.' She takes my hand as though she's helping me across the road, all the time looking at Sherry, waiting for an introduction. Never would she talk to someone without an introduction.

'This is Sheridan.'

'Sheridan, Sheridan! Lovely to meet you.' She gently shakes a fallen curl from her eyes. My mother's hair is her pride and joy. My sister, Gemma, and I have known and accepted this from the earliest of days, before memory. It is beautiful, and timeless, an idea that is increasingly pitting them against one another.

Sherry holds out a hand but hers are pre-occupied with the door handle in one and my hand in the other. 'Hello, Mrs Keeler, you must be Heidi's sister?' Sherry, you fool, you've entered a homestead devoid of humour. Didn't you feel a chill as we walked through the garden gate?

'She just called me "Mum", young man. I'm her mother; her sister's inside. Come! Let me get you kids a drink.'

Sherry smiles at me for reassurance. Sophisticated charm is not a language understood in this land of the literal.

We enter the kitchen, spotless and unchanged since I was a child, probably since my parents first moved in. The only item from this millennium is the washing machine, replacing the wheezing old one which shook like an Apollo capsule on re-entry.

'Tea?'

'Yes, thanks, Mum.'

'One sugar please, Mrs Keeler.'

'Please, call me Tess.'

Well I never. My mum rarely gives others permission for that level of familiarity; either Sherry has clicked with her or she's relaxing her barriers.

'Come, let me have a look at you, Sheridan. Heidi keeps her sister and me at such arms' reach, we hardly know her.'

'Mum.' I throw my arms open, not as an invitation but in surrender.

'Nonsense.' She walks up to Sherry, takes both of his arms and holds them out a little, walks around him, looks him up and down as though he's a farm animal at an auction, or a slave.

'Not bad, Heidi, not bad at all. Good arms, broad shoulders, kind eyes, strong jaw. What do you do, Sheridan?'

'I'm an optometrist.'

'Educated, professional, skilled. Financially sound?'

'Mum!'

174

'Yes, ma'am.'

I'm horrified. Sheridan's loving it.

I take over the making of the tea to take my mind and eyes from the embarrassment.

'Sheridan is an unusual name, why did your parents choose it?'

'I have no idea.'

'Both of Sheridan's parents died when he was young, so—'

'Oh my . . .'

The last thing my mother needs is more death in her life.

'It's OK, Mrs Keeler. Tess. I've not known life any other way.'

'Like someone born blind—'

'Mum!'

'Exactly.'

'Don't be so squeamish, Heidi.' My mother shoos me away. 'Anyway, "Sheridan" is a damn sight better than Gary.'

'Bloody hell, Mum! Really? We're going to go there, now?'

'You settled for too long, made excuses, and failed yourself. He reflected poorly on you.'

I pour the boiled water into the cups without much care, squeezing the teabags against the side to extract as much tea as possible and dispense a little aggression. 'You see, Sherry, my own mother thinks I'm a failure. Now you know why I come here as infrequently as I do.'

'You see, Sherry, my daughter doesn't quite listen to what I'm telling her. Gary reflected poorly on you, not that you were a failure. He was a poor decision you made. You are still my beautiful, brave, strong, determined daughter, but this doesn't mean you always make the right decisions. Doesn't mean any of us do, that's for sure. You are worthy of more. You always deserved so much more.'

She has this habit, my mother, she can deconstruct me until I'm completely defenceless and exposed, then build me back up so I'm stronger and more confident than before, whilst I'm expecting, and almost wanting, her to put me out of my misery. She never gives me what I want when I want it.

Of course, Sherry thinks he's just witnessed a close, touching moment between mother and daughter. His eyes widen and his smile softens.

'You see, Sheridan,' my mother continues, 'she's never been able to make tea properly. A teapot is alien to her, "takes too much time", "means more washing up". Heidi, my darling, the best way is not necessarily the quickest or the easiest.'

'Tea is tea, whether it sits in hot water in a pot or in a cup.'

'Oh well, Sheridan. What she lacks in finesse, she makes up for in other ways. I doubt a young man like you is too worried about a decent cup of tea compared with a good arse, right?'

Sheridan's silence is quickly interrupted by the sound of my own mother slapping my bum!

'Mum!'

'Just remember, I gave you that. Your father had a fat, hairy arse. You wouldn't be round here if that was the case, would you, Sheridan?'

'No, ma'am!' Sheridan's teacup is shaking on its saucer as he tries desperately to contain his laughter.

My mother is smiling. I'm not sure when I last saw her smile. 'Let's go into the lounge and see your sister. Don't tell her I just did that.' She taps her nose as she walks past us.

Sheridan and I look at each other as though we're both strangers who have just been magically transported into this house. Might my sister have let a little joy into her life too?

'Hi, Gemma, you all right?' A redundant question but let's get the formalities over with.

'Yeah, you?' She's of the same mind.

'Yeah, fine. This is Sheridan. Sheridan, this is Gemma.' I sit next to her on the sofa, in the middle, the sacrificial barrier. Gemma's grief is permanently poised, ready to strike like a lizard's tongue.

'Hi, Gemma.' Sheridan offers another hand of friendship but is ignored. I silently direct him towards the sofa. I haven't told him anything yet. Gemma can spot the subtlest sign of sympathy a mile off, and hates it.

176

'So, Gem, what's new?'

She plays around on her phone. No one texts her and she texts no one. All she does is play solitaire, all day and every day. The cards, like friends and opportunities, have all shuffled off and disappeared. The aim of her life and the game becoming indistinguishable; to file everything away until there's nothing left. I get no discernible answer.

'Gemma, your sister is talking to you.'

Nothing. We've been put away in our place; suited, in numerical order. At least I got two words out of her.

Whilst my sister ignores problems and people out of existence, my mother is soon sweeping up after her, apologising. It's not only useless boyfriends that can reflect badly on you, but also depressive daughters. Keeping up appearances is an expensive business and my mother is still paying for it now.

'Sorry, Sheridan. Our Gem has been going through a bit of a bad patch recently.'

'Recently?' This has awoken her. Of course, Mum knew it would. 'I'd say nine years is more than a patch.'

'Mum, not now.' I try to part them.

'Sorry, Sheridan, my daughter believes shutting out light and life will ease the pain of losing a baby. For nine years she still hasn't realised that moving on is the only thing we can do. Remaining in the moment of your greatest pain only brings you more pain.'

Gemma replies, 'Maybe pain, all the time, is what I want.'

'No one wants that, darling.'

'I do.'

'Mum, Gemma, do we have to do this yet again, now? Sheridan doesn't want to hear this, and I certainly don't. Again.'

'Tell that to Mum, I was just sitting here minding my own business.'

'That's all you ever do!' Mum leans forward in her chair, placing the teacup down onto the coffee table. 'I'm still mothering you at twenty-four! Paying for you, cooking for you, cleaning up after you, reminding you to take your medicine. Bloody hell, I have to remind you to take a bloody shower sometimes!'

177

'Ignore me, then! I keep telling you to ignore me, shut me out, let me do my own thing.' Gemma stands up, sweeping her long, greasy hair behind one ear. I used to envy every strand of her beautiful brunette curls, now they're twisted and split by her thoughts. 'I don't want you to put yourself out for me, wasting your time.'

'My darling, you're no burden, it's the wasted potential breaking my heart.'

'It's the wasted potential that's broken my heart!'

'Is this what it would've wanted? To see you rotting away like this. You know you're not the only one who's had to cope with the loss of an unborn child.'

'Yes, you keep reminding me, but mother nature took away yours, not the lies and pride of your own mother!'

'I did no such thing! Your father! You know that.' My mother sits back, waves the accusation away as lightly as if someone had accused her of forgetting to put a sugar in their tea. 'She's just lashing out at me, Sheridan.'

Gemma retreads the well-worn path of the argument for a new audience. 'God forbid, Sheridan, that the fine upstanding Tess Keeler should have to confront the members of the local tennis club or the congregation of St Mary's with the shame of an illegitimate grandson or granddaughter. What was it, Mother, the fact you'd have a pregnant teenage daughter or that you'd become a grandmother in your forties? And for what? You see, Sheridan, she never considered the consequences because now she has to confront the members of the local tennis club with the burden of a husband who left her shortly after his legacy was cut short, a daughter who rarely visits, and another daughter who hardly showers or goes out. Double fault! Maybe her short-sightedness is something you could look at?'

I look at Sheridan. He is virtually frozen to the sofa, become a statue, not daring to move a muscle or let his face reveal the machinations within his mind. The beauty, fragility, and wonder of procreation has never sat well with my family. It's a miracle we've made it this far down the evolutionary tree.

'Short-sightedness, indeed. Sheridan, this girl fixed my broken heart . . .'

'Mum! Don't. Don't involve Sheridan in this and don't look for an ally. We're not taking sides. In fact, we're going to go.'

'No, no, don't. Please don't, Heidi, I'm sorry. We're sorry. Aren't we, Gemma?'

Gemma gets up and leaves the room. 'Welcome to the family.'

'I'm sorry, Sheridan, please stay for dinner.'

Sheridan daren't move, nor breathe a breath, nor think a thought.

'No, Mum, I'm not staying here while Gem sits upstairs again, missing another dinner. Either you let her get on with things in her own way or you're going to end up losing the both of us.'

She reaches over to touch my hand. 'Don't say that, love.'

'Mum, I don't want that to happen but it's heading that way. Gem may not be as resilient as you were but that's because we're all different. Isn't that right, Sherry?'

Sherry answers like a robot walking on eggshells. 'Yes.'

'Mum, is she still seeing her therapist?'

'Yes, it always involves talking her round beforehand but afterwards her mood lifts ever so slightly.'

'And she still takes her meds?'

'Yes.'

'So, she's doing what she has to. It may not be as fast you'd like but she is progressing. The blame game, the one-upmanship, the confrontations aren't helping.'

Mum slumps down in her chair; every visit is déjà vu. 'It's not the end of the world, you know? There is hope. She was my salvation, Sherry. I had Heidi and then there was another, between Heidi and Gemma. I lost it, painlessly, almost imperceptibly. I had no choice in the matter. Stolen. Then Gem came along. Beautiful Gem. Gave me hope, gave me meaning, lit up my life. It's so hard to see her suffering like this.'

'I know, Mum, it's hard for me too, but we have to be there for her.'

Mum reaches for the TV listings magazine, a sure sign this

179

conversation's over. 'Hmmm . . . I like him . . . oh good, the second episode is on tonight too.'

'Good TV tonight, Mum?'

'Yes actually, for once. There's the final episode of a drama Gemma and I have been watching.'

'Good.' I put a hand on Sherry's knee, letting him know the end is in sight. 'Mum, we're going to go now.'

'OK, love.' She puts the magazine down as she gets up. 'Sorry. Sorry, Sheridan, you seem like such a lovely boy, please come again? Gem and I will be on best behaviour, promise.'

I give Sherry's knee a little squeeze to reboot him from his processing paralysis. 'Yes, Mrs Keeler, that would be nice. Soon I hope.'

'Next week, Mum. Sunday, we'll come round for a roast.'

'Excellent idea, that would be lovely!'

We get up, I go upstairs to quickly say goodbye to Gemma and then we step out into the evening air. Up and out of the rabbit hole, back into the English countryside.

I wait until we're in the car. 'So. That was my mum and sister.'

'Holy. Fuck.' Sheridan's whole body and soul sighs. 'Is it always like that?'

'What, mother and daughter arguing over whose lost unborn baby is the most heartbreaking? Oh, only about fifty per cent of the time.'

'Is Sunday a good idea, I mean, if you don't think it is, just say.'

'It'll be fine. Once they've initiated a stranger into their world, then they seem to relent.'

Sherry finally starts the engine. 'Good. Right, you ready for a complete change of conversation?'

'Yes, please! First though, I owe you a dinner tonight, let's go to that new Mexican in town, my treat.'

'Great shout. Now, I've got a surprise for you.'

'I hate surprises.' Seriously, I do.

'I've entered you into the Wigthorn Open House Art event in three months.'

'You did what?'

'You know, the open house weekend where artists open up their houses so members of the public can view their work.'

'And why would you enter me into such an event?' Don't control me, don't push me into corners, don't think you know what's best for me.

'You're a photographer, you've got a flat with a bloody studio, it's perfect!'

'You're a bloody idiot!'

'I knew you'd say that.'

'Invite total strangers into my own home to judge and criticise my passion? My private hobby? And when my personal inner sanctum has been desecrated by all and sundry, then what? What do I do then? Where do I go? Seriously, take me home. Forget dinner.'

'Oh.'

Chapter Twenty-one

17 MONTHS BEFORE TODAY

Next Sunday never happened, not for Sheridan anyway. My life is being lived on my terms, I'm not being dictated to nor am I under any obligations. It's not his fault, he was only trying to push me out of my comfort zone, the problem was, he did it too well and I reacted. Maybe over-reacted, since I've hardly spoken to him in the past three weeks, but now I've found something worth hanging on to, I'm going to cling to it with all I've got. If he can't see where he stands in all this then that's his problem, not mine.

I'm finally in the slipstream of a dream, in the wake of a goal, on a path to a destination; photography colours my black and white life. I don't care for exhibitions, front covers, or making a sale, I just want to capture a moment. Grasp one immaculately composed and flawlessly lit moment from this fountain of the infinite. I just want to know if I'm any good.

'Excuse me, sir, I love your hat, would you mind terribly if I took your photo?' 'Terribly', a painfully polite term I've picked up from binge-watching period dramas. It goes down well with the older folk.

'Well, I don't know.'

I look pleadingly towards his wife, imploring a sisterly camaraderie. It pays off.

'Don't be a killjoy, darling. This young lady only wants to take a photo.' She winks at me.

Before he's had a chance to answer, I'm up close, crouched slightly, allowing the sun to peer over my shoulder, washing away the shadows from the brim of his hat. I click, it doesn't feel right; he's posing, too self-conscious. I ask his wife, 'You must have bought this hat for him?'

It gets the intended response, he's offended that I assume he's not capable of buying such a sartorially sharp item. He glares into the lens, his wonderfully green eyes contrasting against his tanned, weathered skin and white eyebrows. *Snap!* That's the one.

'Thank you, sir.' I give his wife a card with my new website and logo on before walking off.

And that's my new act. I've honed it since that lunchtime with Sherry. It's become a crutch, a ritualistic warm-up, something I can rely on; finally. I still can't quite believe it's me walking up to these strangers asking to take their photo. It just isn't me, or rather, it wasn't. Now I lament all those years of beautiful, inspiring, spellbinding faces I allowed to pass me without the slightest attempt to capture their unique image.

And yes, I have a logo. Stick that in your camera bag, Ansell Adams.

The sun is shining and the wind has died down so I head to the beach to see what opportunities have washed ashore. Seeing your hometown with fresh eyes is not an easy thing to do, especially when the town itself is run by bureaucrats incapable of one creative, imaginative thought between them, who are as stale and in as desperate need of rejuvenation as the town they're running into the ground. No one stays, even the sea leaves twice a day.

Prime real estate plots in the town centre are wastelands due to no more than a Cold War era stand-off between bean counters and the planning department resulting in nothing getting built, no bills getting paid, and no tax revenue being generated. The short-sightedness is infuriating, and the sentiment spreads through the town's populace quicker than the smell of the seaweed, Sherry should go test the lot of them. I read the other day that Dubai has a golf course – in the middle of the fucking desert! Wigthorn built a retirement complex in the centre of town whose residents have nothing better to do than complain about every new building project within a five-mile radius which isn't a bingo hall.

Two old women sitting on a bench along the promenade are just too much of a timeless, corny, seaside image to pass up. It's one thing Wigthorn does well. One of the ladies is even knitting. I have to take a photo as no one would believe it otherwise.

'Excuse me, ladies, would you mind terribly if I took a couple of photos of you?' I hold up my camera to allay any possible confusion.

'Of course, love.'

The knitter pushes up her purple rinse. 'Does my hair look OK, Doris?'

'Lovely, Edna.' She raises her eyebrows at me.

They both pose beautifully. *Snap*! I have the definitive 'old ladies on the promenade' photo. Leibovitz, Capa, Rankin, have you got such a feather in your cap?

The ladies start laughing with more mischief after each shot. They are so welcoming of an unexpected detour in their day that I decide to push myself just a little further. 'Ladies, would you mind if I direct you in a couple of poses, play with the old-fashioned idea of a couple of ladies sitting on the promenade?'

'Huh?'

'What was that, love?'

Relax, Heidi. 'Would you like to take some funny shots?'

'Ohhh! That would be lovely!'

'It's normally so boring sitting here.'

'Great, let's have some fun!'

Edna and Doris turn out to the best, most pliable models I could ever hope to work with. They're up for anything, as long as it involves sitting on a bench. I get some great shots of them looking at each other seriously, looking out over the sea pensively, thinking hard, looking confused, crazy faces, angry faces, one of Edna knitting Doris' hair and some beautiful close-ups. The ability to concentrate and play with one subject rather than the drive-bys I've been getting used to is another ball game. It's the difference between a pork pie and a roast dinner. Being able to experiment with both subjects and the technical set-up of the camera opens up a whole new realm of possibilities. I'm slowly pushing myself from documentarian to artist.

I thank the two of them and continue to walk along the promenade, my camera safely packed away, preoccupied with thoughts of how I can further explore a more personal, experimental form of portraiture at home in my studio. After all, it's been sitting there doing nothing for the last couple of months.

I'm interrupted by my mobile phone vibrating in my pocket; it's another text from Sheridan.

H! Talk to me, I'm going crazy here!

Good. Let him stew on it a little more. I'm not as mad with him as he thinks, the problem for him is that I'm finding the less time I spend with him the more photography I can get done, and I'm enjoying that more than his company at the moment.

My camera doesn't overstep the mark. It helps me focus.

It won't be for much longer though, for as much as I love my camera and hunting for moments to capture, it doesn't satisfy all my needs.

My phone vibrates again, this time to signify a call. It's Sheridan; I answer only to tell him not to call again.

'Heidi! Don't hang up!'

'Sheridan. I'll call you tomorrow, I'm busy right now.'

'No, no, I'm only calling to let you know that someone . . .'

I hang up. My muse has gone, my mojo has dissipated. I'm going to buy a bottle of wine, some chocolate, and head home to examine the day's haul as it's projected onto the studio wall while I'm slumped on the sofa. A steaming hot bath and then an even steamier hot book later on in bed might come close to satisfying the needs a camera can't quite reach; Sherry and his kin aren't wholly irreplaceable. Godspeed android technology with their digital desire to serve, listen, and their off-switch.

I approach the entrance to my small block of flats with wine and chocolate in hand, camera bag slung over my shoulder when I notice a man hanging around outside, looking at the range of doorbells as he dials on his mobile phone. I breeze past him, avoiding eye contact and stick my key in the lock. This alerts him.

'Hello, excuse me. You wouldn't be Heidi Keeler, would you?'

'What do you want with her?'

The man slips his mobile into his pocket. 'I'm sorry, I don't mean to startle you. I'm Richard Clements, I help organise the Wigthorn Open House event. I'm just doing the rounds to check up on everyone taking part.'

'Oh, that won't include me then.'

'No? You've paid and everything.'

'Yeah, my boyfriend thought he'd take it all out of my hands and rush me into something I don't want to do. He seems to enjoy throwing me into situations out of my "comfort zone".' I add the quote marks aggressively, hooked fingers like an eagle clutching a struggling a rat. 'He's in the doghouse and I'm not doing any kind of event.'

'You seem quite adamant.'

'You seem quite perceptive.'

'You take photography seriously though?'

'And?'

'Why not do it? You've got your camera with you, you've just been out taking photos, right? That's great! That's exactly what we're after, local enthusiasts. That's all. Nobody's expecting the next David Bailey.'

'That's lucky.'

'Can I level with you?'

'Level away.'

'The number of this year's exhibitors has shrunk from last year, we've only got three other photographers. One is obsessed with birds, the other is drawn to sunsets, and the third only takes photos of inanimate objects so he doesn't have to engage with anyone, a little shy.' Imagine that! 'All three of them are over sixty. This year we're really wanting younger artists to take part, which means you. Recent social media activity and local ads have attracted a few more participants but we're still down on overall numbers, especially photographers. I need you, Heidi, your town needs you.'

'I need to go.'

'OK. Look, just let me see a couple of your photos and I'll tell

186

you honestly what I think. If you still don't want to do it, I'll give you a full refund, in cash, right now and you can keep it a secret from your boyfriend and spend it on a takeaway or camera equipment or whatever you want. I can't say fairer than that.'

'You're very persuasive, Richard.'

'I know, it annoys the hell out of my wife.'

'OK. Come on up.'

I feel comfortable letting Richard in. Inviting strange men into my flat is not a habit I'm accustomed to but his short, slight stature, the grey hair, leather sandals, and passion for local arts dim any threat by a considerable margin. If anything untoward happened, I'm sure a firm swing of my camera bag would take him out.

Richard is such a sweet older man, I can't believe I've already assessed 'taking him out'.

We walk into my studio.

'Oh, my! This is just perfect. Heidi, this space is ideal. You are a dark horse now, aren't you?'

'It's just a lounge without the lounge bits in.'

'I know, perfect.' Richard walks around the studio, filling the empty walls with imaginary framed, enlarged photos that don't exist. 'So, let's see what photos you took today.'

'I haven't been through them yet, I can't let you see all the crap ones.'

'You're not used to criticism, are you?'

'No, not really.'

'It's the only way you'll get better. So let's get started, download everything you've taken today.'

His enthusiasm is infectious, no matter how hard I resist. I find it hard to imagine how he's been losing local artists and not gaining them by the dozen. I download the photos from my camera onto the laptop, then plug in the projector and start a slideshow on the wall.

This impresses Richard even further. 'Oh wow! This is great, Heidi! You've got a great set-up here, this would be the best domestic destination on the whole open house tour without a doubt.'

I half-heartedly protest, 'Shut up.' I invite Richard to sit down on the desk chair as I stand and we watch the slideshow progress. I have a remote control in one hand, swiftly moving it on when a photo I really don't like flashes up.

'You know Frank's Frames?' Richard asks, keeping his eyes on the slideshow.

'I know the shop but not him.'

'He could frame ten of your best shots with a fifty per cent discount if you allow an advert for his shop under each frame. I can get further funding from the local council's arts budget and maybe some more sponsorship from local businesses, plus a discount from a local printer. You could have eight in here, one by your front door and one on that wall space by the kitchen. Plus, you choose whatever other photos you want to display on this projector, it would look fantastic.'

'I would have to spend money?'

'I'll try my absolute best so you don't have to, but maybe you'd have to put your hand in your pocket for twenty pounds per print, no more though.'

'Two hundred pounds, OK.'

'But you could sell one print for two hundred pounds.'

'Sell a print?'

Richard turns on the sofa to look at me, the slideshow scrolls on. 'Yes! The open house isn't purely a non-commercial activity for the local community, we allow the evil tentacles of capitalism to suckle upon our fragile bosom: advertising, sponsorship, buying, selling, promotion, we let them all tarnish our artisan virtue.'

I raise my eyebrows at Richard; do tentacles suckle? 'All right, Richard, lay off the schmaltz.'

He smiles. 'You could make a profit. But, of course, you're probably not interested in that.'

Hold your horses, Dickey old boy.

He stares at the slideshow, the old women making a funny face stare back. His smile grows. 'Now that's a great photo.'

'Thanks.'

'You like portraiture?'

188

'Yes, I think so.'

'Excellent. You're very good. Very good indeed.' Richard stands up quite suddenly. 'I've seen enough. You're a fine photographer with an excellent body of work. Wigthorn would love to see your work, it would be a shame if you hid it away. So what do you say?'

Why does flattery always work so well? Why am I so weak?

'OK.' I breathe out. I feel good. And surprised. 'Help me with getting the framing and printing costs down and I'm in.'

'Great! Great!' Richard's eyes almost get lost in the wrinkles on his face. 'Choose your top thirty photos and I'll be over next Thursday to help you narrow them down. I'll also be able to give you more news on the cost side of things.'

We shake hands. I show Richard out.

I walk back into the lounge which is now a studio and will soon become a gallery. If something as immobile and static as a room can change so much in such a short space of time, maybe I can too?

Chapter Twenty-two

16 MONTHS BEFORE TODAY

'Before you go, could you come into the office?'

'Yeah, sure.' I'm finishing work a couple of hours early to visit Frank at Frank's Frames to decide which frames to use for my short-listed photos. I've chosen the final ten, shown them to Richard who recommended I only change one, and I've also gone through them with Sherry who would've agreed with anything I said. I'm feeling kinda guilty about putting him firmly into second place recently, but not too much. I did start making things up to him last night. I'll make him his favourite meal tonight, if I'm not getting the sack. My manageress is probably going to give me my monthly dressing-down with regards to Chloe and I overly conversing. She'd love to hire robots. Silent robots.

I enter the office, her face already tells me it's not good news.

'Please close the door, thanks, Heidi.' This is normally how it goes. 'Take a seat.' The script never changes. 'I've got some news for you, good news in fact.' OK, now I'm discombobulated or whatever the posh word for 'WTF' is. 'As you maybe aware, Candleina is experiencing a period of expansion and the plan is for a new branch to open every month this year. Now, these new branches are going to need staff and head office are aiming to relocate some experienced, existing staff to these new branches, promoting them into management positions. This is where you come in.' She smiles at me, as baffled as I am.

'I've only just started my assistant management training though.' It comes out as a protest. I suppose it's meant to. Why am I protesting a promotion?

'Yes, and you've been doing well.' Have I? You've never given me any indication of my positive progress. 'Claire, the area manager, always has a good word to say about you.' That's because she has human emotions and talks to me. 'Claire and myself have recommended that you be relocated to one of the new branches and put into a fast-track assistant management programme where you'll work and train under an experienced manager or area manager and head up your own branch within a year. How does that sound?'

On the dream job scale, it's not exactly ranking up there with Cadbury's Chief Taste Tester or LastMinute.com's Five-Star Hotels Reviewer, especially as I'm in the middle of organising my first photographic exhibition, but that's not what company people want to hear. 'It sounds great!'

She doesn't want to offer me this opportunity and, to be honest, I'm reaching for a dream far higher than the heady heights of 'branch manager', but as a back-up plan, it's not too bad.

'This is just an introductory meeting to sound you out about the idea. We don't expect an answer straight away, especially as they haven't selected which of the new branches you'll be offered a place at. It'll involve a move outside of Wigthorn, most probably London or the North West as that's where the expansion is being focused.'

'Not Paris or L.A.?'

I'm not deemed worthy enough of an answer, not even a knowing smile. 'I'll speak to you in more detail next time Claire's down.'

I leave the office far less invigorated about elevating myself up the career ladder than I should be. The distraction of this stupid, local, small-fry exhibition is just too much of a life changing event for me to concentrate on anything else. Both the exhibition and the promotion have come at exactly the wrong time: together. Since the promotion has been offered to me through no effort on my part, I'll continue to give it that amount of attention; the exhibition is the priority.

As I go out to meet Sheridan on 'our' bench, Chloe pulls me aside just by the entrance, 'So? What did the Managerbot 5000 want with you?'

'Not much.'

'You're lying, so it must be good. Tell me.'

'She offered me a promotion.' I offer this reluctantly as I think she was slightly put out at my being offered the assistant management training before her, not that she'd ever vocalise it.

'That's great, Heidi! You deserve it, well done. Where?'

'I'll find out more next week, that was just an "are you interested-type" meeting.' I adjust the bag on my shoulder. 'I have to go and meet Sherry.'

'OK. You keeping him on a tight leash?'

'Always.'

'Good girl.'

I find Sherry waiting on the bench, early as usual, a big smile on his face as I approach. If he had a tail it would be wagging furiously, I'm sure. That sounded horrible, I didn't mean it to be. He's faithful, loyal, happy to see me, happy to be with me, and it feels good. It's getting stronger every day, intensifying and pulling me in, becoming a part of me. If I lower my defences any further, I'll never be able to walk away unscarred. I realise the conflict here, but we're surrounded by conflict, right? We're all individuals; self-sufficient, desolate, forsaken.

'Heidi, come here.' I try to suppress a smile as he devours me in a hug, his mock dirty voice whispering cheeky nothings in my ear. My defences fail, hard.

'I haven't got off work early to mess around with you.' I give him a playful pat on the bum, giving it a gentle squeeze, assessing its scrumptiousness. When he loses that, he's going to have to work ten times as hard to get my attention.

'Yeah, I didn't think I'd be that lucky.'

'You could do with the rest, old man.' I interlink my fingers with his as a mitigating gesture; we start walking aimlessly down the street.

'Rest?! I'm a red-bloodied stallion, I've got the stamina of a teenage warrior.'

I pander to his delusions and give his bicep a squeeze. 'You're my little gladiator! So strong!'

We walk in shadow as the day closes in around us, heading towards Frank's Frames, when the realisation hits me that I'm going to have to show my photos to Frank. Of course I am. Obviously.

Sherry puts his arm around me. 'I've booked us a table at the Hola Cubano!, have you ever been?'

'Yeah.' Is Frank going to laugh at my photos?

'Oh, you never mentioned it, I thought it would be a nice little surprise for you.'

'It is.' Is Frank going to renege on any potential sponsorship because he doesn't want his fine frames and exquisite reputation tarnished by association with my uninspiring images?

'Yeah, but not as much as it could've been if I'd known, if you'd told me.'

Hang on, something's gone awry here. 'No, but that would be quite hard for both of us. We've both been brought up here in Wigthorn and we aren't hermits so we've probably been to most pubs and restaurants in town. Maybe if you'd booked somewhere out of town—'

'You're saying I'm unadventurous?'

You know when the male ego hits a bump in the road or experiences a speed wobble, that's what we have going on here. Tread carefully, for his sake. 'I'd love to eat Cuban food. Thank you for booking a table, it sounds great.'

He removes his arm from around my shoulders. 'Now you're patronising me.'

'OK, just a little, but what the hell's got into you? Can we get these bloody frames sorted then enjoy an evening of food, drink and maybe continue where we left off yesterday?'

The promise of sex usually gorges the male ego enough to tuck it back into it's slumbering bed. We turn a corner, on to the street where Frank's Frames is situated as the sunlight paints everything in front of us in perfect colours: no glare, no shadow, no darkness. That magic hour in the afternoon. I get my camera out of my bag, it's now a permanent fixture for moments such as this. It's difficult to take a bad photo in this light. Composition is another matter but I'm well past questioning my ability to frame a photo, especially since I can artistically crop it at a later date. I give Sherry my bag and start taking photos.

Sherry doesn't adopt his assistant role easily. 'What are you doing?'

'Taking photos, what does it look like?'

'But I was talking.'

'You can still talk.' I crouch down, framing a dustbin against a bright orange wall.

'You don't take me seriously, do you?'

'Of course I do. I've just been given a street with perfect light and I've an exhibition to host in a couple of weeks. An exhibition you entered me in.'

'I'm only asking for two minutes.'

'We're going for dinner later, right? You'll have my undivided attention then.'

'I wanted to tell you something now though, in private, while we're alone.'

Oh Christ, he's not going to propose is he, here, whilst I'm taking a photo of a bloody dustbin? I lower the camera and look up at him. 'You're not going to propose, are you?'

'No.'

'Good.' I continue snapping. He steps in front of me, the sun covering him in perfect colours, all I have to do is frame him.

'Why is that good?'

'You're in the way.'

'I don't care. Why is it good I'm not proposing?'

'I'm not ready. We're not ready. Hell, *you're* not ready.' I keep hitting the button, framing him in the centre, in the right third, the left, focusing up close, manoeuvring him against the background of a sky blue wall, a red garage door. Dancing around him and his questions.

'I wanted to tell you something.'

He stands still in his own resignation. I focus in further, eliminating all background, cropping out the outer extremities of his head; hair, ears, chin, leaving only his face. I lower the camera again to give the impression of my total concentration but remain aiming the lens at his face, continuing to click the shutter.

'Tell me.' *SNAP!*

'Not when we're arguing.' *SNAP!*

'We're not arguing.' *SNAP!* 'Jesus! You're building this up a bit aren't you?' *SNAP!*

'I love you.' *SNAP!* 'I'm in love with you, Heidi.' *SNAP!*

'Oh.'

Oh? All you're going to say to him is *oh*? You have to say more. I'm not sure if I love him though, I can't lie to him. No, you can't lie but you have to say more than *oh*.

'Let's go.'

'Where?'

'Frank's Frames. Help me choose?'

'Of course.'

'Good, let's go.'

Chapter Twenty-three

15 MONTHS BEFORE TODAY

There . . . I think that's it . . . hmmm . . . down a touch on the right. OK. All ten pictures are hung, the slideshow is on, and the flat has been mopped, tidied, polished, and organised within an inch of its life. Everyone I know is going to think they've stepped into the wrong flat.

Doors open at 10 a.m., leaving me about 30 minutes to get showered and changed. What do I wear? This isn't the first time I've posed the question.

It's only a local open house event, not opening night at the Tate Modern. I need to go for an artistic look but not dishevelled or crazy, I'm a photographer not a painter. We're on the creative but technical side of the artistic spectrum, like architects but without the brain power. We struggle with light, not gravity. No one dies if we get our numbers wrong.

After a quick shower, I brush my teeth, then blow-dry my hair before pulling it back into a messy bun and applying as much make-up as I can in a huge effort to ensure it looks like I haven't put in much effort at all. I eventually choose black flats, loose black cotton trousers and a halter neck white top in order to prioritise temperature control over appearance during these highly nerve-wracking times, although, if I may be so bold, I look pretty damn good.

I add just a smidgen more make-up to strengthen the mask my boldness is hiding behind, when my phone alarm alerts me to the fact it's 10 a.m.

I brace myself for a stampede.

. . . and keep bracing . . .

I check my phone, it's 10:02.

I open my front door; no one. I ring the doorbell to make sure it's working; it is. I walk along the hallway, down two flights of stairs to the front door of the building ensuring all my signage is in place and readable; it is. The most disorientated travellers could find their way up to my flat, even if they weren't intending to visit, the sheer thoroughness of my directions being too tempting for them to resist.

I stand by the main entrance for 20 minutes; only one resident passes me on his way out and says hello. Only *hello*, he doesn't even comment on the signage.

I head upstairs and put the kettle on.

I'm squeezing the teabag against the side of the mug, suffocating the inner voice of my mother complaining, when I hear an inquisitive, real-life voice, 'Hello?'

A visitor! Oh, shit! Act calm. I head for the door, 'Hi, come in, come in, please.'

A women in her mid-forties walks in and stands in front of the first framed photograph, her husband follows behind, viewing the photo over her shoulder. She consults her 'Wigthorn Open House' guide. 'You must be Heidi Keeler?'

'That's me, welcome to my humble abode.' Humble abode? Seriously, no one says that, it's not even ironic anymore. It's post-ironic, post-funny, post-quirky; just crap. Note to self, don't say it again to any more visitors.

The husband talks over his wife's shoulder like a timid parrot. 'This one is great, love the faces. Your gran and a friend?'

'No, two ladies I saw sitting on a bench on the seafront. I asked them if I could take a photo and struck up a bit of a rapport with them. Got a whole bunch of good shots but this is my favourite.'

I chose the one of Edna knitting Doris's hair as the first photograph to be seen by visitors as it's more of a conversation starter than the others. It's light-hearted and an invitation to visitors; this is not the house of a painfully artsy photographer whose images are so twisted by irony and obscured by technicality they each require a lengthy explanation to hide the lack of talent. This is a humble abode.

'You're so brave.' The wife looks at me with what can only be described as awe.

'Brave? What do you mean?' It's only two old women, hardly the Kray twins.

'Asking strangers if you can take their picture.'

Ha! Imagine being scared of such a thing. 'It's nothing, you get used to it. Please, come in, the rest are just around the corner here. If you've got any questions or want to talk about any of them, just let me know.'

I tear myself away and finish making my tea, not because I'm thirsty but because I need to allow visitors to view the photographs on their own terms and not with me hovering over them explaining each one into a meaningless lump of banality.

It's not easy though.

The morning goes too quickly. A steady stream of visitors come inside, about ten an hour, so there's always someone in my flat. Every single one of them are complimentary. My mother helpfully informs me that none of these visitors are art critics and they're far too polite to criticise my own work to my face, in my own home. Thanks, Mum.

I take refuge in the fact that three people say my photos are better than the other two photographers' on the tour. Also, there's the small fact that one person buys a framed print. Actually buys one! Gives me a fifty-pound note as a deposit and says he'll be back on Monday to pick it up, after the weekend open house event ends.

My sister, wanting to balance out my Mum's truthful yet cold critical comment, notes that, technically, I'm now a professional photographer. I give a little 'squee' and hug her. She's right, the tiniest ray of sunshine emanating from her tells me so.

Each photo has a small card accompanying it with the title and price. Crossing the price out with red pen and writing SOLD across one of them was an experience I won't forget about in a hurry. Before I'd finished writing 'sold' across the card, I'd already hypothetically spent the £250 on a new camera bag.

Richard visits to see how things are going, telling me my exhibition is one of the ones people are talking about the most. He also offers to hold the fort to allow me to visit the other houses on the tour. I'll take him up on the offer tomorrow, on Sunday, when I can go with Sherry.

I've set up my camera on a tripod in front of a plain backdrop, next to the slideshow, so I can take photos of visitors if they volunteer. I might as well take advantage of strangers actively entering my studio free-of-charge. I've stuck a sign up informing visitors of this little interactive part of the exhibition but only when a couple of kids came in and were immediately bored by the photos on the wall, did it take on a life of its own. To stop them distracting their parents, I sat them both on a chair and took some photos, but only when I walked around the camera, taking photos with the remote button, did their eyes light up. How am I doing that? Do you just press one button? Can we have a go? That was it. Forty-three photos later, the parents finally peeled them off the chair, tore the remote from their hands, and left the flat.

One photo is a gem. I'm ethically divided though, I didn't actually take the photo.

Sheridan texts to say he's on his way. My stomach is turning, my head is spinning because I'm in the middle of a dream and I so want Sherry to be here to share it with me. I don't fully realise how much I need him here until I read his text. I reply telling him to hurry up, I have something I'm itching to get off my chest.

I'm waiting by my front door when I hear footsteps coming up the stairs following the signage. An older gentleman walks around the corner with his wife and another couple, a double-date tour of the Wigthorn open houses. I direct them into the flat so I can resume my sentry duties.

I hear another set of footsteps ascending the stairs, I will them to be Sherry's. They are. As he turns the corner, I call his name, run up to him and wrap both arms around him. 'Sherry, come here.'

'Wow!' Sheridan composes himself as I drag him into the flat. 'I hope you haven't been giving every visitor this kind of welcome.'

'No, only you.'

'So, how's it been going? Still the worst idea in the world?'

I'll let him have this one 'I told you so' moment. Just the one, though. 'It's been amazing. Everyone is so friendly and generous with their comments.'

Sherry gives me a reassuring hug, 'You're an excellent photographer, Heidi. Maybe now it's finally sinking in.'

I flash him the fifty-pound note. 'I sold one.' I hopelessly try to contain my emotions.

We both fail. He gives me another hug, lifting me up and spinning me around. 'No way! Heidi, that's brilliant! You've just turned pro!'

The four visitors who arrived previously look around at us as we briefly disturb their gallery viewing.

'Which one did you sell?'

I lead Sherry by the hand to a photo I took one evening of a group of kids mountain biking on the South Downs, they were all standing around at the bottom of a hill taking the piss out of someone who'd fallen off.

'Great choice, that's a wicked photo.' Sherry glances down at the little bit of card with the price and title. 'Sold. Look at that. Bet that was enjoyable?'

'Not bad.'

'Have you taken a photo of that?'

'No! Good idea.' I grab the tripod with my camera on it and line up the shot.

'No, no, you set it up, but I'll take it. You've got to be in the shot too.'

'OK.'

Sherry gets behind the camera with his finger on the button. 'Smile then, you've just sold your first photo!'

'I am smiling!'

'Get closer.'

'You're meant to move closer or zoom in, not me!'

'Man! You're a horrible model.'

'Thanks! Just take the shot!'

SNAP!

I double-check the shot; not bad. He's right though, I'm a rubbish model.

'So, ten photos at two hundred and fifty pounds each, you could be rolling in it by tomorrow night.'

'It's eleven photos actually.'

'Eleven? Some last-minute changes?'

'One last-minute addition, that's partly why I was so eager for you to come over today. Come on, let me show you the extra one.'

The four visitors interrupt me in the nicest possible way, thanking me for opening up my flat and complimenting my photos. Sherry gives me a little nudge in support. As they leave I lead Sherry by the hand, once again, out of the studio/lounge and into the kitchen where I have my 11th photographic print standing in the centre, pride of place, on an easel.

I stand aside, revealing the image to Sherry.

He stands there in silence. I can see his eyes searching the image for something to focus on, his face frozen in concentration, his mouth slightly open, a frown ever so slowly crawling along his forehead, his head tilting in an effort to gain a better view, adjusting the light, losing shadow. He looks lost. I think I understand why; he's never seen such an enlarged, detailed, high-definition photo of his own face before. It must be quite shocking.

I grab his hand. 'What do you think?'

'It's . . .' He squeezes my hand back, bending down to kiss my forehead. 'It's . . . It must be me.'

'Of course! It's an extreme close-up, but it captures a special moment. It's not only a great photo of an extremely handsome young man, it's also a great moment. Do you remember?'

'I can't quite place it, my mind's a big blur at the moment.'

'This is the exact moment you told me you loved me.'

'Is it? Wow.' He gives me a warming embrace, kissing the side of my face as he whispers into my ear. 'One of the pitfalls of dating a photographer, right?'

'I'm afraid so.'

Sherry looks over my shoulder at the photo, I give him a minute to look at it without me examining him for feedback and putting him in an awkward position. He rubs my upper arms as he steps back to creates a bit of room between us. 'This one doesn't have a price.'

'No, it's not for sale. I'm keeping it for myself.'

'Oh.' Sherry smiles. 'Are you sure you want that ugly mug hanging on your wall?'

'Sherry?'

'Yes?'

'I love you.'

Sherry looks intensely into my eyes, his head slowly listing from side to side, searching for secrets. As soon as the moment veers from passionate into the first, outer suburbs of awkward; he kisses me softly.

'I love you too, Heidi.'

Chapter Twenty-four

14 MONTHS BEFORE TODAY

'Are you OK, Heidi? The colour's suddenly drained out of you.' Chloe puts an arm around me and leads me away from the till.

'No. I feel awful.' Candleina's aromas are conspiring against my senses. 'And . . . constrained.' My breasts are conspiring against me too.

'Why don't you go into the toilet, let them hang out for a bit and don't bother putting that bra back on either, it's obviously too small.'

'I can't do that.'

'Oh give me a break, Heidi. You're not exactly smuggling a couple of melons under there, are you? No one's going to notice.'

'Thanks!'

'Just get in there and chill out for a bit, I'll grab you a drink and tell RoboManager to hold the fort for a bit.'

I take Chloe's advice and retire to the toilet for some respite. I undo my blouse, release the clasp on my bra, my breasts breathing a sigh of relief. They noticeably relax in front of the mirror, relishing their freedom before giving me an evil stare and it's then I notice each breast is effectively sitting upon a deep red line indented into my skin. I follow it around my ribs and behind my back where the bra clasp has also branded itself against my skin.

This is all I need, weight gain.

I sit on the toilet seat, my legs consciously relieving themselves of my increased body mass, and slump my head into my hands. I sneak a glimpse of myself through rigid fingers, my swollen boobs resting against the creases of my stomach. I undo the top button of my trousers; I'm expanding by the second, soon I'll explode like a rotting whale.

As the memory of a previously viewed video of an exploding, rotting whale plays through my mind, my stomach takes a turn for the worse. I swiftly stand up, flip up the toilet seat, fall to my knees, hold back my hair with one hand whilst clamping my swollen pendulous boobs back with the other and start heaving. I grab a handful of tissues to help muffle the sound and wipe away the tears. Once the worst of it is over, I fill the basin, wash my face, and rinse my mouth out. The smell of the face wash attempts to play games with my stomach but there's nothing left to play with. I dry my face and sit on the closed lid of the toilet with my head in my hands, again. I undo the flies of my trousers.

What a time to get ill. I'm meant to be having a meeting today about a promotion and then treating Sherry to a night out. Chloe mentioned there was a bug going round but I'm not so sure, I think it's a reaction to the stress of the exhibition; an aftermath, a release. But it's a price worth paying. I've sold five framed photos and got a commission for another two. If the opportunity to be part of another exhibition comes along, I'm sure it'll be a lot easier with the experience and confidence I've gained . . . Oh God, that's done it, I've got to go again. Maybe I wouldn't –

Knock, knock! 'Heidi, are you in there?'

Crap, it's the ManagerBot 5000. 'Yeah, I'll be out in a minute.'

'Are you OK? Chloe just ran out saying I need to hold the fort.'

God forbid you'd have to do any actual work. 'Yeah, fine thanks. I'll see you in the office in a minute.'

I rinse my mouth out and sit back down on the toilet, again. Now I have the dilemma of having to eat because I'm hungry and my blood sugar is dropping – but weigh that against the fact eating will probably lead me back here again. I've got an important meeting I need to get through, maybe a quick drink of water and a chocolate bar will get me through? I need to grab my bag too and reapply some make-up, I look washed out.

Knock, knock! 'Heidi? You OK?'

It's Chloe. 'Yeah, fine.'

'Let me in.'

'I'll be out in a minute—'

'Let me in, now.'

I swivel round and quickly check myself in the mirror and put my blouse back on, minus the bra. 'What's up?'

'Sit down.'

I sit, looking up at Chloe with both hands on my knees.

Chloe crosses her arms, her weight shifting to her back leg, the front foot pointing at me. 'Sick again?'

'Yes.'

'For the third morning in a row?'

'Oh be quiet, Chloe, it ain't that.'

'Got a headache?'

'No.'

'Blocked nose?'

'No.'

'Cough? Runny nose? Sore throat?'

'No.'

'So, it's not a cold. You're just vomiting in the morning and your boobs have grown and become extra sensitive. I wonder what they're symptoms of?' Chloe produces a small plastic bag from her handbag. 'Here, use this.'

I open it. 'Oh come on, Chloe! This is a bit too much.'

'Just pee on it, will you. I'll turn around if you're shy.'

Chloe turns her back on me which makes it easier to protest. 'This really isn't necessary, I'm ultra paranoid about this kind of thing.' I roll up my sleeves, literally, and divulge our 'arrangements'. 'Look, I've got a contraceptive implant, have a feel if you want, it's got another couple of years of life so it's nowhere near expiring. I couldn't afford for my life to sink any further with Gary because of a split condom or a forgotten pill. I would've got the coil if they'd let me but this was the next best thing after a hysterectomy. I wasn't going to let Gary destroy my future as well as my present, so I got an implant. You know that phrase "Sometimes it's better the devil

205

you know", everyone forgets that first word: sometimes. Sometimes means "a minority of the time", so, that phrase is actually telling people: most of the time you should leave a shit situation. I can't argue with that. Anyway, I insist Sherry uses a condom. I haven't told him I've got the implant so he can't talk me out of using a condom, and you know blokes, as long as they're getting it, they don't complain. It would be virtually impossible for me to get pregnant right now.'

'Virtually. So with such protection it should be a doddle to pass this test, right?'

'It's not worth doing! The implant is like ninety-nine per cent effective, condoms are about ninety-eight per cent, so my uterus is locked up like Fort Knox.'

'"Life finds a way", *Jurassic Park* told us that. You just said you've been stressed out about the exhibition.' Chloe lowers her voice, 'Give me one reason why you're sick and your boobs have swollen, and I'll take the test back to the shop.'

I can't, even though my uterus has been metaphorically fossilised in amber for the past few years. I'll pass this test. Get Chloe out of my hair, out of this toilet and get on with dealing with this ultra-rare swollen boobs/being sick in the morning condition. 'OK, turn around.'

'You're such a prude.'

I open up the pack, briefly reading the instructions as a formality. I've done this once before with Gary, Jesus fucking Christ, was that a low point in my life, wishing a dream would just quietly and quickly die in my hands. Luckily, the dream was never there to turn into the inevitable nightmare.

I squat and pee whilst poking the plastic device into the stream. I notice Chloe's head peek around as she hears the tinkling of water. 'Go on, girl, give it some!'

'Bloody hell, Chloe!'

'Oh be quiet, we've all done it before. This ain't your first time, I'm sure.'

I give her a look. 'Hold this.' I pull my knickers and trousers back up and wash my hands, again. How long have I been in this toilet for?

'So, what are you going to do if it comes back positive?'

'I have absolutely no idea. The thought only entered my mind when you entered this toilet.'

'Seriously?'

'Yeah! I've got a better chance of winning the lottery than being pregnant.'

I sit there in silence, contemplating the odds of an implant/condom regime failing. Who do you sue? Chloe's right, it's not impossible but hardly likely. I then contemplate what horrific disease awaits any woman with similar symptoms to mine. Maybe, on the face of it, being pregnant would be the better alternative?

No, of course not. That would be a nightmare.

Chloe blows on the testing device.

'It's not a bloody Polaroid, don't start shaking it.'

Chloe checks the clock on her phone, 'Oh look . . . hang on . . . our two minutes are nearly up.'

I stand up and lean over to look at the strip, Chloe snatches it away. 'What are you doing?'

'Interested now, are you? The line is appearing . . . oh.' Chloe's eyes look up from the plastic device to me. 'I think you better sit back down.'

'Stop winding me up. Fucking hell, just give it to me!'

I take the test from Chloe, sit down, compose myself and take a breath. There's one line in a round box saying the test worked and then there's another line in a square box stating a positive result. It means I'm pregnant. I double-check the picture on the box and the instructions.

A line in a square box definitely means I'm pregnant.

A pregnancy is an affirmative result when the square is bisected by a line.

The square box of your life is brutally dissected when the sharp, sudden line of pregnancy impales itself.

'Fuck.' I eruditely conclude with linguistic finesse.

'You should buy a lottery ticket tonight.'

Knock, knock! 'Heidi, are you still in there?'

Oh, fuck off ManagerBot 5000!

Chloe takes control. 'Yeah, we'll be out in a minute.'

'Chloe, is that you? Who's on the shop floor?'

There is a bun in the oven. I'm knocked up. 197.9% protection is not enough. Sherry must have Olympic standard swimmers. The UK has one new citizen on the way, what happens now? Do I have to tell the government? A doctor? Schools? 'Chloe, do I have to phone someone about this?'

'Yeah. Sherry.'

Chapter Twenty-five

13 MONTHS BEFORE TODAY

'What do you reckon?'

Sherry gives me a twirl in the designer jacket he's been drooling over for the past few weeks since first being sold it in a magazine. Sherry is by far the most fashion-conscious man I've ever met, which in itself isn't a negative, by Christ, there's plenty of shell-suited losers in this town. Hell, I've been out with a couple of them. No, it isn't the money he spends, nor the time he spends down the gym crafting his abs and quads, it's the fact he's so non-narcissistic with it. He never looks at himself in the mirror. And he should. I don't get how a man can conceal a close approximation of a model's physique under a £1000 tailored suit but still have a dusting of icing sugar on the tip of his nose or an errant patch of unshaved stubble just under his nose.

I suppose you get men who spend big on their hair but never go to the gym, or have no style, or always wear trainers, over-groom their beards and eyebrows but dress too young, or worse, use fake tan. I guess what I'm saying is: no one's perfect. Am I? Fucking hell, how beige is that? No, what I mean is, I've never seen anyone imperfect in this way before.

'Yeah, not bad.' It looks good but that's not the feature most catching my eye, I tug the price tag towards me for clarification. 'How much?'

'Onlyyyyy thhffyy.'

'You what?'

'Four hundred and forty-nine pounds ninety-nine.'

'Jesus! You could replace my wardrobe for that.'

'We'll go to Ikea afterwards and get you a new one then.'

'Very funny.' I flick through the jeans on a nearby rack as a distraction, occasionally picking out the price tag to properly gauge how fashionable and desirable the items are.

All couples have a situation where the roles are reversed from the stereotype; clothes shopping is ours. I'm no slouch, I'm no square, I'm just skint. Sherry is paid more than triple what I am, which is deserved, he's a university-educated medical professional; I sell candles. I'm not jealous, I'm proud of him and he deserves to spend his hard-earned money any way he sees fit. I especially don't complain when he buys me something or takes me out. I'd love to go Dutch all the time but we both know I can't afford it and he doesn't mind – well, he's never said anything. He silently, diplomatically and subtly pays for the meal, the cinema tickets, the train tickets, makes up stupid little anniversaries to buy me a gift, repays a little act by me tenfold.

I appreciate his generosity and the humility and subtlety in which he does it, but my pride still nibbles like a hungry moth trapped in an empty wallet.

'OK, I'm having this one.' Sherry takes one last look in the mirror before taking it off and chucking it onto the purple chesterfield sofa sitting between us and the changing rooms. 'Right, I need a couple of polo shirts and a new pair of jeans too.'

I step away from the rack of jeans, the prices growling at me. The jeans hanging from each hanger morph into a utility bill of equal value; a pair of distressed narrow fit blue jeans shapeshifting into my annual water bill. This whole rack could pay for my upkeep over the next couple of years and give me satellite TV and contents insurance, plus a Mediterranean holiday.

Sherry goes straight for a pair of jeans that could pay my electricity bill for the next three months. For some reason this sparks me off. 'Are you sure you really need another pair of two hundred pounds jeans?'

'Huh? I need some jeans, that's all.'

I do know what sparked this off; the hungry moth has chewed

through the wallet and is now starting to consume a pound of my own flesh.

'But two hundred pounds worth of jeans?' I flick through the rack, frantically searching for a £20 pair of jeans. I quickly come to the realisation I'm in the wrong store for £20 jeans. 'What about these ones, ninety pounds. They're the same colour, same cut, just a different brand.'

Sherry looks at me with soft eyes. 'Do they have them in a thirty-two-inch waist?'

Damn his diplomacy and understanding, all my energies were geared up for a full-scale assault. I find a pair of 32-inch waist jeans for £90. 'Here.' I shove them into his personal space.

'Thanks. I'll try them on.'

I check my phone, Chloe has texted asking where I am. I reply telling her I'm currently in Harold's Menswear watching Sherry spend a small fortune on clothes he doesn't need. I sound like his mother. At least I sound like *a* mother.

Sherry goes into the changing room, closing the curtain behind him. 'Are you OK?'

'I'm fine.'

Sherry's head pokes through the curtain as he curiously crafts one raised eyebrow. 'Do you think you're fighting with a rookie here? Fine doesn't constitute an acceptable answer.'

'Who says we're fighting?'

'I do. Now tell me what's up.'

'If you don't know then maybe you don't really know me at all and what's the point of carrying on?'

'Whoa, whoa!' Sherry pulls open the curtain, standing there in his designer boxer shorts which no doubt cost more than my whole outfit. 'What's going on here?'

He stands there in a stupid pose; legs bent, a crooked back, pulling a stupid face. I'm not really mad with him so he manages to draw out a smile, I try to twist it into a frown. Damn him. 'Just put some bloody overpriced jeans on, will you.'

He closes the curtain. 'Heidi, TALK TO ME, WOMAN!'

'You know you're not going to be able to buy designer clothes for the rest of your life, right? There's going to be new responsibilities, new priorities.'

'Yeah. You're still not talking to me, I hear a lot of beating around the bush and quite a bit of dillying and dallying but nothing specific. What's your point?'

'It's all this materialism, it's a waste of money. It's great that you earn good money and I'm very proud of you, I just don't want to see you waste it on rubbish and regret it later on when you might want . . . *need* to spend it on something more meaningful.'

Sherry comes out of the changing room wearing the new jeans. 'What do you think?'

Is he listening to me? Am I over-reacting? I'm bloody pregnant! I'm not over-reacting but this situation hasn't been planned, discussed or even broached in the broadest sense. He's going to think I've trapped him, the poor shop worker getting up the duff with the well-off, professional, optometrist. He always wears a condom. I never insist on it, he voluntarily covers up in a gentlemanly manner, responsibly because he's a medical professional, he knows the risks better than anyone. I'm thinking too much. What do I think? The jeans. The jeans! Not the baby, the jeans. 'They look good, better than the other ones.'

'I haven't tried those on yet.'

'I just know, plus you save yourself over a hundred quid.'

Sherry stands in front of the mirror, looking at them. 'They don't look too tight?'

'Not really, why? Do they feel tight?'

'A touch.'

'You're putting on weight?'

'No, the sizing must be all screwed up for this brand.'

I get another text from Chloe asking if I've told Sherry about 'our pregnancy' yet. I ignore it.

I put my phone back in my pocket and walk over to Sherry, smiling at him in the mirror, reaching around his waist to feel if there's any room to be found in these jeans. There's no breathing room at all. 'Hmmm, looks like you better start eating salads at lunch.'

Sherry holds my hands as they rest on his stomach and looks back at my reflection. 'Are you sure you're OK?'

'I'm just thinking of the future.' I give him a little squeeze. 'When you look at yourself in the mirror, what do you see?'

'That's a tough one.'

'Yeah, but we all have to do it from time to time, assess where we're at and where we want to go. You know what I see?'

'What?'

I talk to myself in the mirror. 'I see someone who's ready to move on to the next step and settle down, get serious. I'm sick of floating around from day to day, I need to start making some more positive moves. My photography exhibition gave me a taste of what life could be like if I start making things happen and don't wait around for things to happen.' I catch Sherry's eye. 'I don't want to be like my mum or my sister.'

'Good.' He smiles at me. 'Are you saying you want to get married or move in together?'

'What do you want? Don't try and guess what I want. When you look at yourself in the mirror, what do you hope will be staring back at you in the future?'

'My own face?'

Sherry laughs nervously. I don't think he's taking this seriously. 'No, I mean, where do you see—'

'Yourself in five years? Is this a job interview?'

'You know what I mean. Can you see yourself being a father or a husband, living with me, becoming a branch manager or moving onto something different? What do you want out of life?'

'A good-fitting pair of jeans, these are starting to pinch a little now.'

'Don't try to get out of this, Sheridan. If we can't be honest with each other then what hope do we have?'

'This got serious all of a sudden.'

It wasn't sudden, Sherry, my darling.

I hold Sherry's stare in the mirror. He's looking back at me skittishly, trying to dance his way out of the fire. He looks at his jeans, his shoes, me, back to the jeans, his shirt and then slowly he looks up. His eyes skip around, searching his reflection for an ambition they can both agree on. Sherry's not focused; he either can't see a future with me in it or the inevitable, approaching heavy footsteps of responsibility are making him nervous.

I remain silent.

Sherry speaks. 'Do you want to know the truth?'

'Of course.' I answer immediately so he knows my silence is space for him to think, not that I'm ignoring him.

'When I look into my eyes, I can't see anything.' He turns around and looks directly into my eyes. 'I can't see what you see. I'm sorry.'

I hug him; honesty shouldn't be punished. 'It's OK.'

He holds onto me because he doesn't want me to walk away. I hold onto him because I don't want to collapse.

Sherry whispers into my ear. 'There's something I need to tell you, regarding me not being able to see myself. When I say that, I mean it literally.'

'There's something I need to tell you too.'

'I thought there might be.'

'Sherry, Heidi!' Chloe strides through the store towards us. 'What are you guys doing in here?'

Sherry says hello to Chloe before disappearing over to the counter. 'I'm going to see if they've got these in a thirty-three.'

'Too many burgers, big boy?' Chloe cackles and delivers me a wink. 'You're going to need to keep your strength up.'

I grab Chloe's arm and lead her behind the rack of jeans, our backs to the rest of the shop, 'Shut up, Chloe. What the fuck are you doing here?'

'You still haven't told him, have you?'

'I'm waiting for the right time.'

'Well, the right time better happen in the next few months or he's going to figure it out for himself when you're eating coal dipped in honey or smelling rubber mallets and have got a massive bloody stomach!'

'I'm not sure he's ready.'

214

'Don't second guess him, Heidi, tell him in plain English: *I'm up the duff, I've got a bun in the oven, I'm preggers.* He has a right to know.'

'I know, I know, but what if he doesn't want it, then what?'

'Then you cross that bridge when you come to it.'

'But what if he insists that he absolutely does not want it. I'm not getting rid of it, Chloe. I'd much rather raise it alone than fight over whether I keep it or get rid of it. I'm keeping this baby no matter what.'

'OK, OK, but you can't hide it, he's going to find out at some point. You love him, right? He loves you, why wouldn't you tell him?'

'I'm not so sure now, maybe I just thought I loved him. Maybe I needed to think I loved him in order to move on. Maybe it was a rebound thing, but this baby changes everything. Whatever I have in here, I love more than Sherry. It comes first, no matter what. If he doesn't want to be a part of it then fine, but I'm not subjecting my baby to a father who never really wanted him in the first place.'

'You know it's a *him*?'

'No, just a figure of speech.'

'Have you even been to a doctor yet?'

'I've got an appointment.'

'When?'

'You don't believe me?'

'Honestly? No. You're not acting rationally, Heidi, get a grip. You're labelling Sheridan as being irresponsible but from where I'm standing you're not the standard bearer for responsible living at the moment.'

'He doesn't want the same future as me! He just said as much. I'm not a gold digger, I'm not going to ruin his life and drag him down with me, I'm not going to be the source of regret he sees in the mirror every morning.'

'Sherry may be a little strange at times but he's not a monster, he's not unreasonable. He's an intelligent, understanding bloke.'

'That's what I'm afraid of! My sister got talked round from having her baby and look how that turned out.' Chloe's not listening to me, her ideals are plugging her ears to the reality. 'I'm not going to tie him down either. He never asked for this so I'm not going to put a gun to his head and demand child maintenance or anything like that. I don't want his money, I don't need his charity and I don't want to manipulate him with guilt. I gave him the opportunity to tell me what he really wants without bias, and he told me.'

'You have to tell him, Heidi!'

'Tell him what?' Sherry stands on the other side of the jeans rack with a pair of 33's in his hand.

Chloe butts in. 'Heidi's got some news for you.'

I look at Sherry. He has a kind face, even now. He knows I'm hiding something, something important, but still he looks at me as though I'm the only one who means anything to him. He has more self-control than anyone I've ever met, it must come from the confidence of knowing who you are and what you want. That doesn't leave much flexibility for change.

'I've been offered a promotion at work.'

Sherry's face lights up. 'Great, well done.' He hurries round to give me a hug, then pulls back to look me straight in the eyes. He's looking through me, his eyes appear to have glazed over but he's not lost in a daydream he's just not focusing on me. He's trying to focus in me, drilling into my brain or into my soul, to do what? Maybe he can detect a lie or he senses something more? Maybe he knows the truth and is trying to change my mind already? Either way, it's too freaky for me. 'What are you doing?'

The look disappears in an instance. 'I'm happy for you, this is brilliant news. I'm so proud of you.'

His calmness and confidence may belie a deeper willingness to change me; get me to see what he sees. That's his job after all. I wonder how far he'd go?

'The promotion wouldn't be here though. I recently found out it's going to be in Chester.'

'Oh.'

Not that far, then.

Chapter Twenty-six

ONE YEAR BEFORE TODAY

I head into town for a meeting with my area manager and someone else from HR, hopefully I should get the final say on where I'm going. Probably Chester, but there's been some reshuffling in the exotic North West so it could be a number of other places. Never been up that way before and don't have any compulsion to check out the area before I start a job there either, the main attraction is no one knows me and I can start afresh.

We can start afresh.

Sherry's been bugging me, of course he has. 'Bugging' is unfair. I've been a bitch. Ignoring him, palming him off, being vague and unresponsive. I'm going to break up with him, I have to end it. I've been avoiding him because I'm scared he'll talk me round. He's so rational and sensible and textbook, and for two people who have only been together about eight or nine months having an unplanned baby is so irrational, non-sensible, and non-textbook. He's intelligent, cleverer than me . . . than I . . . better with words, able to construct arguments I can't wiggle out of. If I tell him the truth, let him know I want to keep this baby, I need to keep it, he might not agree and find a way out for both of us.

I don't want a way out. I don't need choices or options; I need space.

I need to lie.

I need to lie to my family too. The Keelers don't coo over babies, we cry. We mourn them. I can't be around a sister who will be a confused mess of jealousy and eagerness, I also can't ignore the possibility she may completely reject me, feel I'm flaunting mother-hood in her face. I also can't be around a mother who talked my sister into having an abortion as she'll probably over-compensate. This child of mine is in danger of being over-loved. My fear is not of being alone but of being smothered.

From a little side street lined with a couple of small coffee shops and an off-licence, I walk out on to the pedestrianised High Street exposing myself to the predators on the savannah. I can hear the jungle drums sending along the latest headlines on the retail grape-vine, 'Assistant Manager gets pregnant, optician says he didn't see it coming'. That's what my head is screaming at me but it's all fantasy. I've only told Chloe and she wouldn't have told anyone else, I know she wouldn't. I'm not going to let fear feed my paranoia and start distrusting my closest friend.

I head towards Candleina, keeping my face shielded from Twenty20 across the road, but I can't resist a quick glance up to Sherry's office window.

Damn!

I see Sherry in the window, looking straight at me. He disappears leaving the blinds shivering in his wake. OK, OK. No avoiding him now. Brace yourself.

I sit on 'our' bench, facing Sherry's shop and wait for him. Within seconds of sitting down, I see him march through the shop and out the door. He's not angry; is he ever?

'Heidi.'

'Sheridan.'

Sheridan sits next to me, a hand reaches for mine, I decline. Small, simple gestures without the strength to move a pencil, can also have the power to redraw your entire future.

'Are you ignoring my calls?'

Now's not the time to build bridges or to be kind. 'Sheridan, I'm already late for a meeting. I want to talk to you, I need to, but not now.'

'When?'

'Tomorrow lunchtime?'

'Heidi, I love you, what the hell's going on here? Why are you ignoring me?'

'Sherry, not now, please.'

'Let's go away! Let's get away from all this; this town, this country, somewhere we can relax, get some peace and quiet, just you and I. I'll sort it all out, a week away, how does that sound? South of France, Malta, Dubai—'

'No, Sherry. There's no running away from this.'

'From what?' Sherry goes for my hand again, more determinedly and holds on to it.

'Sherry, please.'

'Is there something about me you don't like, have I got something written on my face?'

'Don't be ridiculous, Sherry. Look, I have to go.'

'Heidi, I'm not sleeping properly. I thought you were the one, you know? I still do think—'

I can't let this go on. My child is No.1, Sherry has been reframed into the background, my priorities have refocused. 'I have to go to a meeting now.' I have to leave in order for my heartlessness to appear more grotesque. Sherry has to see my face twist into a deformed gargoyle, I need to see my own disgusting reflection in his eyes to know he believes me.

'But I don't understand.'

My hideousness is multiplied and distorted further by the tears forming in his eyes; a kaleidoscope of contemptible repugnance. Tears form in my own. I have to go. I stand. 'Sherry, we'll talk more tomorrow lunchtime. Meet me here at one p.m., I promise I'll be here. I'm sorry.'

I walk away, a couple of tears rolling down my cheek. I only want to hold Sherry and nurse him from the hurt I'm causing him, but I cross the street and enter Candleina, the welcoming odours helping to separate me from the twisted reality I've created and left behind.

Temptation overwhelms me. I turn to see Sherry slumped forward on the bench, his elbows on his knees, his head bowed down like he's going to be sick. It makes me feel sick just watching him

219

from behind like this, seeing him in pain, knowing I've caused the pain, knowingly. I've knowingly lied to cause him pain.

I actually feel sick, I rush to the toilet.

'Are you OK, honey?' Chloe follows me in.

I flip the toilet lid open, fall to my knees, and let the full disgustingness of my true nature exit my body to explore its rightful home, the sewers of Wigthorn.

Chloe holds my hair back. 'You haven't been sick for a few weeks now, everything all right?'

'Chloe, promise me you won't tell Sherry where I am or where I'm going. He says he doesn't want anything to do with the baby. I can't let him talk me out of it.'

I can't stem the onset of tears as I sit on the floor; my hair a tangled mess, smudged make-up streaking down my face and the taste of vomit in my mouth. Lie to a friend too, why not? You've lied to Sherry, why not Chloe as well? The cruelty of my lies strike a blow against myself as well as the unfortunates standing in my way. I'm glad not to be getting away with anything; there's honour in paying for your crimes without complaint.

Chloe grabs some toilet roll and sits next to me. 'Anything you want, darling. Here, don't cry.' Chloe wipes the tears from my face and kisses my forehead. 'You can do this on your own, no sweat. Auntie Chloe can even help out every now and again, if you'll let her.'

I smile at Chloe and give her a hug back. 'I'm treating Sherry like crap so splitting up is a decision we both come to together.'

'But he's not biting?'

'No.'

'Looks like you're going to have to play the big bad wolf and end things, then.'

'I know, but how?'

'You don't want to give him any hope of a reconciliation sometime in the future. I dumped a guy once by saying I couldn't offer him anything, it's like a refined version of the old "it's not you, it's me" line. You're taking the blame yourself while also saying we're not a match, we have nothing in common, and there's no future in our relationship. That's the sort of thing you want to say, right?'

'I suppose so.'

'Look, Heidi, there's no pretty way of doing this. The firmer, harder, crueller you are now, the easier it is in the long run. If you fanny around now, you'll be fannying around for ages. Time, my love, is one luxury you don't have.'

'I'm seeing him tomorrow lunchtime.'

'Tomorrow lunchtime it is then.' Chloe gives my shoulders a brief massage like I'm a boxer. 'Come on, time for your meeting, I saw RoboManager go into her office with a couple of HQ-looking bods earlier.'

'How do I look?'

'Like crap. Here, have a mint, you need it.'

Chloe helps tidy me up until I look like a viable candidate for a branch manager's position. I can hear a couple of voices behind the office door, I knock and then enter. A few brief introductions and pleasantries later, we get down to business.

'. . . and so this brings us to where we'd like to assign you. We're so sorry about leaving the actual location of your branch until virtually the last minute but we've been having to juggle a number of personnel in your position with spouses, children, infirm parents, et cetera, with a change in direction of business expansion. Whilst the North West is still the focus of the majority of our new branches we're also looking to expand into the Midlands, North East, and the South West. The business is planning a lot of new initiatives over the coming years, not just expansion but diversification, personal grooming treatments, furniture fragrances, and more. Now is a great time to get on board the management fast-track programme.'

I nod to show I'm listening. I've hardly said a word in the last half hour. I've hardly managed to construct a coherent thought in the last few days.

'So, how does Plymouth sound?'

The other HQ bod cuts in. 'No, no, Jackie, Plymouth's not vacant any more, remember?'

'Oh yeah, I'm so sorry. I mean, Newcastle.'

Newcastle. Never been there; big city, lively, on the coast, a long way from here. Perfect. 'Sounds great. When do you want me to start?'

'Well, we've discussed it with your manager and if it's OK with you, as soon as possible.'

SHERIDAN

Chapter Twenty-seven

TODAY

'Sherry?'

I was hoping to enjoy the anonymity of being a faceless stranger in a new town a little while longer, start again, begin a new story, airbrush history, bury my old life within a chrysalis and emerge reborn somewhere else, but it's not someone knowing me that's released a swarm of butterflies inside my stomach. I recognise the voice.

I grip the door handle to steady myself, the aromas of Candleina toying with my sense of time; dragging me into the past, pulling me back into the present, blurring the future.

I turn around. Standing at the other end of the shop floor is Heidi. She hasn't changed one bit; still beautiful, still attracting me, still the other half of me. My brain binges on a cocktail of chemicals, I remain motionless in thought and movement. Somehow, when I least expected it, I found her.

'Heidi.'

Or rather: she found me. I walk towards her, I can't do anything else. Before my brain has assessed the situation my legs have automatically started bringing us closer.

'What are you doing here?' Heidi asks, as she steps forward from a group of women crowding around a pram. The light around us dims, external noises fade, the remainder of the world slides in shadow.

'I just moved here, got a promotion with work.'

'Snap!'

We hug, she kisses me on the cheek.

'The Twenty20 across the street?'

'Yeah, you know it?'

'Of course. I work here in Plymouth too.' She points to the floor. 'I took a promotion but got a last-minute change of location. I was heading to Newcastle but someone's dad died and I got rerouted.'

'So we're working across the street from each other again?' I give an apologetic smile; I must look like an insane stalker right now. 'I'm sorry, I had no idea you were here, no one back home would tell me anything about where you'd gone or what you were doing or even why you left. I'm sorry, I'll see if I can get another transfer—'

'Sherry, Sherry, shhhh.' Heidi holds both my hands at waist height, drawing herself closer. 'I'm the one who should be apologising.' She looks down. 'I'm so sorry, Sherry, I've been so selfish and stupid. I couldn't see what was right in front of me.'

'It's harder than it looks sometimes.'

'Yeah, I suppose it is.' Heidi brings me in for another hug but this time she melts into my arms and shows no sign of letting go. I close my eyes as I bury my face in her hair, inhaling the intoxication of nostalgia and hope; one pulling me back, the other pushing me forward. The here and now twisting into a confusion. 'I'm so sorry, Sherry.'

'Tell me what for, I don't understand what happened. What did I do wrong?'

'Nothing. You did nothing wrong. You were never anything other than sweet and wonderful to me. I got scared and paranoid.' Heidi sniffs, I feel her body shiver. 'I lied to you, Sherry.'

'I don't care.' That's wrong, I do. Have some balls! 'That's a lie, I do care.'

The baby in the pram cries a little and Heidi looks around, a woman bobs it up and down while all the others soothe it with sing-song baby talk. Heidi turns back towards me, then looks down submissively, playing with my fingers. 'I thought getting out of your life would be the best thing for all of us.'

'Why would you think that? I was in love with you, I thought you loved me too. Why would you think I'd want you out of my

226

life? Nothing could be further from the truth. I've been looking for you ever since you left, I'd virtually given up all hope.'

'I was confused.'

'You could've spoken to me, you could've opened up to me. Am I such an ugly monster that I would've abandoned you?'

'No, no, of course not. It wasn't me I was worried about though.'

Heidi's eyes are welling up. I'm taking out my frustrations within two minutes of finding her. 'I'm sorry.'

Heidi steps back, wipes her eyes. 'Sherry, I can't lie any longer, I have something to tell you.' She flashes a brief smile. '*Someone* to show you.'

She steps back towards the group of women who, in turn, step aside and let Heidi through to the pram. 'Excuse me, ladies, let me introduce my son to someone.'

My head becomes an incalculable mass of numbers, digital rain tapping against my brain; months, ages, dates, addition, subtraction, gestation, absence, abstinence, odds. Nothing adds up. Nothing makes sense.

'Your son?' I whisper mostly to myself in an effort to ground my feet.

Heidi takes the baby from one of the other women, handling it with expert care and dexterity. The distress on the baby's face immediately disappears in the arms of his mother.

'Sherry, come here.' Heidi struggles to contain her joy. 'Sherry, this is our baby. This is Jack.'

I look at the back of the baby's head as Heidi holds him against her chest with his head resting on her shoulder; fine blond hair, chubby limbs, and a red baby suit. I take a step forward but this is surely some mistake, I can't hold a stranger's baby.

Heidi smiles at me, beckoning me closer. 'Sherry, Jack is yours.' She walks right up to me, bumping the baby's back against my chest, almost dropping him into my arms. 'I'm a terrible person, hate me, despise me, but please don't hold anything against this little guy. He's yours, I swear. I never cheated on you and I haven't been with anyone since, please, Sherry, just hold him. He's yours.'

I reach out my arms, more as a reflex action rather than parental desire, I've never been good with babies. Heidi twists him round and places my hands in the correct places. I take the weight, he's so light. His head rests against my shoulder as I focus on securing his body against my own chest. I gently touch his blond hair.

'I don't know how we got here but I'm glad we're here. I tried calling you this morning, can you believe that? Of all days! I call and you turn up!'

'I let it go to voicemail because I didn't recognise the number, that was you?'

'Yes! I wanted to try and make amends, get in contact and tell you all about what's going on. I left a message, it's a garbled mess but it's the same garbled mess I'm telling you now. Before you walked in here, I was hoping to get in contact with you, I just didn't think the wait would be so brief.'

'You're better at finding people than me.'

'I think happenstance should take the credit, not me.' Heidi and I both look at Jack peacefully resting in my arms. Never mind how he got here, he got here and we're both responsible. We smile at each other. 'He's got your nose, Sherry, and my sister thinks he's got some of your mannerisms.'

That's when I realise I haven't actually looked at him yet. I place both my hands under his arms to pull him away so I can get a good look at him. I take his weight and slowly lift him up into my eye-line; wispy blond hair followed by the soft skin of his forehead, then the skin gets softer, I'm scared it's going to continue getting softer until his skin softens completely into a blur because he's my son!

I close my eyes. What have I given you? What genetic mutation have I created and passed on?

He starts fidgeting, sensing the void between us.

'Open your eyes, Sherry.' Heidi rubs my arm. 'Don't be afraid.'

I open my eyes and lift Jack up further, following the smoothness of his forehead down, down, down until the finest blond eyebrows that ever existed.

I've never seen my own.

I lift him all the way up so I can see my beautiful son face-to-face. I can see him, all of him. I smile uncontrollably and he begins to smile back: a big, dribbly smile. I kiss his forehead and give him a hug, then just hold him out in front of me, staring at this boy I helped create. How could Heidi think I wouldn't want to be a part of his life? What kind of person am I?

Maybe . . .

I bring Jack closer to me until our noses are touching. He stops fidgeting and holds my gaze. This baby boy, only a few months old, stops and looks directly into my eyes. I stare back into this cobalt blue canvas and see my own reflection explode into creation within the expanding universe of his pupils. As the darkness grows from the lack of light, so does my reflection. As the blackness deepens, so does the clarity. What I saw in Kevin's eyes was a Platonic cave shadow compared to the detail I see in Jack's eyes; a real boy stepping out from an ill-drawn caricature, but this heightened self-realisation quickly pales to seeing the face of my son. I've travelled all the way to the moon only to be overcome by the view of home.

'Isn't he beautiful?'

'Yeah, he's *so* beautiful.'

'He's smiling, Sherry, he's smiling at you. That's right, Jack, this is your dad.'

Was that the first time he saw his own reflection? Do we have the same condition? Are babies even interested or capable of *knowing* the concept of reflection? Either way, we've got each other now.

'The girls all think he's got my mouth and nose but he's definitely got your eyes, can you see it?'

'Yeah, yeah, I can.' I kiss his forehead again: I don't think I'll ever tire of that. 'He's got my eyes.'

Heidi puts an arm around me. 'I know now's not the time and the place but I hope you can bring yourself to forgive me at some point in the future. I still love you, Sherry.' Heidi withdraws her arm. 'I'm sorry, you've had enough dumped on you today.'

Jack starts crying. 'Come here, give your old man a hug.' I bring him back to my chest, back to the warmth and the reassurance of a heartbeat. It'll be tough at first but we'll get through it, Jack, I'll show you all the little ways of dealing with it, the turns-of-phrase, the shortcuts, what to avoid. Not everyone can see themselves, not even those with a mirror.

I stroke Jack's back and he quietens down with his head in the crook of my neck, I smile at Heidi, the girl I thought I'd lost. 'You come here too, give me a hug.' I reach out my free arm, Heidi walks in with both her arms around my waist. 'There's a bench outside, let's catch up and figure out where we go from here.'

Heidi raises herself on tiptoe, kisses me on the cheek and Jack on the back of the head. 'Sounds perfect.'

'There's something I need to tell you too.'

'OK but first, wait there—' Heidi quickly bends down to get her camera out of the pram, playing with the settings as she stands back up. 'Let me get a photo of you two.'

The End

Acknowledgements

Thanks to my beta readers; Claire, Damo, Molly, Vanessa, Mum and Dad.

Thanks to editor Sophie Playle for critiquing and knocking this novel into shape for submission.

Thanks to Katrin Lloyd and Accent Press for picking it out of the slush pile.

Thanks to Jess Whitlum-Cooper and Headline for publishing 'How We Got To Today'.

Thanks to editor Greg Rees for really getting stuck into the final edit and making the novel even better.

Thanks to my Mum and Dad for having books and reading in my life from day one.

A special thanks to my wife Claire for her support and encouragement.